GULLIBLES TRAVELS

BY JILL JOHNSTON

Lesbian Nation
Marmalade Me

GULLIBLES TRAVELS
WRITING BY
JILL JOHNSTON

New York **links** London

ACKNOWLEDGMENT

thank you to danny moses for publishing more of my work and being a friendly editor and a friend and to carol fein for her essential behind the scenes detail labor and to carol dear alias strawberry for her love and her tremendous design for this book and to dianne hunter and rena patterson for their encour, agement and intellectual consideration and mythological per, ception of the work and to winnie and richard my youthful and approving parents and to betty anne clarke my concerned and amicable agent and to gregory battcock my unwilling teacher in the ways of not being serious and to all the women who send me letters or less demonstrative support as well as a few men and to the village voice as usual for continuing to tolerate or abide me as a recalcitrant daughter and especially diane fisher and joanne lawrence at the voice there who read my copy every week and talk to me on the phone.

p.s. thank you god for making us in your image.

CONTENTS

PART ONE

PART TWO

PART THREE

PART FOUR

FOREWORD

it is all a change.
writing is changing.
the writing is changing.
changing is such good writing.
                    —jill johnston

to exist is to change
to change is to mature,
      to mature is to go on
      creating oneself endlessly.
                    —henri bergson

With the appearance of *Gullibles Travels* on the heels of
Lesbian Nation and *Marmalade Me,* Jill Johnston emerges as
the most vital and original literary personality of our time.
Vanguard feminist, and disruptive, innovative artist, she is the
vortex of a sensibility shaping itself into a renovative cultural
force.

In this new collection of essays Jill Johnston celebrates
herself in motion. She says, "i'm almost always anxious
to leave soon after i get there, in order to see what the
next place is like." From the Red Baroness at one with her
speeding BMW, to the pilgrim in search of Agnes Martin,
Jill shifts from persona to persona as she lives from week to
week and moves from place to place. She is a protean figure
who seems to roam the global village in search of experiences
to synthesize into an expanding succession of selves.

Jill's moving vehicles of the earth and air are vehicles as
language is a vehicle for self-projection and self-discovery.
She creates "backgrounds to project a central figure." She
is a radiating "composite creation" moving through outer
spaces carrying her image through various guises. "Whither

we rides, and why, we do not know, only that the business
is important and pressing. in the unstable compound of fable
and fact that passes for our lives." She is a wandering
innocent at home and abroad, a picaro in high denim dyke
gear, Hermes in aviator shoes, Wonderwoman. She reflects,
"i dream all my selves into autofulfilling facets of each other.
i move around from room to room depending on the light."

Dadaist disruption is Jill's special vocation. She is traveling
Saturnalia, a mobile theatrical event, complete with costumes,
multiple role playing, and festive release. Her very appearance has a magical aura attracting the wrath of the Dragon
Guardians of Normality, necessitating quick shifts to make her
escape. An innocent junket to the Guggenheim Museum
carries her to jail. Trapped in a Michigan airport between a
preying seductive mother and the blue uniformed arms of
the law, Jill metamorphosizes from Enraged Amazon brandish-
ing unladylike language to New England Injured
Dignity.

Jill's adventures and misdemeanors provide material for a
weekly updating of the process of "becoming who she is" in
print. She says, "we write ourselves into the future by
re-inventing the past." She identifies with Apollinaire, the
man in the black derby, her Animus. Born an illegitimate son
of a Polish mother in Italy, Apollinaire changed his name
and turned his life into a public performance, "arranging his
own incredible revisions of himself." Leaving herself behind
for a fiction, Jill proposes to "exploit like Apollinaire our
expansive personalities by celebrating them in our works and
saying that around this composite creation unites a conflagration of dream and reality." Jill shares with Apollinaire
a mutual will to refashion the self in chosen images. In
opposition to the bondage of fixed and determined identity,
they project the freedom to escape the limitations of the
past.

The self is not a single homogenous entity but an evolving compound of multiple identifications. Self-creation through the elaboration of invented pasts shapes itself for Jill Johnston into a mission of synthesizing a new female identity, giving birth to the myth of the heroine.

Born the illegitimate daughter of an English aristocrat father and a rejected American mother, "more orphan than not," Jill is an avatar of the archetypal hero of humble origins who rises to great fame after a succession of adventures. Jill's identity is mythic. Her image is collective. She finds herself in women, and she offers her self-projections and ongoing metamorphosis as a redefinition of the female principle. She is "turning in circles and saying the whole world is moving."

it's not y'know as if i believe that any of us is where we want to be particularly, why would we stop any place in any case, we do keeps on movin, we as womenfolk can't as i see it be all that smug and satisfied about wherever we're at anyhow until the ascending female principle is better established at large.

Like her prototype, Odysseus, Jill is a storyteller as well as a shape shifter. *Gullibles Travels* begins, "these are some stories of women. i intend to adhere to the subject." She incorporates the stories of women into her narrative, and she reflects and transforms their images as part of her expansive self-revision. By absorbing women's conversations and bringing them together as parts of her "weekly resurrection" in her *Village Voice* column, Jill mediates and communicates a collective voice speaking women's language. Her stylistic composites, her "ideal cunnilinguistics," like her composite identifications, serve the function of disrupting and reformulating the terms with which women perceive and structure their own self-images. This is the most fundamental of changes.

Dianne Hunter
Rena Patterson

NOTE

this is a collection of writing which is writing which very often appears to be about something or other and may well be, i'm sure it is, many things interest me, but my enduring interest is the act or the process of writing. i have some illusions left about subjects, that subjects are important, the importance of a subject seems to me to reside in how much we want to save it, is it worth saving, is the world worth saving, etc., how much concern would we lavish on the survival of the whale nations forinstance, or are we looking forward to a natural death, and given such concerns what is the proper mode for any individual of expressing them if not directly participating in the operations or politics of change. for a writer is writing a vehicle for the subject if the subject is political persuasion. all these matters may be interesting.

sometime in october 1973 i drove to danny's house with friends dianne hunter and rena patterson where we laid out all this work around the floor of a big room to sort out the sequence as we might want it for the book. several of us off and on during the afternoon would move the pieces around correcting somebody else's positioning with (in)adequate explanations until as if by the magic touch of an invisible outsider or as though selected by a process of randomized divination the apparent satisfactory concoction assembled itself and then we only needed a title to know what it was all about. there were many titles. the titles are not necessarily what anything is about, or one might say the work is a collection of titles. more accurately of lines and titles. rena suggests that my preoccupation with lines and titles is significantly related to my obsessions with heritage and genealogy. lines—lineage. titles— legitimacy. on the other side of the lines and titles is the self without any personal history, the self created from nothing. i knew some of the pieces only by title, those that seemed to be about so many things, and i was pac- ing around all this flotsam thinking what a lot of stuff it was and what was it about, and danny mentioned the fox and the hedgehog, how the fox knows about a lot of things and the hedgehog knows about one big thing, and i felt somewhat relieved to hear that i might be a hedgehog since at least as danny suggested the center of the work is undoubtedly the self. anyway there were many possible titles:

A Book of Possible Titles
Book of Dark Predictions
A Heavy Serious Title
Keep Write Except to Pass
A Very Moving Book
Writes of Passage
Easy Writer
The Loneliness of the Long-Distance Writer
Admission Accomplished
Rotten to the Encore
Wait Till I'm Gone
I Take It All Back
Fully Assembled & Ready to Go
Contribution by Admission
Copious Notes of a Retarded Daughter

Memoirs of an Aggressive Dwarf
A Writer's Snotbook
Writing Into the Sunset
Lesbian Empire

Translation Please
Explanation to Follow
Journals of a Defeated Amazon
And So On
As I Was Saying
To Be Brief
I Could Go On
Etc.

Jill Johnston   November, 1973

PART ONE

collage —carol dear

THE RED BARONESS IN AMERICA

these are some stories of women. i intend to adhere to the subject. the mood is both strong and vulnerable, tentative and expansive. (not) all the parts can be moved. i planned originally
to share some stories of my cars. and other peoples cars. the
best car story i remember from eighth grade was by harriet
beecher stowe who said the automobile would divide humanity
into two classes: the quick and the dead. my friends indicate that
i'm so one i should be the other and that's because my present
vehicle was made by the germans. i now drive instead of just
going from one place to another. i don't drive and daydream
any more. i don't know if the germans imagined their jugger-
nauts hurling 75 or 80 mph on country amerikan winding
roads, possibly all they had in mind was a normal cruising speed
of 90 or 100 or so on their own hiways, but whatever the conditions the product they've turned out says drive me. esther
tells me that's no excuse. she didn't explain for what. i suppose
for risking my life. i don't take it lightly myself. i take my new
career as a racing driver seriously. i approach the launching
pad with intent to speed and nothing else. i pass everything
else that moves on four wheels at double dispatch. i don't even
see the things that don't move. all i care about is passing everything that moves and breaking my own speed records for arriving anyplace including any aimless trip whatsoever. i take
adverse conditions into account too. i made it one night from
hartford to new jersey in one hour and a half in a blinding rain
storm even though i had to pause or slow down momentarily
while a vw bug in front of me went into a wild spin and a half
and i paused extra to admire its trajectory across the three
lanes spinning like a top in each lane and miraculously escap-
ing bodily contact with three other onrushing vehicles and ending up dead still facing in the right direction in the emergency
pullover lane. i've already bragged about my three hour and 15

minute record maiden trip from washington d. c. to manhattan. i have no intention of repeating the trip just to outdo myself. i'm just writing about cars. these are some stories of cars. i intend to adhere to the subject. the mood is free and confined, regular and irregular, rectangular and unmanageable. i planned originally to share some stories of women. everything which is necessary is in her. and what is not in her is not necessary. she was turning in circles and saying the whole world is moving. she represents herself as a sphere. the news was beginning to spread. there were more friends, more flowers, more cars! she was invited to write a column in a city newspaper called the brakes. she wanted to call it just motor. i mean motor. the word motor sums up everything you need to know about cars. i don't use fancy words like engine. i would however toss dymaxion around in architectural company. the same thing over & over & over again. how important the third over is. the important thing about my life & times right now is its quality of risk and speed. i haven't been so fast since i played right wing soccer. a study in contrasts is what it's all about. the way one might enjoy taking up soccer after playing croquet every year until you were 13. i've been driving tinlizzards since i sat on somebody's lap to steer their heap when i was nine so i deserved something dangerous and foolish and impractical at 15. i was brought up on gingham and seersucker. the last allaround washnwear type thing i had for a vehicle was that rectangular underpowered dinosaur they call a vw camper which made it across wyoming at an all time high of 25 mph. other outstanding features of my great house on wheels were its motor spattering oil capacities and its ability to turn over on any bridge on which the wind was above breeze warnings and its general reliability under stress on remote turnpikes for just breaking apart. i had one fine trip in this house. i parked it for a week on an island off maine overlooking some reefs and seaweed and holed up inside to write very comfortably as though i'd discovered the allpurpose self reflecting box with a window on the ocean of the world. when i wasn't doing that i was struggling on the outside with my feet touching the ground with this survival equipment by hudson's called coleman's, these frightening lanterns and stoves, the lantern i busted immediately and presented the remains to a friend, the stove i gave away to the stranger who relieved me of the house one day on a local street i accepted the first comer for whatever he seemed to have in his pocket. i told him it was a famous house because it had appeared in esquire. that seemed to really turn him on. i wished him luck in his camper phase. we all have these camper phases even if you don't actually get one. everybody likes to get into somebody else's and rummage around checking out the compartments. the reason i liked it all originally was for its compartments. i didn't enquire into its efficiency or anything like that. this german number i have now is efficient completely by chance. that is, i had no idea i was obtaining the darling of amerikan afficionados in european models. it's not that i didn't know it would be faster, *any*thing would be faster, nor that i didn't know it would be more reliable than a rambler pickup, but nobody told me it was a racing car favorite of the nazis. the model by the way is a bmw 2002 stands for bavarian motor works and i feel exempt from any responsibility of collusion with an unpopular nation state since i never did know where bavaria was and for some time i thought the b stood for british. the reason i thought of it at all was that three or two years ago i happened to see this exquisite backside of a medium small orange number parked on a west side street and it occurred to me right then that i'd get one. i jumped out of whatever tinlizzard i had at the time and found its identifying insignia. i'd never heard of it. a bmw. a british motor wench i surmised. anyway the romance was all visual. the only thing i like better now visually is anything else german with a lot of chrome. i really dig chrome. and in 5000 years when i'm finished with my creditors i'll have this one painted the silver blue metal flake job. oh lord wonchu buy me—a mercedes benz . . . my friends all drive porsches, i must make amends. oh lord wonchu provide me with a mechanic for free. for any- one considering seriously becoming a racing car driver i have to offer this inside information that an 8000 mile check on a small bavarian affair costs $135. which may be nothing to nazis and nebuchadnezzars but for myself i can't reconcile that sort of price of a tuneup to the $50 i once paid outright for a '51 pontiac that i'm still sentimental about. i can't believe i abandoned that one on the street just because of its radiator. it wasn't even a motor problem. i don't remember what was wrong with its radiator. i remember getting after a suitable interval an allamerikan prone sprawl of a desoto that wouldn't go in reverse and which i abandoned within three weeks. i remember hearing a story about a car that would *only* go in reverse. i know lots of car stories. i know lots of car and women stories. all the cars in the world are driven by people. all the people in the world are women, except some of them are men, whose mothers permitted them to make them. the mood is soft and dynamic, relaxed and concentrated. (not) all the parts can be moved. i suppose if it were possible the hiway engineers would've constructed some special bypasses over around or under their tunnels for women, i heard that a woman mining engineer in colorado won her case for enter- ing a tunnel, apparently they don't permit women in tun- nels out there, possibly here too except for driving, and i for one go through them very fast, i timed myself last week in the new haven tunnel it was a five second run. it's more ex- citing to pass everybody in a tunnel too. and there's no ex- cuse as esther said. and esther wouldn't drive with me. once rosalyn said she wouldn't drive with me either but she didn't remember why. i've only destroyed one car and that was my mother's. i've never hit an animal. i've only knocked two peo- ple down and it was all their fault. and i have only one speed- ing ticket in my german racer. i suppose they know i'm out practicing. I don't know why they got me that one time. i was doing 80 at 2 a. m. on the merritt and this pleasant pig who probably didn't know who i was pulled me over and said did you know you were doing 80 ma'am. of course i knew i was doing 80. what'd he think i'd be doing at 2 a. m. on the merritt parkway. he apologized and punished me at the same time, so undoubtedly he was confused. not all of them i'll have to admit are so charmingly ambivalent. most of them in fact actually are on the lookout for these ex favorites of the nazis and they cruise up and down everywhere just especially to hunt us down. the only times anybody ever stopped me in my house was for having long hair and/or when my son was in the passenger seat. my son by the way was instrumental in the purchase of that house. the fact is that one year i was homeless and very upset about it and richard who was nine and driving along in a tinlizzard for an outing said casually why don't you get one of those things with a box in the back and i thought he meant a trailer, i'd always associated campers exclusively with trailers, so i didn't take it seriously for a year until when i was on the coast and saw zillions of these boxes that sort of went with the driving equipment and thought that was for me, i had no intention of retiring into a trailer at the age of 15. trailers and retired nuclear disasters were the same thing. anyway so i had my camper phase. during my truly big trip, a three month junket to the coast and back, i slept in it a total of three nights. when you have a car that you *can't* sleep in nobody wants you to stay in their regular plumbing and electrified houses and when you *do* have one they're quite eager for some reason to put you up, so the true benefits deriving from a camper are those of increased and unlimited visitation rights, something to consider if you prefer squatting in other peoples houses the way all the women i know do. there's a history of good luck with cars in my family. my grandmother never owned one. my second cousin eddie had a fine ford with a rumble seat. and my mother made her first fortune driving a model-t when a rich man's son oscar somebody piled his motorcycle up on her running board ramming the handlebars into her head causing her to sustain a concussion for which the rich father of the son paid my mother 10 grand in those times was a fantastic sum and she became an adventurer by taking a boat to europe. she didn't drive again for dozens of years. the only other story i remember about the early days was being compelled to go for sunday afternoon drives with my grandmother in martha and elsie's black chrysler and reading the funnies and throwing up. i never thought i was destined for the racetracks. except for eddie's rumble seat i didn't take cars seriously at all. there was nothing to it then anyway. there weren't any japs or germans. there weren't any rpms and the word handling was unknown. the thing about a foreign efficient car is that it *handles*. i told jane all about my car history so that when i acquired this current juggernaut she used it against me and acted as though i didn't deserve having something that *handled* or something that had such an overqualified motor that a number of its incidental details were fucked up in a royal way like when a certain type of person sat in the car it wouldn't start or a certain type of other person got in the car the key would get stuck in a door so you couldn't put it in the starter and stuff like that and in fact she didn't think i was *capable* of *handling* this fabulous piece of machinery as a mechanic put it and that's because she happens to be a true car freak and that's because she owned a morgan. i always thought a morgan was a horse but now i know better. i know a *lot* better. i can't identify them on the road, but i display an interest in them and i intend to get one when esquire or the vw outfit people come across for that photo i posed for they didn't tell me was going to be an ad for those lousy campers it looked as if i had nothing better to do than to advertise what a wonderful house i was leading in my life when in reality it was a minor miracle i'd survived to have the photo taken at all.

the vw people wouldn't recompense me a cent for all my broken down motors or the mental cruelty i experienced as a snail being a sort of beast of burden carrying all these compartments around. kaput. i'm paying everybody back by being a terror on the roads. and they'll never get a picture of me. i go too fast. i take other drivers on too but basically i'm practicing to be faster than myself. i don't like to pick up challenges by strangers but i've noticed i can't very well ignore certain dudes who think their crummy dirty dent chrome dodge is a match for any german. the thing is there isn't a dude under 70 who won't start driving with his prick as soon as he registers that a *woman* is on his ass and then he turns into a goddam bombardier. but it's a solo flight most of the way. i go too fast for most anybody to determine *what* sex (if any) is causing the wind and they assume it's a male anyway unless otherwise proven and if they do see anything i suppose it's a longhair marine so essentially after all they're pretty polite and move over and make as much room as possible as soon as they hear the blast and recognize a nazi racingcar driven by longhair marine. okay i've taken care of some car tales and some women too. i didn't say i had a very important sexual experience in my camper, so i guess it was worth it. the most exciting thing is to think of anything, then you don't have to do it. i never expect anything to materialize anyway so i have basically a good time. the components exist in a peculiar idiosyncratic space. and i experience the other stories as my own so that in effect i can imagine i've done everything. the most impressive car story i ever heard was from lois hart who told me she had her nervous breakdown in a '51 chevy. i wouldn't ever forget it. the way things shake down currently is that jane got a saab and esther drives a vw squareback and gregory leaves his mg in garages to go abroad on boats and phyllis b. totalled her bug two weeks ago and bertha's is in north carolina and i saw the ex old man of an ex lover of mine in a bentley one day and i saw her

mother in a taxi and sheindi says she's getting a learners permit
and richard wants a license next year and rosalyn probably
still doesn't drive and i don't know what my mother has and
ingrid said her favorite job was a '51 chrysler and the only
other human i know who has a bmw 2002 is brenda hyphenated and i take it back i forgot so does simone and the wheels
i want next is a bavaria four door six cylinder sedan maroon
with folding wings and a rocket fuel jet propelled engine for
short trips to the moon whenever i'm in the mood.

january 11, 1973

AT THE CROTCH OF DAWN

September 14 arrived surprise lake at 4 p. m. i thought it
could've been called lake suddenly since you come upon it
suddenly. and life is fool of surprises. the united flight boston
to seattle september 7 contained a whole fastpitching softball
team called the kawanis club and i've never flown in a plane
full of goon boys who yell things like let me outa here when
the plane is landing and taking off. and i've never flown with
a couple celebrating their 58th wedding anniversary. and i've
never flown with carol strawberry. and i've never been in point
roberts which snowshoe tells me is probably the most inaccessible piece of land attached to the continent. to me the most
inaccessible peace of anything i've been to was this surprise
lake 4800 feet above sea level and nobody flew me there. it
may be one of those points from which the desire to travel is
more interesting than traveling. i didn't want to stay there
long myself. about 5 p. m. i said i thought one night would
do. i was cold and i felt strange and we'd forgotten to pack
in mayonnaise. also i wanted a martini. and snowshoe was
cooking up beef strogonoff with sour cream out of a package
and the mushrooms she was frying to go with the package
fell in the dirt so i had to wash each one off individually in
the lake. and she wasn't happy herself that she'd forgotten a
jello cheese cake mix she says she never goes without. she
showed me the guide book with pictures and maps and told
me if we kept on going today, that was the next day, these're
some of the things we'd pass by. i'd already passed by the
whole snoqualimie national forest on the pacific crest trail
system and i thought i might have to have the cartilege in my
right knee removed like my left from when i fell out of bed
once. i kept referring to my knees. the day after when i
couldn't walk, i kept referring to my calves. that particular
trail was not recommended for cow travel. or rather horse. i

wanted to know what mountain we were climbing and snowshoe said all these mountains have names but she'd have to
look on a map to see what they are, none of em are famous
mountains, tho that's a very human way of looking at it, tho
what i meant to say was that what she told me mainly was
we weren't climbing any mountains at all, we were hiking. i
deduced therefore that for an outbacker like snowshoe who by
the way was carrying 40 lbs. next to my three that climbing
4800 feet which she said is a lot more than our eastern mt
washington which is our highest is a sort of a stroll over a
slightly rising mole. she stopped to rest quite a bit on the way
up though. i asked if every trail goes to a lake. she said no to
peaks and meadows and shelters but lakes are the favorites.
i could see why. they're not polluted by humans and they sit
all still deep blues greens like a nest in a steep bank of branch.
way up are these white vulva gulleys that're snow passages.
way up were these meadows of stone heaps that avalanche
down in the winters of snows. way up top of all that're the
peaks that snowshoe doesn't know the names of. the mountain
you can see around pt. roberts and vancouver is mt. baker. all
i know about vancouver is you can walk to the beach from
almost any part of it and you can't ever get lost cause you've
always got the mountains to guide you. i saw the whole thing
with embalmed freighters in a still life harbor out of jane rule's
picture window and what she told me is that toronto is a city
and vancouver is a womb with a view. i have no idea what
toronto has to do with it. as i said i arrived at pt. roberts and
that's where snowshoe came in her mother's toyota corolla
squareback to take me down to gold bar and turn me into a
rockicrucian mountaineer or rather a mere hiker whose knee
cartileges would split and have to be excised and whose calves
would assume a permarigid condition who anyhow would
never be recommended for travel on any more horse trails.
snowshoe arrived at the crotch of dawn while i was in the arms
of carol strawberry with whom i flew united as i said. s. told

me my horoscope for that day was i was not supposed to make any binding contracts, and the next day was auspicious for travel and romance, so she guessed i'm supposed to travel in romance on a free lance basis. every shroud has a silver lining. we accept whatever situation arises. i'm enjoying being sentimental. and i had to pack my fresca bottle out of the snoqualimie national forest. i wouldn't've packed it in if i'd known, three lbs. is a lot of lbs. climbing five miles, and s. had plenty of these packages with flavored powder for our drinking supply. she says it's a joke in the outback that anything to drink is good. we drank this grape mix all the way up. only city bunnies like me drag in their fresca bottles. there was a yuban can somebody'd thrown in a small pool this side of the lake that s. wanted to pack out too, but 40 lb. is already a lot, and i wasn't adding to my three, which included the empty fresca bottle. on the way there were all sorts of mushrooms, even some papery thin orange ones, and white white white ones with fluted undersides like jane rule's white crepe pants. there was marmots pikas chipmunks no bears no snakes. i looked a pika straight in the eye beside the lake surprise. i said i'd like to study biology again, basically to find out how every-body reproduces. snowshoe said she just wants to know what to eat. at bottom we never know how it has all come about. i didn't actually see a marmot. i heard one whistle. i thought it was a boyscout leader, then the same whistle on the way out past the same place a cemetery of rocks and trees from ava-lanche and s. informed me the marmots'll lie out in the sun and roll over on their tummies n tickle themselves and play around then when they see somebody coming they'll whistle and dive for cover into the rocks. a good smart life. i can't even remember to take my mayonnaise along myself. nonetheless i have the cents to take a plane to the most inaccessible piece of land attached to the continent. when you cross the border around here there's a white peace arch that says Children of a Common Mother. that means canada is the legitimate child and we're the bastards. after being legitimate on king george highway for about 20 minutes however if you're going to pt roberts you cross another border into the u. s. a. again into our natural bastardy, pt roberts being a u. s. possession. four candles one bowl of salad one woman sleeping. analogies, affinities, correspondences, and repercussions. the feeling of strangeness which she conveyed, and yet of having known her always. i was immediately attracted to her because she was beautiful, eternite, infini, charite, solitude, angoisse, lumiere, aube, soleil, amour, beaute, inoui, pitie, demon, ange, ivresse, paradis, enfer, ennui, embrasse, etc. . . . as sacred as 36,000,000 new born poodle dogs. switchback or sailboat tacking. in the woods snowshoe said oh by the way if you see any snakes don't worry 'cause none of them're poisonous. as for the bears, they're not grizzly. anyway i was pretty involved in these huge trees. i said there wasn't any lake, meaning we'd never get there. i said it's raining and s. said we call this sprinkling. i said my feet were falling off and s. said if i had the equipment very soon i'd get right into it too. i said lookit these enormous leaves, which were sun dappled, and s. said if i think they're big here i should go out to the olympic rainforest, the leaves there're like the amazon basin. coming down i kept saying we should be recrossing the footbridge soon and s. said it's a foot log not a foot bridge. i said we were making it down in double time and s. agreed. although that was about three hours fast walking, or fast for trails not recommended for horse travel. the last 16th of a mile when we emerged from the trail onto a gravel road stretch crossing a crick and a railroad track back to where the toyota corolla was parked my mind told my body it was through so the remainder was a terrific sludge. i mean my mind had told my feet it was over but they had to go another 16th of a mile. this indicates to me that you could travel tremendous distances on foot and not mind it a bit until your mind registered the end, distance being absolutely relative an all. and space. the moving thin line of white far below was raging torrent, all you have to remember is your jello cheese cake mix. all i had to remember was the thing i never liked about camping was when you got to the campsite. then i never knew what to do. that's why i said to snowshoe i felt strange. i like just moving along, paddling down the rivers or trudging up the trails, oohing and ahing over the wilderness. but at the campsite i would feel dirty and sticky and useless and stand there poking at the fire and not looking forward to a night on the hard ground in a blue nylon tent flapping madly in the glacial wind and wishing i was looking out somebody's picture window at a bunch of embalmed freighters in a stilllife harbor. sdrawkcab spelt backwards spells backwards. the last thing on the way out were the great martian-like towers of the electrical transmission lines that stalk across the earth under which we passed on the way in and i heard for the first time the hum-ming sizzling drone of the wires that had turned on la monte young as a boy in the west. if the winged victory of samothrace had kept her head she might've smoked a cigarette in a long jade holder. i got back to the cabin in gold bar and had a mar-tini and a mayonnaise sandwich.—this is snowshoe's postscript that i asked her to write: time passes slowly up here in the mts. steel guitars and stars, mountain lakes and blackberry ramble. hey jill is this a letter to you? anything i can say is only about existing on a different time scale. four and a half miles up the trail is not the same as four and a half miles down the trail. leading a reasonable existence comes down to leading an in-visible one. the singular technology of wilderness. surfboards, a co-op senior pack, bluet camp stove, poly bottle in the side pocket. we did spend a lot of time talking about trees. cedar trees and fir trees. the whispers tell of growing in a softly breathing world, a hundred years just to become young. richard and i lying on the snow, goofing on acid and getting drawn into the life trees swirled across the mist and dripping snow. the world we have is not the world we want but the forest seems satisfied. how remote. the nervous bustling trivial 20th century. where have you gone lita lepie? it was a long distance search. a long distance hike. an alpine lake with a happy personality. lake surprise. find it if you can. enough of salvation, back to civilization. go ahead and listen to helen reddy when you get back home. its so cute it'll just make your mind fall out. mind did. luckily as a rockicrucian that doesn't bother me at all. none of this is scary energy. like bears in the cascades. dark space outside the tent and no flashlight. i still believe you could relax and laugh with them and the bears would really dig ya. i talked with one when i was eight, it was cool. i'm in my own pocket. save our mother ocean. maybe my mission in life is to pass out surfer t-shirts to my friends. you're gonna laugh but we're gearing up for action. mind trips even. being in this time is being in no time at all. possession in a past space, and peace in another. hello lake carol lake diana lake robin lake vicki lake trina lake sandy hurricane heather mt debbie mt francis lake circumspect lake becky lake white cloud lake jane trapper pass surprise creek hidden lake mt alison mt betty lost river & lake jill. goodbye from lake laziness.

september 27, 1973

16

THE RIGHTFUL AIR TO THE THROWN

yesterday somebody said cultural baggage is like climbing into a canoe with a footlocker. i'm thinking i'd like to take a canoe trip. i saw an aluminum canoe last week wrapped around a rock in an old crick river and i thought of trying to salvage it. i was never into buying a canoe. my canoe experience came along with the rest of the equipment at these camps i went to once where you didn't count for much if you didn't learn how to kill yourself mastering certain incomprehensible feats like paddling a canoe alone into the middle of a lake and tipping yrself plus boat over into what they called a swamped condition in which you were obliged to somehow make your way back to shore sitting in your swamped or submerged canoe, which you would then empty and ready for some other such wondrous adventure. i hated camp. i only liked going someplace with a suitcase. we always used to be going places with suitcases. and footlockers. going to camp was an interminable train ride with a suitcase with a lot of other unbearable children. at camp the only way you didn't notice how unbearable we all were was by never stopping being a camper, meaning learning all the tricks they made up to keep you very busy. another important canoe trick was maneuvering your boat across a great distance in a straight line by standing on the tiny deck of the stern and bending yer knees rhythmically while flapping yer arms as though you were a huge bird trying to land whereas what you really were doing was something called bobbing. whatever you did in camp it seemed it wasn't worthwhile unless it was really uncomfortable. you could ride horseback but in order to learn how to do it you had to go round and round in circles in a dusty old ring with somebody yelling at you to adjust your feet or your back and making you feel unworthy of animals. then if you learned you could go on a great adventure called a breakfast ride which meant arising at dawn to go trotting off into the sunrise in a line to eventually die of stomach cramps and stitches and hunger until the leader decided they'd found the proper clearing for a breakfast you no longer felt like eating. if you wanted to get away from the camp more seriously you had to sign up for a three day mountain trip and if there was one thing i didn't understand as a kid it was walking up steep hills with a pack on my back for nothing. i preferred carrying two heavy suitcases a mile to a train. at least i could sleep in a bed when i got where i was going. probably the worst thing about camp was the enthusiasm you were supposed to manifest over the prospect of sleeping out under the stars. there wasn't anything i despised more than sleeping under the stars. ten breakfast rides were preferable to one night under the stars. if i went on a canoe trip now i'd arrange to sleep every night in a motel. i did have a thing for canoes. i think i actually enjoyed swamping and bobbing and gunnelling and docking and jumping etc., otherwise why would i've ended up as a canoeing counsellor when i grew up to be 18. recently i read in a feminist publication where a woman thought of me as her ultimate camp counsellor or something and i had to shudder to think what that meant. i hated being a camp counsellor as much as i hated being a camper. it must've seemed like the only alternative to spending the summer in woolworth's selling socks and safety pins. we might've been better off at woolworth's. in return for the sun and water you had to play nursemaid to a cabinful of suburban brats of whom you were one. i did it badly and i wasn't a good canoeing demonstrator either, by which i mean mostly that i was required to assume responsibility for two and three day canoe trips up and down unpredictable rivers about which the report was made that my trips were masterpieces of disorganization. all i remember is being burned to death by the sun and despising sleeping under the stars and being amused watching the campers washing the tinware in the river and floating it downstream to a rinser. i liked floating downstream myself. that has nothing to do without it. i attach no excessive importance to these recollections from various stages of childhood, but it's convenient to collect them here at any moment. riding along at random she comes to a deep river. arriving at a place where the road leads no further. leaving the stars to their fans. i had a dream i jumped into a body of clear pleasant water to swim to "the other side" and shortly as i was swimming some snakes appeared and i panicked and turned round to swim back, swimming thus through these snakes, who were very threatening while desisting from harming me and apparently i made it back. melusine. occasionally i attribute motives to you i might not have. we look on with resignation at all the xstrawdinary things the unconscious produces. when the self is steeped in a kind of fluid universe, as at the hark of the absalute. aqua permanens. the rightful air to the thrown. the clouds and me and the crick river were all running in the same direction some day. and the road that leads further, and a number of rocks were having a meeting, i thought so. and i needed a canoe to get back by the river past the house with a dog the size of a woodchuck zarking my heels. i saw an aluminum canoe wrapped around a rock and i thought of trying to salvage it. i was never into buying a canoe. i've considered however the difference between the wooden and aluminum and aesthetically i prefer the wooden especially for its gunwales. i asked a friend what she remembered about paddling and she said the funniest thing she remembers about paddling was when jill became the captain of a four-man life raft in the middle of the stillness of a small pond by taking up with the old jay stroke from camp days. and we'd just gone out there to flop and sun. feather. sweep. reverse. pull-to. jay stroke. all that fancy stuff. and i was still a rotten counsellor. i liked being a camper better because the counsellors were so important and such good demonstrators of tricks that campers were bound to be having crunches on them all the time and this was a preoccupation that made all the other discomforts occasionally bearable. also as a camper, at least in this particular place, one qualified to race at the end of the season in the 18 seater *war canoe* of yr own blue or white team. 18 campers with paddles, and a cox.

it wasn't at all like the henley regatta, but very exciting. the
ultimate trick. and i preferred the racing business with lots of
other people. i hated racing alone. my greatest humiliation was
this swimming meet in which i raced the crawl for my team in
the outside lane meaning the lane closest to the raft and the
rest of the lake. it was just a single lap race and i used to bury
my head and do it across without breathing. so that's what i
did and the next thing i knew i crashed my head into some
object and came up gasping to see that the race was over and
i was out near the raft someplace having collided with an official rowboat. i went up to my cabin directly, giving way, no
doubt, to a fit of uncontrollable sobbing. i packed my suitcase
and footlocker and wondered how i could catch the next train.
all campers of course in a sense were being detained. we knew
the name of the state we were in and that was about all. oh
and the name of the lake. but you couldn't leave unless somebody came to get you except when it was definitely all over
and they transported you to the station for the interminable
train ride home. before they did that they had to reward you
for all the tricks you learned and the races you won. you might
receive little pieces of felt with the camp insignia on them. and
you had to sing a lot of corny camp songs. and you almost always had to cry, even though i hated it i cried, i suppose it
was just sad standing there in a circle singing some gooey sunset & canoe song and realizing that in ten hours you'd be playing hopscotch or cops & robbers on the suburban cement with
some other unbearable children. or at the least that more than
probably you'd never again see this counsellor you'd picked
out to have the ultimate crunch on. certainly in any case it was
all about girls. in which case it don't make no never mind. we
were all girls swamping and bobbing and docking and jumping
and sleeping out under the stars. i attach excessive importance
to that recollection. that has everything to do without it.

april 26, 1973

THE GENIUS I'VE SQUANDERED IN BED

I want some old violins old wine old people old buildings and some young ones homesick for infinity. Goodmorning, I responded politely, altho when I turned around I saw nothing. I am very busy finding out what people mean by what they say I used to be interested in what they were what they looked like I am now interested in what they say. Please remember your own lines. I make them up, I don't have to remember them. I know, she says, you're operating on about ten levels at once writing two books and two pieces and three letters and two lists and this record book with everything neatly organized all over the room and she went about organizing her part of the chaos. I'm going out to get a fresh air of breath. The ice is still forming a ceiling over the stream. The men are still going up in trees on ropes with saws and mutilating the branches. The rest still looks like a postcard whatever isn't white is black and the white makes the black look blacker or the black white whiter. There's a nuclear family in that car with the woman driving. We talk about our mothers sometimes. Marsha always used to forgive hers because she was right and she M. was wrong and now she's permanently disgusted. Jane says she's her mother's posthumous child. She was born 20 years after she died. Mine shut herself up in an impregnable silence. I'll marry myself to the mozart basson concerto. These Elusivian mysteries. Marsha never mentioned a father. Jane's had a widow's peak and that's all she remembers except for gray eyes maybe and he came around once or twice like visiting royalty and invaded the mythological vacuum her mother created to explain and insure his absence. He is familiar to all of us and not a very interesting or important person. I like to talk about my grandmother's boarder. His name was Mr. Shoemaker and he was a drunkard but he walked straight and sober through her living room to go upstairs to his bedroom

and out the same way is what he amounted to. Ecce hobo.
Marsha's mother took in some boarders, the italians had stinky
feet and the germans burned holes in the furniture. Anyway
we're all mutant forms—happy products of the failure of the
nuclear family. I meet this tree and embrace it and put my
arms around it as if it was an old-fashioned woman. Y. wanted
to know if I really thought all men were unredeemable, after
all they've done some pretty interesting things, like say einstein
. . . and I said E equals mother cunt squared, his particular
relativity was a wife who left his boxlunch outside the study
door every day. The author of totem & taboo himself frankly
acknowledged that he didn't know where the actual arena of
the drama he sketched could've taken place. None of our
mothers were much into the old and new testicles either. Or
they reacted a lot in the margins and stuff. Mine was a heathen
she said although she sent me to be baptized when I was eight
and made me go to some strawberry festival at a community
type church place and sent me off to a high episcopalian establishment where they confirmed me and left the rest up to me.
I went to confession once. They gave me a small booklet of
sins and I chose ten. I never confess although I don't keep
secrets either. Jane's mother actually was somewhat religious,
but not pious. She was into the rationalists c.s. eliot and t.s.
lewis and lewis's science fiction too rather than the books of
the common prayer. Before she died my grandmother was trying to find out something about all of it. She wrote out a
prayer on a scrap of paper for instance. What did I say yesterday about my grandmother opening the tops of the bottles
for me? Wouldju please remember my lines too? I make them
up sometimes, I shouldn't have to remember them. I'm busy
finding out what other people say or mean by what they say I
used to be interested in the looks of them and who they were
I am now interested in what they say. In new definitions perhaps especially. Penis envy is the envy of a man with a little
penis for the bigger penis of another man. A feminist is a

woman who wants a better deal from her old man. Aggression is when a cannibal eats another person and he isn't hungry. A victorian phallic mother is a woman who comes after you with an enema bag. She moves rhythmically to the accompaniment of her own daydreams. The idea that pleasure could be an end in itself is so startling and so threatening to the stricture of our society that the mere possibility is denied. Flying still seems a drastic means of traveling. I'm going out for a fresh of breath air. I go skid on the ice and mail a letter to suzi and to rolling stone. I said to rolling stone why don't they print a photo of a female rock star with a nude man in the background. Or a male rock star with the same. Like say mick jagger with a depressed anonymous naked man in the background. And also how do they come off covering the women on their scene exclusively by men. And why can't they call their rag the male rolling stone. I'm a real revolutionary. I write lines and letters and books and pieces and lists and records and even copy down some ladys room graffiti: "I like grils." The next person crossed that out and said "you mean girls don't you?" And a third person said "what about us grills?" When you think of all the genius I've squandered in bed. I need a movement omelet. I need a bee exterminator. I need a gazebo. I need a superficial excursion. I needed to know if she was really serious about pretending to be ignorant about not being in business. Or I needed the line about richard's question about her seriousness and pretending and ignorance and being in business or not seemed irrelevant to the monopoly game itself. She remembers when she went through her thimble stage. I was fond of the boat or the shoe. I like to talk about the games sometimes. The best was a square board that came with a few sticks and a bunch of small wooden doughnuts combining which—the board sticks and do-nuts—you could play about 75 different games. The other best was a rubber cup and a rubber disc and two dice and for each player a string with a colored wooden ball at the end and I don't remember what happened then. I played marbles on the rug too. And asked my grandmother to open the bottle tops. She was the butch I guess. She had arthritis but she could open bottle tops. I couldn't do a thing like that. I could read and play ball and marbles and toy soldiers and cops and robbers and climb trees but I couldn't do any knots or screws or plugs or wires or anything like that. I suppose I had my revolutions all mixed up to begin with. Next time I'll contrive to be ordered to do what I really want. But it won't be mechanics, even so. Jane said she thought I was just playing the dumb femme, not fixing the light. So she wouldn't fix it. Then she fixed it. Then Marsha fixed the other one. Then I said Marsha must be a mechanical genius because she seems to do everything and she replied that wasn't true, that I was just subnormal. I'm going out for the fresh air. I need the air and the picturepostcard black and white snow escape. I want some old violins old wine old people old buildings and some young ones homesick for infinity.

january 27, 1972

MARY KISSMAS & A HIPPY NUDE YEAR

there is no god and mary was his mother. the steam was coming off the roofs and i thot we were on fire. she couldn't undertaker anything. too much light darkens the mind. there's some tactical insignificance about doing anything but living. what somebody found was incontrovertible evidence that it all means zero. that phrase predicts the pattern of our ruin. what it is that one becomes is that that that is that it is. certain movements we make can be distinguished clearly as being simian or reptillian or piscine or bovine. soap bubbles and the forces which mould them. people only pay attention to what they've discovered for themselves. i knew i had gangrene or leprosy of the legs and one night we remembered a childhood disease called impetigo so i rushed to the doctor who said it was poison sumac or oak or allergy related and i wasn't suppurating but giving off the serum of the cells. i applied the yellow stuff out of a one half ounce of cortisone or mycolog creme nystatin ceocymin sulfate gramidcidin triamcinolone acetonide in an aqueous perfumed vanishing cream base with polysorbate 60 alcohol aluminum hydroxide concentrated wet gel titanium dioxide glyceryl monostearate polyethylene glycol simethicone sorbic acid propylene glycol ethylenediamine hydrochloride white petroleum polyoxyethylene fatty alcohol ether methylparaben propylparaben and sorbitol solution and wrapped my legs in paper towels held together with scotch tape and went on living. we went to eat at the boston union oyster house and saw this creepy adventure flick called deliverance. i went to the 46th street docks to see gregory go away on the cristoforo colombo and eat champagne and drink fish on cracker and meet gregory's mother's stockbroker and watch the helen mcallister tugboat push them all out to harbor. i went to princeton and purchase to talk about my former life. i distribute my body in different parts of space. i internalize a series of unanswered

questions as a builtin mystification abt my elemental identity.
i regard a neat bundle of wood for a desk divider. i swear at
the ice on the driveway. i summarize the five months of my
death state. i make numerous complaints about my feelings. i
decide to modify my part into a more likeable character. i try
to clear away the rubble of understanding. see that it doesn't
happen again. i produce a new explanation and pray to make
it improbable. each of us cld rediscover the possibility of doubting our origins despire and in spit of being well brought up.
i hazard being original one day and say oh i'm making a living
being bad. check that. cheque that. it's like we're in this summer camp without adequate supervision. we do exactly what
we please and then right it up as well. i practice detachment.
i don't read the papers. i note the visitation of two cows and a
black horse . . . a promising practitioner of naturalism. in her
posthumpus ascent to lasting literary esteam she still contrives
to dismay her readers in approxmire the same protortion that
she impraxis them. in 1893 alibaba was robbed by one of his
40 thieves. on page 144 of orlando virginia woolf says orlando
professed great enjoyment in the society of her own sex, and
leave it to the gentlemen to prove, as they are very fond of
doing, that this is impossible. which is almost as political as i
wished to be today. get yer flexible flyers and we can go belly
woppin together. mary kissmas & a hippy nude year. the most
unforgivable character i met in new england recently was one
virginia fuller tucker mcilvain perkins aged 64 born 1909 the
third of three sisters who stood on her head on television in
1944 and was pronounced legally sane by the state supreme
court and whose mother said she didn't have any imagination
and who was knitting lots of red & white santaclaus stockings
formerly of scaneateles says the best way to pass the time is to
waste it. she's done so many things besides standing on her head
on television i axed her what was the most important thing she
does and she said circulate. whenin aye was a kiddling. like
my good bedst friend. she's a very shellfish person. i blamed

jane for my leg disease or jane's mother who caused jane's face to brake out in a disfigurement the day after she told her she looked pretty and what a nice girlfriend her brother had how she washes the dishes and everything i analiced dis way dat her mother was running a straight trip around her and if she was pretty that meant she too could be straight like her brother's girlfriend and wash the dishes and everything so right away she developed a facial disease to make sure she wouldn't have to be pretty and straight and i caught it on my legs where it turned into poison oak or sumac so i wouldn't have to be straight either and i showed it to everybody i could in order to gift the impersian of being permanently unattractive. those very dangers most dreaded can themselves be encompassed to forestall their actual occurrence. it is notwithstempting by meassures long and limited. venit ut vinceret. she was not educated to be a mother like her mother and like all other mothers who were educated not to be themselves but to be like mothers. a disease is a defense or a deflection. what one should note here is the invention of a discipline of disintegration. she spent another night with a terrible storm raging in her head. she said there was a white cat in a white cadillac with two black people looking out the window. she said a friend of hers was being held against his will in a chinese cookie factory. she says she meets herself coming out of the center she's moving toward. she says she gets tong tied in the face of all this glibness. she says she didn't say this at all and i'm making it all up and that it's extremely unamiable nonsense and i'm a selfindulgent abuser of langwedge and she (?) (writes) i have often resented yr articles for their sloppiness and unintelligibility which she attributes to my frustration and anger not being able to write like a "nice girl" and i throw ketchup bottles in restaurants too and i'm throwing a massive electrickoolaidacidtest for feminists and the oknoid state is the normal state of the well-conditioned endlessly obedient citizen and it requires a good deal of patience and hardwork to be exquisitely sloppy and

immortally unintelligible. magna cum cura. potentissimus au-
dacissimus messissimuss. electra is alone/ on the coast of france
tonight/ she never writes. by being loved one is placed under
an unsolicited obligation. to be eaten doesn't necessarily mean
to lose one's identity. jonah remained very much himself even
within the belly of the whale. i throw last year's rainbow scarf
over my red and black chequered lumber jacket over a striped
vertical candycane shirt over a red and black horizontal striped
undershirt. i walk into midmorning mist my shoelaces trailing
snakes in the wet grass. i've never been impressed with cata-
tonia as a lifestyle. i experience confusion and express bemud-
dlement. i exercise creative modesty based on exhibitionism. i
argue in order to have the pleasure of triumphing over me.
i interiorize these contradictory signal systems. i stop and see
two three four men in orange in kayaks rushing down the
river as if they're in a hurry. i tell jane i'm going to tell everybody she cut a vertical for a bookcase three inches too short.
and she castrated her cat too. and she hates her brother. and
she was reading orwell's the clergyman's daughter and she said
only a man could say a woman has monstrous breasts. that's
zs polliptical as i wisht to be tomorrow. i sd to gregory on the
cristoforo colombo gregory you look really good today if i was
straight i might even find you attractive but then what would
i do with a faggot and his mother's stockbroker claimed i dis-
missed the line as soon as i said it but i didn't i was so pleased
i repeated it and repeated it so i could remember it so i could
speak it abroad long before the sentence is executed, even
before the legal process has been instituted, something terrible
has been done to the accused who is now happily by then in
lisbon or turkey or venice now finally we may be able to begin
to say what it is. what somebody found was incontrovertible
evidence that it all means zero. all that asnide, trust in god,
she will provide. she's a pretty good carpenter but you can't
ask her to come and make bookcases for you. she's the one who
is here who is not all there. she is the one who risks meeting

the lunatic in herself. she is the one who resorts to inappropri-
ate types of rationality to defend her positions. she is the one
who jumps out at you in a new england hotel and says she's
virginia fuller tucker mcilvain perkins circa 1909. she is the
one in a sterile room saying you have oak or sumac or an allergy related mother disease. she is the one who is nine years
old who says her name is now a jennifer harris instead of
whatever it was the day before whatever was the name of her
father. mary kissms. what it is that one becomes is *that* that
that is that it is. certain movements we make can be distinguished clearly as bovine, say. i dreamt a fabulous muscular
woman was crouching ten yards behind an enormous brown &
white dappled cow seated like a dog facing a hurdle and that
the fabulous woman took off as tho in a race and sprang onto
the back of the cow and somersaulted twice and sat upright on
the haunches of the cow who took off in turn for the hurdle
knocking down a board in the jump after which the woman
was seen striding off in her tall muscular legs. i was still using
cortisone and paper towels and scotch tape so it wasn't me. and
all i wanted to do for a week was to go with jennifer to bunky
parker's birthday party. there's some tactical insignificance
about doing anything but living. soap bubbles and the forces
that mold them, as i mentioned a long whirwind ago . . . ceux
qui parlent de revolution . . . sans se referer explicitement a
la vie quotidienne . . . ont dans la bouche un cadavre!

december 21, 1972

GREAT EXPECTORATIONS

tuesday jan. 23 i got on a united flight 769 at newark to go to grand rapids. going to grand rapids was like going to timbuctoo or kalamazoo. it's the sort of place you've always known about and you don't know why, i suppose it has something to do with the name, the name stuck in your mind back when you studied the really important places in geography such as boston or raleigh for being capitals or tobacco centers or something and you just happened to remember places like kalamazoo or tallahassee because they sounded very weird. grand rapids doesn't sound very weird or anything but i can't think of any reason i might know about it except for its name. it's a mythical city like the others. i was actually supposed to be going to this place called allendale to do a talk thing at some obscure college and the woman who invited me was supposed to pick me up and drive me there from the grand rapids airport. i like airports a lot and i'm afraid of strangers so i told this woman on the phone from new york that i'd be arriving at grand rapids at 6 p. m. when in reality my plane was arriving at 3:30, that way i could enjoy myself in the airport and finish my book and find out about grand rapids and observe all the other anonymous strangers. frankly i prefer total strangers to the kind of strangers who expect to make your acquaintance. i like to address them in a familiar offhand way about the time of day or the price of eggs and see what happens. the trouble is in most places in the country you're not supposed to strike up a conversation with strangers, so usually they look at you funny as if they think you're crazy or they look right through you pretending they didn't hear you or they say one thing very short and snappy making it clear they're not interested in associating with strangers. i don't mind too much though. i like to just look around, and overlisten conversations if i can. the first thing i did in the airport at grand rapids i asked the waitress behind the counter in the coffee shop why grand rapids was grand and if they had a rapids there. her name was lorna doone and she didn't know but she asked me about my accent. she thought i had a new york accent. she said that after i told her i came in from new york. that was the extent of our conversation. i started talking to a woman across the counter and she wasn't unfriendly particularly but i stopped because a teenage woman was whispering about me to her mother or her aunt or somebody and i got paranoid. that's why strangers don't talk to each other, the tradition is carried on by the children and the younger people and they're not very inhibited about letting the offenders of the tradition know that it isn't done. i had a good time anyway. i went into the bar and sucked on a couple of martinis and overheard some fragments of a few gruesome stories by a small crowd of rubberneck business jerks sitting next to me at a round table. i wrote down whatever i heard. i go to the people for my stories. a while ago in new york a black woman asked me if i went out among the people and i said right away that i was the people myself and i could tell by the tone of her voice that she thought i was playing with her mind or something and i wish i'd told her that i really do go to the people, at least whenever i happen to be among them. for example on one of my numerous flights from airport to airport this trip around i happened to be sitting next to this type who interested me for some reason, possibly because of his raspberry tweed jacket and his tie that had all these colors running together, more probably because of what he had inside this case he was carrying which he opened up on his lap. it looked like a folded up shovel and there was some other hard indeterminate object and a lot of papers and letters and stuff, and then he started using a calculator and i was more interested than ever so i started in a conversation and i practically interviewed the guy right on the plane. i wanted to hate him naturally, but i found it very difficult, he was totally sincere about everything he said. he was apparently completely happy about being a sales promotion representative or whatever he called it exactly. he was beaming about it in fact and he wasn't threatened in the least by my hostile questions. he said sales and products is what makes the world go round and after a while i got to believing it myself. he said he had one objective in life. what was that, i asked breathlessly. to be the best sales representative he knew how to be he said. and he has a son in college who's going into the same thing. and he has a daughter who thinks she's going to be a nurse. and what does your wife do i asked, as if i didn't know. and then at one point i asked him what his wife might be doing at this very moment and he consulted his watch and said well right now she'd be serving lunch to his son who'd be home from school. i felt then as though i almost hated him and i asked a lot of hostile questions about his products and his attitudes toward them in order to press my advantage but he came off with flying colors. he said certainly he believed absolutely in his products, otherwise why would he be selling them. and besides he gets to choose his own products, if he doesn't like something he doesn't have to sell it, he'd like to sell calculators for example because he believes they're something that can do people some good. the main thing is that he intends to excel in his chosen field. he was in fact at that very moment on his way to a meeting in milwaukee at his own expense to learn something new about his field. i had to say to him finally that i didn't understand why we were getting along and i could only imagine it was because he happened to be the same sign as me and i get along with my own sign and it turned out that he actually was not only my sign but only two days away from me. we were getting off the plane by that time and the last thing he said however was that he gets along with most everybody. he was beaming and waving goodbye, so i realized there was no excuse for not hating him and i wondered what was happening to me. i didn't have to wonder too hard. i had the usual quota of horrible revolutionary experiences on this particular trip, so my sales promotion friend was just some freaky unnatural exception. i almost became a "future stewardess" for instance. i got onto this north central plane from chicago to madison wisconsin i believe it was and as i walked back to the lav i noticed a little boy holding a silver pin of some sort that he got from a tall graysuited steward in a moustache standing in the aisle over a black bag at his feet and i wanted to know right away what it was the boy had been given exactly, i found out it was a "future pilot" pin in the form of a cheap wooden pair of wings painted silver so i asked for one immediately and was presented with some *gold* wings that said "future steward-ess" on them, i'm not kidding. i said c'mon man, whadya think i am anyway, and i handed them back and got the "future pilot" number. i know there's one thing i'm *not* gonna be in my next life and that's a flying waitress. i don't know about being a pilot, but i like the silver wooden wings. and i told the story wherever i went, to all those strangers who logically ex-pect to make your acquaintance. one thing about being in the air for some reason it isn't totally taboo to talk to strangers and since they're *complete* strangers and you feel pretty cer-tain you'll never see anybody again it's a very satisfying ex-perience to make these short artificial intimate communications with alien creatures who feel the same way about you. i wasn't dying to see this woman who'd invited me out to her college, i had some reason to believe that she had great expectations of me. i think she actually expected me to save her or something, i really do, or at least to fall in love with her, which is the same thing i guess. i didn't know this or suspect it until about the third letter i had from her in which she said she thought she loved me although i might be too tough for her and then i was afraid to go. it gets me how anybody can decide they love somebody or think much of anything else about them when they've never even laid eyes on them. i don't think i even ever thought that way about ingrid bergman. the thing is though that i could tell i really liked this woman, from her letters and poems and everything, and i didn't mind coming along to be outrageous for the revolution on her behalf in the middle of amerika's great wasteland and all, but i can't see being *personally* the object of anybody's expectations in the name of the revolution, i see myself as a medium for transmitting the ideas and that's about all. otherwise i hope to get away from it all and to be transported around from building to building or air-port to airport like a visiting sales promotion expert and to be idolized a little bit from a distance and to hear something new about the world. so i was sort of drinking myself to death in the airport there at grand rapids by the time 6 o'clock rolled around and my woman was due to meet me. the culture en-courages women to instigate the crimes of passion for which the woman is then condemned. i'm trying not to expect very much from other women myself. i expect a lot from myself but if anybody condemns me i want to be the one to do it. i like to trot out my credentials as a cosmic personality in the hopes of not being considered anything in particular at all. this is close to that old forgotten feeling that you can't stay on the earth for another minute. anyway i guess i have to say i survived grand rapids and allendale and my sponsor and all her friends and i went on to bigger and worse things in madi-son via chicago and in ann arbor via milwaukee and detroit. i even found out what grand rapids is all about, as i suppose everybody else knows they make furniture there and they go to church a lot, church is a big thing. that's what barbara the poet told me on the drive back to the airport after doing my tricks out at her college. some people say there was a big cloud of literal consciousness repression during the '50s, well i don't see how the world is that much different, it's true that a lot of amerikans have blown their heads out on one thing or another, but anyplace you go in amerika outside of freaksville on a few city streets or deep in the boonies on a clump of god's lost acre you see the same old people in permanents and sears dresses and patent leather pocketbooks hanging on their crewcut beer bellied old men about whom you know damn well they'd *never* talk to a stranger, so i don't see how anything has changed significantly, although sometimes i'm more optimistic i didn't feel optimistic a bit after i was almost arrested for disorderly contact or rather conduct in the grand rapids airport on my way back out of there. i was standing at the north central ticket counter with barbara getting a ticket for chicago and madison and asking the saleswoman how the planes were today, i always do that, as a matter of form i ask if the planes are nice and safe today, it's sort of a superstition i suppose, and they *always* smile a little patronizingly and say yes the planes are fine or something like that, they might even mumble a line about the excellent record of the airlines, anyway they know it's a game and they figure i'm a harmless nut, sometimes i even throw in that they must think i'm crazy, just to vaguely apologize for asking their indulgence; well for some reason this woman in grand rapids was very uptight about my questions concerning the safety of her planes and the more defensive she got naturally the more alarmed i became, especially since i was querying her in particular about the two recent crashes at chicago, where i happened to be landing, and at one point i asked her *why* she was so uptight, i don't remember what she said, she was scribbling out my ticket, and around that moment some pinstriped business dude came up along behind me prac- tically snorting down my neck and saying something like you're holding the rest of us up too which wasn't true and i swore a big mess of stuff at him and also told him to get his fucking dirty feet off my jacket and the woman handed me my change and we walked away all puffy and huffy when i realized i didn't have my ticket. then what happened barbara walked back to get it and the woman told her she couldn't give me a ticket and she was calling the security guards, can you imagine that, i was really floored and wanted to get the hell out of there so i lined up across the way at united who would also take me to chicago, and the men there said yes and smiled the usual bemused smile the planes were fine today, but along came these scary characters in their navy blues and guns and holsters hauling us back to some office, it was maddening and embarrassing and upsetting but i thought i could handle it because i'm very cool with the cops, i really am, and what i did i put on my best wasp new england posture and accent and all and just kept quietly insisting in a tone of injured dignity or something that this man had been extremely *rude*, which he was. of course these security officials were on *his* side all the way, and *he* hadn't even registered a complaint. they kept barking about how he was a "professional man" and when barbara wanted to know what they meant by asking if the official *knew* him the official said "no, but i know his title" but whatever it was his attire made him innocent obviously, and i thought to myself that's how all these business suits in washington get away with their wars, if you're a man in a business suit you can do anything you goddam please, including being rude at ticket counters. anyway the main thing was that "ladies" don't use "four letter words" in kent county michigan. the fact is i guess that i upset the whole airport by being a lady and yelling at this dude that he should go home and fuck his fucking father and that's how i almost got arrested in the middle of amerika's great wasteland of churches and furniture and whatnot. i said listen i've never been in kent county michigan before but i'll probably happily never return and in the meantime here's looking at you or some such inanity and i couldn't wait to get out of there. the incident cost me eight bucks in a different air fare and i was pretty shook up. i was waiting for the plane and standing at a phone booth calling the voice with a margarita at my elbow, and that's not allowed in kent county michigan either, old gun and holster came up and said i'd better get that drink back to the bar. i was sure by that time they didn't like the way i looked which happened to be a lot of dull silver studs and rhinestones on a denim number from the london jeans machine place. i suppose when you go out into the land of the bible belt and all its good citizens you should wear something that's considered to be legitimately color co-ordinated at least. possibly i added a fragment of instant cre-dentials when i acquired my "future pilot" wings on the flight from chicago to madison. anyway my sales promotion friend didn't seem to mind the way i looked. he just commented that i didn't have on a "gown" or anything. that was his idea of being funny. anyway generally it's impossible to look right out in these areas if you want to feel really good about the way you look yourself unless of course you still feel great looking the way everybody else looks and that means being daring in a color coordinated pants suit i would guess. i'm not interested in clothes at all particularly, sometimes i have an "attack" and go out all over the place searching for something i decide i think i really need, otherwise i don't care that much any more, except for my various blue jackets, one day i realized they were all blue, that may be because the whole world is still my board-ing school where the navy blue blazer was the most impressive aspect of our uniforms since they were decorated every year with the chevrons and such of our athletic achievements, i donno, what i'm trying to arrive at saying actually is that when people are arrested for the way they look it seems like clothes are something to really think about. i think if i'd been dressed to the nines like any good housekeeper on her way from city to city they wouldn't've cared that much about my four-letter words for which they said they wanted to arrest me. they said that "ladies" don't use "four-letter words" but the point prob-ably was that i didn't look like a "lady" in the first place. this whole lady culture is getting me down. the ladies look terrible and i'm not attracted to them any more either. they can't run properly should they be in trouble and they smell of cosmetics and they look all stuffed into somebody else's idea of themselves and they can't tolerate the rest of us. if they'd just *smile* and be friendly. how *can* they be friendly when they look so awful. i told gregory about michigan and he said he doesn't think

about the people in michigan, or what they wear, it's all ridiculous, he's given up thinking about it, he just goes out there to
do his lecture, then rushes back to play with his trains. he has
a set of toy trains. and he's back to wearing suits and ties because he can't stand looking the way everybody else looks. it's
pretty confusing. who is everybody exactly. is everybody our
friends or is everybody Them. i guess for gregory everybody
is our or rather *his* friends and the implication is that *we* all
look alike too and going among his friends he has to wear the
uniform of Them out there in order to feel different, which
may be the way you feel really good about the way you look.
there's something in other words about feeling the same and
there's something about feeling different too. i like resembling
my friends and i like looking different Out There and i like
being different from my friends too and very often i wish i
looked more like Them. it's all mixed up i think actually. i still
prefer my stompers to any other type of shoe since i discovered
stompers but i haven't yet succumbed to the street dyke uniform of overalls, i don't care to look shapeless before my time.
i didn't want to get into this clothes business at all particularly.
i was leading up to my encounter in ann arbor michigan and
the ultimate impossibility as i now see it of looking any way
at all. before i forget it i have to say right away that it's all
very well for gregory to get back into suits and ties but what
would i get back into if i was suddenly tired of looking like
everybody else who happen in my case to be sensible revolutionary women who dress for comfort and play and mobility
and with an invisible or aggressive appearing unavailability to
the man. some dykes for example are monochromatically invisible, and some are polemically obvious in overalls and baseball bats. or lavender armbands. or visors and leather chaps. i'm
sort of kidding. i did meet two incredible women up north a
couple of weeks ago however who might be said to've resem-
bled a complete set of dickens bound in cowhide. i watched in
amazement as they gathered themselves together to leave.

leather chaps. leather boots. leather shirts. leather vests. leather coats. leather gloves. leather hats. leather accessories. leather *every* thing. i've heard they even have leather pillow cases and leather candle holders! i want to visit their leather house and read a leather book on their leather bound toilet. some people do manage to be truly different! the thing is they have a leather business. a lot of leather ingenuity goes into all that packaging. i don't like leather that much but i admire the way they appear to be different both from Them and from Everybody Else. and how they can undoubtedly appear with better credibility out among Them since leather is a valued and somewhat unavailable middle class commodity. and they certainly look unapproachable to the man. the straight women by the way in contrast to dykedom seem to be arrayed around on the streets or wherever like decoys. i wonder often what it is that the straight *feminists* want, since they claim to be fighting the same war, the strategy of the disarmament of rapists or men, rape coming in many seductions as germaine wrote in playboy last month, is as serious as i intended to be here, i'm always serious, anyway i wish they'd start wearing overalls and if they did i would too, why should i care about looking shapeless before my time anyway. another good question. and according to the ann arbor auto mechanic dykes i should cut off my hair! that's what i was coming to. a lot of women poured into a room in a building on the university campus on two days notice to view the dyke from new york who in turn was curious to see the fabled stompers of ann arbor who indeed were there. one somewhat femmy woman put her foot in her hair right off by declaring that bed was her own business and a rather fierce dialogue ensued basically over the length of her hair. at last i can tell my wendy wonderful hair story. a year or two back wendy wonderful was at a feminist demonstration where these women on a stage were cutting off their hair, saying that men play with your hair, and wendy yelled from the back why don't you cut off your breasts too, men play with your breasts.

i don't know what kind of a political argument that is, but i identify with the hair problem, and i care about my breasts as well, and i don't like to be personally attacked over my own disarmament solutions. at the same time i appreciate the short hair position. i think the position is that some dykes think that femmy women in their long hair are soliciting male protection as opposed to male assault. i believe it works both ways and many combinations thereof. not all guys want to assault and/or protect any particular woman. i don't want to solicit assault no matter what, i do want the protection they offer from their own kind and that's why i get along with the cops, who're not necessarily your ultimate protectors or anything, i know i know, essentially i don't want anything at all from them except good manners and better contracts. well it was a hairy scene in ann arbor. i was beginning to be overwhelmed by new waves of strangers too. i'd just come in from madison and about 200 women in a chapel, it's really a strain greeting that many people you don't know who appear to know you. the dykes in madison however were a lot more lesez faire. i told all my stories and got away with looking exactly the way i did, or so i assumed since nobody criticized me. i hate to be criticized. also every month i get pregnant and when it's close to delivery time i'm very sensitive. nevertheless i told the most critical of the ann arbor women that i'd consider seriously my use of the word kid to designate a child. i won't cut off my hair and i won't stop using the word fuck to coopt male language to throw it back at them if i have to, that is in every place excepting kent county michigan. actually i appreciate being challenged on political grounds. the tyranny of normal consciousness is a certain political smugness over the rightness of your own current set as well as other types of consciousnesses and i like to add and subtract effects if the spirit is willing like i have a new gallows humor laugh and a new way of saying yes that appeals to me and yesterday i asked jane to cut my split ends. i just don't like any sort of skinhead fascism.

we all went through that as bobby soxers. the thing is there isn't any consistency anywhere anyway. it's a joke. the short-hair stompers and overalls who was criticizing me the most for instance and who was preparing to leave this house where we'd repaired after the room on the campus, i asked her as a matter of form was she going to some other house where perchance of course she lived with her own group of women or something like that, and she looked me right in the eye and said no, she lived with a man. —! see, so nothing makes any sense, or else everything is all about transition. and when we *arrive,* what will *that* look like. most of the time i was trying to relax, like a wet sandwich. there i was draping over a chair at some desk behind my aviator blues telling desultory stories in a mellow alcoholic haze of the bloody marys off the last plane trip when one totally sober stomper said Why are you sitting up there in front of us, Why aren't we in a circle? i wanted to say why did you come here, but i said Do It, and they Did It. and we were then in a circle and i continued telling stories and all but i really began to feel like crying, being pregnant and such, and i wanted to be home, and see Everybody Else who looks familiar. one reassuring thing happened however and that was a religious type (i presumed) in femme boots and a leather fringe who came up and shook my hand and said you're a very evolved being, that's the phrase those people use, she seemed a sort of ascetic variation of the frontier chick (that's barbara the poet), whom i had left two days before in grand rapids, and who had also criticized me, for not reading my stuff lovingly enough she'd said. although otherwise she liked me fine, too fine in fact i thought. she told me before i arrived she'd informed her class that i wouldn't be "nice." she was certain i wouldn't be nice. so she expected it. i suspected she really wanted me not to be in order to satisfy some butch fatale expectations of some sort. she herself was more or less just the way i expected to find *her* according to photos and descriptions and poems etc. tall beautiful romantic frontier femme drag earth mother and mother of two beautiful daughters out in the middle of nowheresville amerika between various impossible worlds. 20 years of a straight marriage done and gone. one daughter off with her own beautiful daughter. the other aged 13 living with her and her transitional mate whom she de-scribed as 17 years younger and who wears earrings and femmy clothes, etc. i called the morning i left new york and said i don't stay in houses where there's guys. i don't know why she'd expect me to be any less uptight than all the women of the midwest who're supposed to be in love with her and be uptight because as she wrote they get pissed off at her for living with this man. not that i was dying to jump into bed with her sight unseen or seen or anything at all including being in love which is a state i don't understand too well these days anyway, but i'll tell you i'm not rescuing any woman personally from a man and moreunder i can't even work up a sufficient attraction to do it. i don't think i could do it for the queen, and that's be-cause i look at a woman who's cohabiting with a guy (*especially a faggot* for chrissake), and i see her as a cocksucker in the literal sense of that term and i have instant repulsive reactions like i don't want to be contaminated or something, i'm really serious. i don't even want to say will you teach me to love you and leave you in just one night. i didn't want to be responsible for anything whatsoever except reading my stuff materoffactly the way i do and fielding the same old questions about how women must have as hard a time getting it on together as women and men and such and as i mentioned being idolized a little bit from a distance and hearing something new about the world. as simone said when she got into my german racer the other day and noticed the raggedy ann and the teddy bear why don't you just tell them you're a little girl. but i always think they know that already. i'm going out to get a set of toy trains too. if they're waiting for me to grow up, i'll make sure to stunt my growth. anyway i didn't feel great about not being able to save the beautiful frontier woman of the midwest. it isn't by the way that she hasn't made it with women before either. the way i heard it in fact she did every thing at once at the end of the old straight marriage. feminism women the faggot the works i guess. a couple of women brought her out sexually and she brought them out politically she said. the question is what next. and i didn't have any answers. she's a good feminist, what's she living with a faggot for. i donno. how should i know. she's scared. me too. we were standing by her car in the parking lot waiting for the old man with the keys to go to the airport, here i am way along in my story and i'm still leaving the grand rapids airport!, there was this awkward silence, so i tugged on her scarf a bit and said whatsa matter, and she moved over and i had to hug her and i even sort of kissed her, it was very embarrassing, i'm pretty reticent actually, and she said oh she was gonna say something silly but then she thought better of it. i'm glad. it was bad enough at the airport when i kissed her again, this time goodbye, and she said she wished i'd fallen in love with her. see what i mean? everything is hopeless. shit, the faggot is her woman for the time being so so what, the whole world is living in the time being. at last i was leaving the grand rapids airport and saying goodbye to the woman the whole midwest is in love with. i've never written totally about one of these college junkets before and now i suppose it's becoming my winter odyssey. i want to convey every detail. the color of their hair and the size of their houses. i had an indian dinner in a wonderful house on stilts at the top of many stone steps overlooking lake michigan when the sun was going down. i met a fantastic woman called rachel in the cafeteria of this thomas jefferson college. i met terry the dyke and copied some of her writing out of her journal into mine. i saw ann wehrer from the old days because she met me at the detroit airport and drove me into ann arbor. i met a woman who was unable to tell me her life in a shorter time than it took to live it. i have a letter here from a woman in madison thanking me for the confusion and the excitement i created. i learned about riot control architecture on college campuses. i threw a male student out of a class at that thomas jefferson place by threatening his life with a coke can. i had a very interesting time. i always do. and i'm almost always anxious to leave soon after i get there, in order to see what the next place is like. i don't like either fulfilling or disappointing peoples expectations. i think expectations are oldfashioned. if i expected a tornado tomorrow what would i do about it anyway. nothing neutral and detached and intellectually pertinent ever happens. you always have to be fulfilling and disappointing. your image has preceded you in an absolute riot of expectations. everybody thinks that you and your image are the same thing. they don't even realize that the only thing that actually exists is your image. expectations are all about images. if i expect a tornado tomorrow i form an image of it in my mind. if i don't expect it why should i think about it. my conclusion therefore is that it isn't wise to go anyplace at all. let them come to you and see how you don't actually exist. you sit all alone in a new england winter reading books and playing vivaldi. you try to get more involved in snow shovels and things, be a little bit more outer directed. a very regular life. an outrageous person who leads a routine life. a big irresistible force that leads you toward whatever the future will be. the force of the unexpected moment. if you lead a daily life and it is all yours. last week sk told me there's gotta be an environment where we can relax and assume that we're all god. this is definitely not the environment on the college circuit. being god means not thinking about anything in advance of its happening. being god means not existing. in the meantime if we insist on accepting invitations to places we have to put up with our images. i've learned a great deal about myself that way. not all of it very reassuring. most of it not very good at all in fact. i leave a wave of disappointment behind me and fly away with terrible guilt tremors. the very act of leaving is a disappointment. that's basically why it's wise not to go anyplace. arrivals and departures in themselves are the original expectant forms of fulfillment and disappointment. the first mistake is existence. that's why we worship god. we don't remember how we got here and we know it was a mistake. then we make things worse by moving around creating expectations, unless you travel all the time without going anywhere the way gregory does. staying still is the earthly form of being god, like a tree. or launching yourself into orbit, like a radio satellite. that's how i got to be god a few times, by launching myself into orbit. a snow shovel or a head of lettuce can become holy that way too. of course we *are* in orbit here on earth, but not enough of us know it yet. people haven't read bucky's operating manual for spaceship earth. or they have and they think *bucky* is god. that means they think he exists. we're all under the illusion that we exist, i am too, when i go someplace i have my own expectations. i'll never be god until i stop thinking i exist. all of this explains why people don't mind other people so much when they're dead. existence is very threatening. of course death is disappointing too. the price of arrival. the kind of god who is said to exist is an icon and icons are always crucified. an icon is an image. there's no hope for images. images come and go. god doesn't come and go. god is my unexpected moment. god is not my expectation at all. god is me in the new england winter getting more involved in snow shovels. i think i can perfect my image by staying home. i love going places though. besides by the time you're 88½ you don't have to go anyplace to have bad things happen to you, they're working on your image all the time. i heard that salinger disappeared into a cabin in the woods forever and i suppose what they say about him is he's some sort of crazy recluse. you and i may think that's a good thing to be but other people have other ideas. other people always have ideas, that's the trouble, the whole world is about other people. other people who don't know other people develop ideas about them, so we all have these big ideas about other people. the other people are the

strangers i was talking about. strangers everywhere. the strangest experience i ever had at one of these colleges was at this
place called albright in reading pennsylvania. for some reason
that nobody seemed to understand including me and the people who invited me i was the keynote speaker for this spring
arts festival, and the reason it was incomprehensible was that
there wasn't a single dyke on the premises that i could determine, and the level of their feminism was cosmopolitan or
redbook advice to teenagers, thus there was a kind of mutual
embarrassment all the way around and in fact near the end of
it my own sense of the unintelligibility of the occasion was
confirmed when a woman told me confidentially that when
they heard that this Lesbian was coming to the campus and she
was going to *sleep in a dormitory* they went around psst
psssting to everybody that they'd better lock their doors, can
you imagine that? well that was one place whose expectations
were completely satisfied, i didn't get to sleep with anybody.
the first thing people think about is sex. that's one reason i
liked that woman rachel in the cafeteria at allendale michigan
so much, all she wanted was for barbara and me to straighten
out her life. i have a letter here from barbara in fact saying
contrary to all my expectations that my visit was just what she
(barbara) needed and she feels like she's getting so strong she's
almost a goddess! it's a good thing i left. i'm terrified of goddesses. she rightly i suppose identifies herself as the Mother,
who has more *power*. i'd seen her already as the earth mother
but i thought that was just a frontier style, women for the
festival of life and all that, the women that is who still bake
bread and string beads and sew patches on their old mens
denims. i know i think a lot of women are confused between
their Mother and their Daughter aspects. it hasn't been allowed for one thing for the Daughters to remain the Daughters. i for one had to pretend to be a Mother before i could
get to be my Daughter again. some children look like ancient
crones and they probably are. i think one of these days we're

going to separate the Mothers from the Daughters so we can
be clearer about ourselves. i want basically to be with my
Daughter clan, with an occasional visit from the powerful
Mother, who casts good spells and stuff. i just spoke to danny
and i asked him if he was the Son or the Father (i think he's
more the Son) and he said he sees himself as the Son being
cast a lot in the role of Father. but i don't want to get into
that. the thing is sometimes i can't figure out what anybody is
supposed to do. in the cafeteria it was very clear. here was a
confused desperate Daughter and her Mother and her Daughter had all the answers. that is, we recorded back her own
words more or less, we heard her and bounced it back until i
supposed she believed her own self. what was happening was
she'd been living up in the hills in a clever original house that
she herself had built with her boyfriend and now their relationship was so lousy that she was afraid to even go there since
he'd smashed some of her sculpture, she's a sculptor too, and
was beating her up sometimes like the very night i was due to
talk there he beat her up and she couldn't come and so forth,
but i suppose she loved the house and the main thing was she
felt some responsibility to a project she'd committed herself to
on the campus and she didn't know what to do. i'm sure she
split. she was living her future already. it takes a while for the
images to catch up. the trouble was she couldn't be god where
somebody was fucking around with her image that way. she
was big and beautiful with strong features and dark eyes and
a builders hands. anyway so i got to feel like i helped save
somebody. and i didn't have to jump into bed or anything. one
reason i flew away from there with those guilt tremors was
that i believe inadvertently i turned on a student and promptly
ran away from her when i realized what'd happened. there
was a neat party at barbara's after i talked and we were all
dancing a lot and i forget that for some women if you have
bodily contact with another woman in the act of dancing or
whatever, it means instant sex or the prospect of some great

romance or possibly even a lifelong marriage, who knows, but i got up to dance with this woman and suddenly she was very hot and bothered and saying things like she didn't know whether she was ready for this, and i untangled us immediately, rather tactfully too i thought, and made some excuse for going someplace else, *she* might not've known whether she was ready for it whatever it was but i knew myself. then the next day in that house on stilts at the top of the stone steps overlooking lake michigan she was there and she said suddenly to the assembled company that she was *very* confused and didn't know what to do, she felt like she was ready to come out, so how was i supposed to feel, and what could anybody do. nothing. i'm sure she's come out. she's come out in her mind so she's come out. i don't put much stock in the images at all as i've been saying. the world is mind. and other people have other ideas, etcetera. who cares about other people. nobody does, that's the trouble. then it comes to you that you can do anything as long as it's not you and you refuse to recognize yourself in the street. the whole matter of focusing on the problem is one of the large penalties for having one. the first point to note about biographies is that we assume an individual can really have only one of them. this being guaranteed by the law of physics rather than that of society. physics is images. as terry the dyke said when a woman in her class walked by us everybody's her business. terry was up there on lake michigan too. that's where i copied some stuff out of her journal into mine. i had an embarrassing scene with barbara there too, although it wasn't the end of the world or anything. she arrived and handed me my cheque in an envelope and with it or rather on top of it a pink candy heart that said kiss me. then she tactfully disappeared. she went into the kitchen to find out from her friend ingy what happened when i threw this male student out of ingy's class. while she was gone i was fooling around with the plastic bag of candy hearts and sort of looking for one myself when accidentally one fell on the floor and it said ask me so i gave it to barbara when she came back but i don't think she thought i meant it and i didn't. after all, she's the powerful Mother. i don't mind being attacked by and mauled somehow occasionally by the Mother, but what's the Daughter herself supposed to do. anyway as i'm thinking about it now and tallying up a few experiences with the Mothers i see that oftentimes what's happening is that the Mother is living with her Son, the hermes or the dionysus, the faggot in other words, the one who refused to become the Father, and come the revolution she begins to perceive her Daughter, the persephone, her daughter the dyke, her lost old self, and she goes out looking just the way the myth says she does, but either it's been so long that she's forgotten how to look, or she doesn't look long and hard enough, or something, i dunno, i know i can't do much myself with the old Son there lurking in the background, especially when the old Mother is sort of challenging me in this ultimate way like that if i don't come across me myself in person she the Mother will then feel justified in giving up the pursuit of her Daughter in order to linger on with the Son. you know what i mean? i could give two other examples of this contemporary drama, but i wouldn't want other persons living or dead to misunderstand what i'm trying to say. it happens always in different guises. i'm just beginning to catch the pattern. the last time it happened the Mother was very explicit and demanding. i thought she was kidding. the trouble was we Daughters were challenging this Mother to death ourselves. it was a mutual mistake. she was coming on to the Daughters, and maybe even another Mother or two, i don't really know who's what truthfully, and she had the Son back at the old homestead. it sounds like grendel and beowulf somehow, i don't know why. anyway it was hopeless, i was enjoying myself with another Daughter, and i wasn't going to save her from the Son anyhow for sure, and she was pretty angry about it in the end, even though we managed to present her with the ultimate Daughter, a seven foot amazon princess, that was hopeless too, since the amazon princess had her own Daughter, and between the lot of us in the end she could feel universally justified in keeping a *harem* of goddam Sons, for all i knew, or cared. i cared, but it's all still too much about images. expectations. arrivals and departures. i'm vowing to make small decisions that're in opposition to the existing order of things. snow shovels and such. it doesn't matter whether you go anyplace or not. the best thing that happened to me this trip around was ending up in albany late at night with just enough cash for a motel, the fine absurdity of going to albany because there wasn't a plane into new york and you just wanted to be in the state of new york so you take whatever they have and that means you don't know *what's* going to happen to you tomorrow . . .

february 15, 1973

THERE'LL AWE WAYS BE AN ENGLAND

well i went to england and i didn't see any feminists nor too
much of anybody else and i was neurotically famished and ra-
tionally cold and determinedly homesick and righteously paranoid but in nine or ten days i figured out the country and that
was what i went for so it was an awful and worthwhile trip.
the first thing i did i went to sleep for six hours on the top floor
of roy jenkins's house on ladbroke square. the next thing i
woke up and called george and peter and suzi and charlotte
and carolee and i forget who else but the only person who
answered was peter who told me there was an r. d. laing soiree
of some sort going on at eight at a paul somebody's house and
i should go and i did i left roy jenkins's house on ladbroke
square and never returned, much no doubt to the relief of
whomever was there who never saw me as i was whisked up
the carpeted stairways as though i was a poor relation of one
of the cooks or something. anyway i took a cab over to this
paul's house and thought how wonderful and clean looking
london is and how all its cars are shiny and sleek in their small
interesting economical designs, no dirty old crates all over the
place, and i came to my first sweeping conclusion about england
as i pondered the outstanding fact that none of its taxis are
bent out of shape, they're spotless and scratchless and scru-
pulously immaculate and i decided this must reveal the character of the english in conjunction with their space which
compared to ours is relatively small. later george told me this
was ridiculous, that the taxis in england are built like trucks
and the english are *always* having accidents, they drive around
like demons as if they know what they're doing but they don't,
and in any case the taxis he would've led me to believe can
sustain the onslaught of a sherman tank and come out looking brand new the way they all look. i've never seen an accident in england, and what rosemary told me was that the

english are very frightened of touching each other. whether benign or repressed the fact is that it's a lot easier and nicer getting around since the people watch where they're going and are forever politely excusing themselves at any real or imagined contact, and i assume this is because their character has been molded by tight quarters and short distances, the pushy ones left long ago to invade plymouth and boston and cross the rockies and develop a real amerikan sense of arrogant limitlessness etc., which i suppose includes a capacity for grand and gratuitous generalizations based on any fleeting observation and delivered with great confidence at the slightest provocation. nevertheless, i did find out what england is all about. it's all about my father, who died more or less when england did. the english are somewhat dead. amerikans may be brash and crude and ugly in a lot of ways, there's no doubt we're a beastly lot actually, but we are alive, there's no question we're alive, even if we're alive with desperation and delusions and crooked impossible schemes for saving the universe and a greedy consuming materialism and a grubby untidy incestuous belligerance, whatever it is and however unpleasant, we are by comparison with a country like england alarmingly alive. all features great & small. can you imagine for instance that as dead an amerikan as andy w. is up in lights over the title of his flick trash at picadilly circus which is like our times square? or what may be equally significant that an amerikan as nervously alive as me arrives in england always possible naively expecting the england of the representation in my new record book in the form of a photo blueprint made by jane of these suffragists around the turn of the century being led away violently by the bobbies outside buckingham palace? i mean that we can't even go someplace, and someplace for that matter which may be quite contented with its demise, without projecting our own agitation and restlessness which we think is being alive. i went quite dead in england anyway, i always catch the spirit. at the laing soiree at paul somebody's house i even exercised a bit of will power and restrained myself by not charging vocally into the excellent silences which at times would overtake the company. the company by the way was a large group of people packed tightly into a living room of a high ceiling, sitting on the floor in curving banks against the walls and facing the master with what i assumed to be a rever- ent attention awaiting the first utterances. i'm sure it was un- amerikan for me to be there at all, it was certainly unfeminist, and although i respected the silences i did find the opportunity to more or less deplore my own attendance by being no doubt brash and crude and hopelessly undeferential and altogether predictably amerikan. old r. d. was getting off some good stuff too, stuff about the impossibility of relationships and all that should cross all race color age and sex lines and interest abso- lutely everybody, and i was certainly interested, and i even tossed in some two cents on the subject, i said if you want to know i said something smartassed about how it seems to me that any form of detachment, i. e. zen or yogurt, is another kind of attachment, a very deep comment, but essentially i realized at some point that i'd hate for anybody to think i really wanted to be there, in other words that i might have any intention of becoming an initiate into the london laing circle, a group of sycophants if ever i saw any. i know i'm full of contradictions on a subject like this, going and then trying to deny that one has even gone, and such, but that's the nature of my involvement in whatever vestiges of admiration i still retain for men, among whom i have to still say i think laing is a pretty good head. i even went out of my way, arising from the london apathy, to go over to his house in belsize park and have tea and cheese cake and admire his 2½ yr. daughter and his beautiful german wife jutta and compliment his style in refusing to take advantage of the authority vested in him at such as these soirees by meandering awkwardly or haltingly in and around his subject without appearing to answer anything. the purpose of my visit may have been however to sort of apologize for my own appearance at the salon by saying that i would consider it humiliating to personally publicly invest any man with that authority etc etc, it's a hopeless contradiction i suppose. possibly the purpose of the visit was to talk to jutta who's a fine person besides being beautiful, and she didn't make me feel as if i had to convert her to anything, she might actually be satisfied living with the most amenable psychoanalyst of the western world. i don't know. i called joe berke too and he thinks r. d. l. is a terrific chauvinist (i suppose berke isn't), and tho' he has great respect for him he can't work with him any more, it's impossible he said to be around him without being a sychophant, and all he talks about these days is what he has for breakfast and how many baths he takes a day. there are in fact now in london two sets of communities, freakout houses modeled after the original kingsley hall, and berke is involved in the set that isn't laing's set, in fact i imagine berke and a couple of associates formed a splitoff community, it sounds like the professional jealousies that arose around freud. we are reminded of the brief nature of earthly power and glory. berke of course is an amerikan, in case that makes a difference, and i for one think it does. i wonder if r. d. would've branched out at all, i mean get all involved in therapeutic communities and other extroversions if the amerikans hadn't sped across the atlantic in the first place in search of the english guru of psychology beside whom i'm suddenly imagining they rallied to the cause and rushed to the barricades of one sort or another, always of course respecting those intermittent silences. i have to say by the way about these silences that they're probably the most alive thing in england, these pregnant silences, silences by which we might enliven our own hysterical gatherings. characteristic again of the amerikan space of which perhaps we have too much. always rushing in to fill it all up. terrified no doubt of what might happen if we don't. we might die. yeah. well, i don't know truthfully *how* dead or alive the english are, but one thing is certain and that is it's impossible

to get to know them. and i think now that that's the real reason i always go dead there. i want to integrate totally with the
situation. i begin speaking a polyglot of english accents as soon
as i disembark and very quickly i become as difficult to get to
know as the natives. i go to sleep more or less, even after recovering from the time lag trauma. not however until after
i've been variously and repeatedly discouraged, learning my
lesson anew each time as it were. the day after the laing affair
i charged with bright amerikan anticipation out of george's
place on dorset square into the gray london winter expecting
god knows what and wound up being dizzy as a drunk dog in
the mill of foreigners meaning english people on charing cross
road walking up to tottenham court in and out of these highly
confusing bookstores buying a satchels worth of history and
the grail, i thought i was going down or taking off, the dis-
orientation was intense, until i brought myself into order by
clugalugging two glasses of milk in a wimpy bar, and began
already to feel chastened by the english chill, if only because as
an amerikan i expect a lot to happen and suddenly all that's
happening is that you're disoriented by streetsful of very polite
and remote dead strangers. their avowed impulses are only
part of their entire attitude. i have no idea what their attitudes
are in the least. but i must admit that the analyses and conclusions i reached were corroborated by one englishman and one
amerikan man, and in a sense by rosemary who reiterates that
the english are simply repressed. i met colin naylor at the salis-
bury pub, he's the editor of arts & artists, and he said very
cheerily that everything is quiet here, under the table, that it's
usually in the form of a nervous breakdown when anybody in
this country begins expressing themselves. and it was george
(walsh), gregory's friend, who said what i suspected when it
occurred to me that england was dead and so was my father,
the two events being causally connected somehow, and that
was that the individuals in england feel however consciously
or un- that their country is a 3rd rate power and that what-

ever they do won't make a difference particularly, which is why you get that muted or "given up" sensation when you disembark, and that by contrast naturally the amerikans do feel that what we do will make a difference and that's because we live in a greedy aggrandizing imperialist pig world power place, which is what england used to be. the whole place seething with savage enthusiasm. yet i don't imagine for a second that the working classes in england have been affected one way or the other by the alteration in their country's fortunes. i have more to say about that, and this and that. anyone may think i went over in this terrible time of year just for the hell of it but i really had a purpose and the trip was successful because i found out what i wanted to know, no fooling around. other than that, i'll probably continue making these devastating journeys, the fantasy is still very much alive. there'll awe ways be an england. (beware the ideas of march).

march 8, 1973

OH VADER & MOEDER GODDELIJK

LONDON: I thought Holland was all about tulips and wooden shoes. I didn't see a windmill either. To the ordinary foreigner Amsterdam is a city of dope sex canals and cyclists. It's the United Nations of hippiedom. The capital of the bizarre. Nobody seems to care or notice. It takes place while anyone else is eating or opening a window or just walking dully along. The Dutch themselves are a decent agreeable people. They don't pretend not to understand you like the French. Their facilities are well organized. Their money is attractive and helpfully moronic. Their manners are embarrassingly modest. They all speak English and if they don't they'll accept your miserable French or participate in a goon show of sign language. They're extremely tolerant of boorish and paranoid Americans. It's a fine place to experience your annual nervous breakdown for a day. In London the opportunities for heroism are relatively meagre since the Empire is over and foreign color is absorbed or quarantined by the British chill and reserve. I did my best wearing the gay revolution button, and thumbing my nose in the airport at some schoolgirls who were at least giggling after me, and discussing with Kate Millett the radical action of necking in the last row of a striptease in London she thought was the only thing to do in that particular sexist context. She said it was depressing. I said it was an experience. I suppose it's counterrevolutionary not to think it's depressing. But we could be defending them at the risk of their lives. The case against such an ancient theatrical tradition could be indelicate and interminable. Anyway the objections of two American lesbians dropping in on a London striptease can't be too convincing. What we might be deploring is the quality here and the quantity elsewhere. One can always make a career out of disapproving of whatever it is that makes life agreeable for somebody who, say, has the power to rescue people from their sexual boredom. Amsterdam is rampant with hard porn and prostitutes and preverities. I had just arrived and had just reeled out of 717 Keisersgracht where phase one of some annual divine punishment had begun and across a little bridge over a canal balancing in a glass the last of the first good bottle of a Dutch red wine when my person was solicited by two whores of Amsterdam sitting on a stoop. Are you a lesbian? —Yes. —Well we like that, especially. Twenty-five gulden for 30 minutes they said. I saddown to talk to them. One advertised herself by frowzing her hair to a calculated disorder and arranging her dress to pop up her breasts. The other was a drag queen or a transsexual and I didn't want to go to bed to find out which. Not that I could make it with a transsexual in any case. I've got enough confusion in my life. But then I thought of my column. It could be a five star sex scoop. I looked at them closely, in particular the drag queen or transsexual. Would they rob and murder and mutilate me after they tied me and beat me and strung me up by the toes? Oh vader and moeder goddelijk, I'd better not, I decided not to die in the line of duty. And my friends across the street were in no mood to support me in an amorous misadventure. I wanted to go back and plead that I had been guilty only of an indiscretion, not a crime, but I couldn't create a confession appropriate to anything at all, so I demonstrated our collective savagery by inadvertently destroying an object belonging to the forebearing Dutchman who owned the place, all because it seemed that the murmuring of disturbing confidences or biting allusions or preposterous inferences had deteriorated into marvelous tirades of insults and denunciations to which one could only respond by a theatrical nervous breakdown. Death in Vensterdam. And I wasn't thinking about the column. Every phrase and every sentence is an end and a beginning . . . And any action is a step to the block, to the fire, down the sea's throat Or to an illegible stone; and that is where we start. I awoke to my newborn day. Naturally we do not know how it happened until it is well over beginning happening. At the Central Station for a room reservation they said to come back in an hour. I was relieved to be done of my compatriots. I walked the streets and canals an eternity of fever and sweat from our sins. Still sick from Paris. Still sick from Toulouse. From America. From Aroosha. From Atrocia. From Caledonia Columbia Corrobonia Ceremonica Caliphobia Carrumba. From A to the Zuider Zee. Drenched and stinking and stewing in the fluids of passions and illusions. And everything as it should turning away quite leisurely from the disaster. The straats and grachts. The Dutch have permanent laryngitis. The Central Station designated a room. A recovery room. An annex to something. A toothless beaming old woman of Amsterdam. A high ceiling. Cool sheets. Persian rugs. Deep brown velvet drapes. Lamps. Tables. Pictures. Paradise. Pass out and shed an old skin in the sleep of abiding afternoons. Arise and go forth and return for the sleep of a thousand and one nights. We shall not cease from exploration And the end of all our exploring Will be to arrive where we started And know the place for the first time. I went for some onion soup. I went for the flea market. I bought a few crummy patches. I stopped at the Rijksmuseum. I wondered if I was strong enough to stand the sight of a masterpiece. I looked at the Nightwatch. I thought how I no longer get off on paintings and dancing or the theatre or anything in a frame. Only rock and Bach and lit. and clit and corny ideas. I found the only gay bar for women in town. The Taboo. I liked M. and so did C. who ended up with me. She said she'd seen me that afternoon in the museum or someplace and had thought if she couldn't find the bar she'd follow me. I suppose I paid for her since the landlady spied her and charged me double. I packed my stuff bag and searched for my cleanest dirty shirt and bought a Dutch-English dictionary on my way out of Amsterdam and sat between a Jewish doctor and his wife from Dayton Ohio on a BEA flight to London returning from Israel with one daughter and three sons of whom one was bar mitzvahed in the holy land the occasion of their trip they told me. The doctor interviewed me on his tape box from Amsterdam to London. Are you off for the summer? —Uh, I'm off—Off for life?—Yes, off for life. Maybe better you should say you work on a book all morning and take out a comma. And add that in the afternoon you put it back again. London at the Gateways tell someone what you do is go around America explaining how all women should sleep together. Again: how do you live? —By my charm and good looks. The English have a weakness for nonsense. The English and Americans have everything in common, except of course, their language. Drink Whitbread Tankard & tame single-handed man-eating crocodiles exert powerful influence over women swim the channel with amazing speed in fact Tankard helps you excel after one you'll do anything well. In Hyde Park on the Serpentine go rowing with Patrick. He never did that before. I wouldn't do it in Central Park either. Patrick is 20 now. He hasn't changed much. His hair is longer. He has a scholarly stoop. His cuffs are still open around the knuckles. He still speaks with eloquent shyness. He's still scarce and possibly anemic. He's still religious but the University is teaching him Psychology. Education may be an admirable thing even in England but we remember from time to time that nothing worth knowing can be taught. I wonder of the outcome. And of the women, who number about 500 here in London as a movement. I went to a meeting with Kate. I pursued the gentle American art of making enemies. They all speak English. They may however pretend not to understand you. It didn't matter too much since I wasn't there to persuade anybody particularly but basically to recover from Amsterdam, the capital of dope sex canals and cyclists. Where nobody seemed to care or notice, and it takes place while anyone else is eating or opening a window or just walking dully along. Death in Vensterdam. One more summer in the line of duty. A step to the block, to the fire, down the sea's throat or to an illegible stone. And that is where we start. Thinking

Holland was all about tulips and wooden shoes and not seeing any windmills either. I awake to the newborn day. Naturally we do not know how it happened until it is all over beginning happening. And everything as it should turning away quite leisurely from the disaster and well over.

63

july 29, 1971

IN EXCESSIVE DEO

Went and bought summore witch books and nerval's journey
to the orient the man at the store said the french were always
going to the orient and I mentioned the english always to
greece and india so i'm reading about greece but not india although the reservation I made was for madrid which may be
because originally I had one for munich whatever it is and by
tonight it may be barcelona or brisbane or basel the english in
amerika tend to go anywhere that's why I bought nerval's journey to the orient because I wouldn't actually go there. Would
we rather be anywhere as long as we are somewhere. Snowshoe
sent a snowy mountain postcard and said she was going away
like a. rimbaud. I guess that means black mistresses and gangrene. Why not go like shelley to italy and die in a boat in a
storm or byron to greece and perish in the war of independ-
ence or keats in his rooms overlooking the spanish steps in rome
actually I thought they were all in love and died drowning in
the aegean off rhodes or mt. athos. Nor did I know shelley
married mary the daughter of mary wollstonecraft who wrote
the vindication of the rights of women and died giving birth to
mary who married shelley and who by the name of mary
shelley wrote the story frankenstein. I thought frankenstein
was a monster, not a book. I wonder who frankenstein was. I
forgot whether shelley's first wife suicided or just died so he
could marry mary. But one has to remember to continue to
forget and remember to remember to avoid that person in the
future although they're still not really people these people out
of books and my memories are morbid. Going away like rimbaud starts you thinking that way why not think about osa
johnson going into the heart of darkness to marry adventure
or iris love finding the head of aphrodite in turkey or rather
the british museum or mary mc-carthy writing home about the
stones of florence I think I'll go to florence I like to say I'm

florence on the phone after florence o'connor who lived next door with her mother and her grandmother and occasionally an uncle jack jane's mother spent the winter in florence and said she liked it all I know about florence is the flood and the plans to resuce the art so I could still see piero and ucello and masaccio and there was a dense book of names dates events about the medicis by jacob burckhardt and I remember a plague but there were plagues all over and the worst was somewhere in 1348 I know it was the worst because I remember the date so much for florence and not going away like rimbaud. I think my mother once by accident was locked up all night in the coliseum in rome and I remember my mother in europe on a horse near wales and very angry that she left me alone in amerika and the last woman who made me cry is my daughter who went away last week to live in baltimore but I gave her some subversive material including patience and sarah and the story of the grimke sisters and I guess I should've thrown in frankenstein who happens to be hades old enough to be the child's father dragging her off to the underworld for that I'll have to become the furious old hag demeter and wander all over the place beating my shrunken breasts and causing the lands to remain barren and mankind to perish until her daughter persephone is returned to her is what'll have to be done if my own mother had done it right I would've stayed childless myself I remember actually she tried and I misunderstood the attempt in maine on an island one summer it was it was not a nice thing I thought for her to be hovering around outside my window in the early morning to see if the hades who was visiting me was indecently in bed with me and I'm sorry to say he was which was the origin of the present predicament of baltimore and the necessity of being demeter as though most of us aren't already clearly what should've happened reading backwards is that my mother should've stayed locked up that night in the coliseum in rome and then her mother my grandmother would've had the gift of her own childless daughter

and so on it was at each stage that something even more alarming happened. A baby is crying it's amplified in the courtyard
and a dog is doing something too. I'm going to madrid or
munich and the orient via nerval. Various people will give
their contradictory advice. Would we rather be somewhere as
long as we are anywhere. Why not be or go anywhere and
say whatever we please about it. I ask jane what was the nicest
thing about greece and she says she thinks it was being on the
tourist deck of a boat coming into the harbor which was a
volcanic crater of santorini which may've been atlantis in the
evening the sun was going down and the cliffs were layers of
black and red and white and she remembers also there was a
time in a little town near the temple of bassae she stood with
a friend in the middle of a cobblestone street at ten oclock at
night and all the windows of all the houses were shuttered
and they watched the moon rise and listened to the goats bells
on the mountains she says so I feel it too eventually every
english person even in amerika goes to greece. I know the men
are bad but they're bad in spain and italy and mexico too and
most places. A man in greece came out of a submarine onto
the beach of the island lesbos and propositioned jane who said
leave me alone I'm a lesbian and he said that's all right, I am
too. In new york here physler told us she said to this man listen
I'm a lesbian you better leave me alone or I'll kill you. I don't
want to give anybody the idea my daughter is getting married,
that hades who's old enough to be her father is really her
father. Her family of one sort or another violently disagreed
about whether she was growing up knowning who she was.
For future reference I'm dedicating my book to my mother
who should've been a lesbian and to my daughter in hopes she
will be. A good friend is writing an article called bringing up
your daughter a lesbian. I may've lost my own chance in order
to bring myself up as one. I can send subversive literature what
else. I could almost envy rosalyn talking about the guilt and
expiation and expense of rachel needing the money for glasses

or for teeth and they don't even ask me for busfare since it would mean the end of the barren crops an such and the beginning of a nice life for everybody why not. Why d'we have to keep going away like rimbaud. I've gone away like rimbaud before but never contracted gangrene and black mistresses. I always have a terrible time in europe even this time thinking of meeting esther in barcelona and susan in madrid and physler in athens and florence in florence I'll be driving along in a foreign vehicle that doesn't work crying about something or other and pleased at the despair I've caused myself by trying to be someplace else. I was supposed to see gregory in venice or nice or morocco no not morocco but nice or venice and I didn't and I don't know what to think about gregory any more but I didn't I was busy writing the dedication to my book. I know sk and carol are in paris and florence and traveling by train to iran. I know suzi is in cadaquez and teeny was going to iceland and john cage and david tudor were going to buy some shoes in figueras which is the town where I saw the bullfight and susan flew to rome to go on a yacht and maybe rosemary will come down from london to meet us in madrid and leticia is going to london where I might fly from athens or munich or denmark to meet everybody in scotland. I might stop off in stockholm to see sontag on the set. I might stop off and have tea with iris murdoch at oxford. I might see germaine in australia and golda in tel-aviv and indira at new delhi and jackie at scorpios and gloria in excessive deo. I've never done it all up right. I was always scrounging around in london looking for the ghost of my father who died in a taxi. One has to remember to continue to forget and remember to remember to avoid that person in the future I plan to be my own childless daughter and be wherever I am there's a real nice pattern of light in your eyes and as she sang her mouth was round and was going around and around, sic transit mater manna manilla manifold.

july 13, 1972

GULLIBLES TRAVELS

athens, or thereabouts: I thought athens was blue until I took off my glasses and then it was yellow and white like other coastal cities and not very good looking although I didn't put any stock in my judgments since I was slumping from not sleeping in the back of the cab it was two in the afternoon but for me it was seven in the morning in new york and the last time I'd slept was 24 hours ago. So I went to this king minos hotel and flaked off at three and woke up wide awake at two in the morning took a bath did my exercises read my greek history book and played with the buttons around my bed by accident I rang for the maid and didn't know how to turn it off so I ordered some coffee and juice when she came and developed the idea of watching the sun rise from the acropolis. The city of athens is really all about the acropolis which was the original city it's amazing I think that the monument of a city is its original city in the form of an enormous fortified hill from which you can see everything that came after it. I don't think I really knew the acropolis was a hill until I saw the thing rising out of the boxes and terraces of the flatlands of a modern city the image of the parthenon out of countless reproductions taking shape of reality way up there against the sky I started out of my slump in the back of the cab and thought maybe the trip was worthwhile after all. I suppose it looks like the first glimpse of the manhattan skyline to a european who doesn't expect to see any indians. I suppose it was like landing in london and seeing the buckingham palace which looked like the 42nd street library. I suppose it was a genuine greek experience and it was certainly more impressive than the view of mont blanc from the plane flying south out of geneva. What was impressive about geneva was the metal check in the terminal depot waiting for the continuation of the flight to athens in new york the check was pretty uneventful I took off my belt and virgin badge and neck piece and passed through an electric eye of some sort and waited while these men at a table searched my stuff bags for the weapons or whatever it was I needed for bailing out and collecting ransom they didn't find it and my friends waved me happily onto the plane expecting a good cut of the take I guess anyway in geneva it was nice being suspected of skyjacking! A swiss dyke in a red dress got me in a big brown booth with a swinging door and felt me up and even grabbed me at the crotch it was a whole interesting introduction to switzerland I felt very special and criminal and wished they suspected me more. Already bertha had told me to watch out for the stewardesses jill on twa they're all queer and I didn't think much of it until after geneva when I began to notice and sure enough this french stewardess with arched eyebrows strapped herself into my empty row for the takeoff and told me how sexy it was in cairo where she was going and other obvious invitations I thought if I wasn't so tired I'd just go on to cairo and forget about athens if she'd only do something about her lipstick. I used up the rest of my energy to overlook it. Anyway I had a good time at kennedy biting jane's white soft muscular appropriate legs and thinking up this poem A woman gets wet like the ocean/A man turns to stone like a stiff I haven't written a poem in years. A woman wrote to me that there are only fragments of sappho because no woman is an island and I thought that was a strange remark. I think it's even stranger that our one historical dyke was a greek considering what we're supposed to know about greece and how the greek men are now I wonder how different they could possibly have been then. I don't know why no woman isn't an island but the reason there are only fragments of sappho is that the men in another time and along the way found it necessary to abolish any competition to their own image the way a new dictator comes along and buries the images of his predecessors except in the case of sappho and any other women we should know

about the process involved the two sexes over a number of mil-
lennia. I saw the clue to the fate of this one in a 1911 encyclopedia under the entry for sappho it said her reputation in
ancient times rivaled that of homer's. I brought homer into
athens by the way. I was wearing the eyes of greece and jane's
brother's t-shirt and carrying the odiad & the illysey and un-
purturd about not being a classycest as leticia used to say I
have a prenatal classy education and that's all you need to
realize how the avars and the slavs devastated the balkans and
the visigoths seized all the byzantine possessions and the barbarians reached an understanding with the persians who sent
an army into chalkidona and the people of constantinople were
terrified and the last greek tribes arriving poured violently into
the greek peninsula conquering the acheans and destroying the
fortified acropolises and killing the kings and seizing the achean
treasures. and everything. I'm still very tired. I went out to
ekali a suburb to see gail and charoula who know lyn and the
holy spirit and others and slept from 3 to 6 p m and from
midnite to noon and from 3 p m to 7 and thought I'd straighten
myself out by sleeping again at 2 a m but then I woke up at 6
so what can you do it's still all fucked up and so is the food.
For food jane said tell them not to soak everything in oil so I
did first thing in the hotel I told the maid to bring the coffee
and juice without oil please and that was fine and then I ordered breakfast down in the lobby at 5 (a m) and said to put
the eggs in water not oil and they did but the milk was caky
and curdling and the coffee was french and the toast tasted
like steamed olive trees or something or so I imagined anyway
I knew the food scene would be hopeless and they wouldn't
have any amerikan mayonnaise I should've brought homer and
mayonnaise. All I really want to do is go to the country and
grow carrots and draw pictures. It's such an ordeal seeing the
rest of the world. Seeing how the citystates of the kings gave
way to the oligarchies and the democracies an such. And the
plumbing doesn't even work, like gail said don't flush the toilet

with any paper in it you know they had excellent plumbing in
crete in 12000 b. c. and now the toilets won't even take paper.
And everything reminds me of everything else. So I might as
well be where all the other things are. Walking out this house
in ekali I thought I was in new hampshire. Walking down this
road into a fishing village I thought it was cadaquez. Coming
back to ekali from the fishing village I looked up at the stars
and said the stars are the same as in the states. Driving into
athens from the airport I thought it could be havana. Looking
out over the city from the acropolis I thought it was just like
los angeles spread all over the place for miles and with these
dry brown stony hills growing clumps of green or it was just
like san francisco except that they didn't put the houses on hills
here but they do have the saronic gulf of the aegean which
could be the san francisco bay of the pacific I liked flying into
athens over its gulf which is green not blue and trying to imagine all its ancient traders and pirates and invaders although
I couldn't possibly I was too sleepy but I rarely do see what
isn't there the way that song goes that's supposed I think to
make you feel all misty and ghosty and did those feet in ancient times walk upon england's mountains green I get that
feeling on st. patricks day on fifth avenue hearing the bagpipes
that's all. So I didn't expect anything from the acropolis. After
all I'm not even greek. I don't know why the english are so
excited about the greeks. I'm beginning to think I should be
getting into some of my own mythology too like some old celtic
goddesses maybe instead of fooling around thinking I have
some remote connection with artemis and athene and atlantis
and all these dark oliveskin black-eyed beauties from the south.
Anyway as I said I didn't expect anything from this big old
hill of the greeks. I just thought it would be great to see the
sun rise before all the people came to the world's most famous
international tourist trap. That's the way I did it at stonehenge.
I saw stonehenge silhouetting itself at 5 a m in the mist on the
amesbury plain and almost managed to see what wasn't there

and that was druids. So thinking of my stonehenge success I walked toward the acropolis in the early morning light of athens after that 5 a m breakfast in the lobby of the hotel and stopped in the village below the hill for an hour to read my book. Was the virgin mary assumed or did she ascend. I'd decided on my way that the acropolis at odd hours was probably like central park and I wasn't any more anxious to be raped by the greeks than by the amerikans who at least don't come right up and grab you when you're minding your business going someplace in public in open daylight it was worse than mexico city where as phisby said of somebody she knew she had an ulcer by the time she got there wherever she was going just from ignoring them I guess they're all from the same race of latin barbarians and the women are invisible although I needn't have worried about the acropolis since if I'd gone as far as the gate I would've found out that you couldn't get in until 7:30 and by that time the international tourists like yourself would be keeping you plenty of company. I suppose it's ironic too that one should have to be thinking of rape on the way to the great temple of the virgin the parthenon but that could be just the point, in ancient times apparently it was the first object of the invading tribes (i. e., tourists) to secure for themselves the protection of the local goddess. And I wasn't wearing my virgin badge. Although in new york I was very cocky or rather cunty walking out of the cleaners the morning of departure the cleaner asked me where are you going and I said athens and he smiled and said how nice and still smiling but you'd better take off that badge or you won't have a good time and I replied without thinking listen I have a *very* good time—with women, and didn't wait to check out the reaction. I wonder sometimes if we can afford to go on not being charming. Or how productive it is to retaliate. Or why I wonder about any of it when all you're doing is approaching the sanctuary of athena parthenos in all its doric majesty which is a hot hill of marble rubble and 46 columns intact or restored and the ruins of six powerful

maidens in long flowing chitons holding up with their heads
the roof of the southwestern porch of a place called the erech-
theum off to one side of the parthenon. I couldn't see the original athena by phidias who apparently was 39 feet high and

wearing a helmet adorned with a sphinx and two winged horses
and carrying in her right hand a winged nike or goddess of
victory six and a half feet high and in her left her shield the
outside and inside surfaces covered with reliefs depicting the
battles of the giants against the gods and of the amazons against
the athenians I couldn't see it but I could speculate what was
going on in this part of the world besides what they say in the
books when the chiefs according to the books were men and the
deity was a woman although it isn't insignificant that the erech-
theum was so called after the ancient king erechtheus who was
supposedly born on the acropolis and raised by the goddess and
enjoyed her special protection and was considered the ancestral
father of the athenians he was represented by phidias in the
form of a coiled serpent beneath the feet of the goddess but
even more significant I think that the god poseidon was also
honored in the temple somehow because of the great struggle
that took place between him and athene for the possession of
attica the olympian gods pronounced athene the winner for
she had made the athenians a present of a plant until then
unknown but the spot where the contest occurred was deemed
to be holy and the dispute was sculpturally represented on the
west pediment and so forth anyway what I'm saying and remembering is that the presence of the god at all and in that
form of the struggle which took place say around 1700 to 1600
b. c. is the clue to the apparent paradox of a male chief and a
female deity was undoubtedly the compromise settlement offered by men to appease the slowly vanishing matriarchies
which survived only in the symbol of a deity to which the men
could appeal for protection and for clemency in their crimes
and assuage their guilt in seizing political power from the
woman much the way the christian religion intelligently intro-

duced the virgin after centuries of pagan resistance to the christ although the dispute still goes on like in england you have christ church and in france the cathedral of our lady which is the vestigial pagan or athenian tribute to the original great mother cult which certainly preceded such aids and comforts as athena who was in a sense a plastic token survivor which may be why I couldn't actually see her at 7:30 in the morning anywhere near or inside the ruins of the temples or around the marble rubble. So much for the acropolis of athens. It was nice seeing the real thing in columns. I liked looking down at the restored theatre the south side of the hill and seeing an actor enter and speak to a woman up in the seats cleaning with a huge broom. I didn't like the flea market or the modern agora the tourist trade in chintzy souvenirs below the hill forming part of the village which looks just like france. I liked a whole lot driving to rafina that fishing village to eat cod squid shrimp & octopus at a table right on the water watching the boats come in from the islands. I'm directly south of leningrad and I don't know what to do next. I never know why I'm here rather than there especially when as I said everything reminds me of everything else. I do like thinking about history for example I keep trying to remember what isadora said about the acropolis I think she and her family camped out in sight of the hill at that time the city was a village stretching out into barren plains and they didn't have any water it was a funny story but anyway there's that famous photo of her in her desperate black at her most romantic arms outstretched amidst the columns which is what I mean about this madness of the english for the greeks and it's still going on. Everybody knows that most of the parthenon is up in the british museum. That elgin fellow just went right up on the hill with a bunch of workmen and walked off with everything they could stagger off with. I think it's worth another war. The wars men make are never over anything more serious and what are they stealing anyway if it isn't the woman. Spolia and praeda are spoils and booty and if you get enough of spolia and praeda you have gloria. Theodosius divided his empire between his sons honorius and arcadius and the first took the west england spain france italy africa and the second took the east the balkans asia and egypt. I'm still very tired. But I'm beginning to wake up. I remember something else about athene that she was an olympian meaning a male creation and really very similar in her function to the christian mary, athene being to zeus what the christ became to mary, the head of zeus equated to the virgin womb of mary, the god giving birth to himself in both cases in different guises, and that the great mother cults exposed by jane harrison were pre-olympian naturally, and here's some neat history that around a. d. 450 when the byzantine empire through theodosius became christian the temple of the acropolis at athens became a christian church! Later on when the turks took over I think it was converted into a harem. Later on a venetian bomb hit the place and 28 columns came crashing down and this doge francesco morosini who did it wanted to take the whole west pediment depicting the dispute between athene & poseidon back to venice with him as a trophy of his great deed. I think I may stay in greece a few centuries to find out what happens next. I think what I really like best about traveling is writing about it. The illysey of gullibles travels.

july 27, 1972

STRAGE DEGLI INNOCENTI

june 17 a note in my record book written in athens should I
go to florence or venice or rome or cadaquez or london or paris
or all of them or stay and go to delphi and marathon and eleusis
and mycenae and santorini and rhodes and lesbos or do that
and also the rest or what. I was waiting outside american xpress
for susan who was waiting for me in madrid so I went to
myconos and delos and flew directly to london to see the rest
of the parthenon at the british museum where certain of the
heads óriginally belonging to their bodies are in places like the
louvre or copenhagen or for that matter back in athens somewhere so you could find a real reason for going places by following it all up. Some people know exactly where they're going
and why. The quest for the lost atlantis has inspired an im-
mense literature. The classical schoolers laughed at schliemann
when he set out for troy with homer in one hand and a spade
in the other. I think now I've evolved two fairly precise reasons for going anywhere one is to find the appropriate location
for an annual nervous breakdown and the other is to practice
not losing vital documents and to manage to experience the
former while succeeding at the latter since the loss of any said
document in a foreign city tends to produce a terror and
anxiety that exceeds the emotional quota for a nervous breakdown. Anyway the improvisation and ingenuity entailed in the
satisfying realization of these two projects constitutes a whole
art form which I should add includes some expectation of being
saved just when all hope has been lost. Flying, for example, is
the ultimate act of trust. Thus any time your crisis is clearly
peaking you know you can get on a plane and feel saved if
nothing more pedestrian like people is available and by so
doing too you can reasonably expect that you've created the
possibility of another crisis just by flying into more trouble of
a strange place weird customs language barriers tourist claus-

trophobias money freakouts directional dilemmas health problems time lags time leaps time laminations and generalized hatred of amerikans who themselves could care less. One project is conservative, the other liberal kamikaze. A person executing both successfully will be seen disintegrating in a huge square amidst the pigeons or on some cathedral steps or in an airport or a restaurant anyplace will do so long as you're raving disheveled hysterical dissociated or simply languishing and dissolving in a pool of your own making it doesn't matter but at the same time you must have all your effects intact on your person or about you well organized and immediately handy including your address book which you can lose as soon as you get home. Not that my address book mattered terribly much on this particular trip. For example arriving rome one person I called who'd been described as "an admirer in rome" was this anna maria marinelli pellegrino who had become unreachable since she had moved from the number given and her husband's first name was unknown to me and there are countless pellegrinos in the roman directory. Also arriving venice I expected to locate mark di suvero but I had two german addresses under his name and for venice it just said studio. I expected actually to see his steel beams crisscrossing the grand canal and a crane in the middle of the piazza although sheindi had told me that all he was doing was saving the city. In that case of course anybody would know who he was. I stepped off the plane and went up to the first italian I saw and said do you know where I can find mark di suvero but they never heard of him nor did anybody else in the entire city including the peggy guggenheim gallery so I decided I must have the wrong city and maybe he was saving germany. You may think by the way just because I said so that I flew directly to london from athens but I didn't I wasn't going to fly north and then south again simply to spend more time in the air although I don't know why not. Anyway it's common form for composers of historical romances to insist that their stories are really true. Any merely corroborative detail is intended to give artistic verisimilitude to an otherwise bald and unconvincing narrative. Sometimes gertrude floundered around without a subject but we know that's no longer necessary. The subjects abound, the problem is how to undermine them by making them increasingly im- portant in diminishing permutations, always maintaining abso- lute fidelity to fact. Atlantis stands for a vanished civilization, not just a buried building. There's no limit to the number of new sentences that can be produced. It may not be so much the new sentences that count as the constant alteration of im- pressions. S(he) who understands me finally recognizes my propositions as senseless. But as to impressions I remember say- ing as prelude to what I plan to say now that the view of mont blanc from the plane flying out of geneva was unimpressive and that was to create an unlikely contrasting intermediary link between the parthenon and the sexy metal check at geneva airport but flying back the other way from venice to paris over the alps the pilot instructed us to look again and this time it was fantastic and I wrote down in my book right away it's the alps that make the world worthwhile which is not to say that I wasn't impressed the first time I was but not so much since my mind's image was parthenon and nothing else measured up even the reality of it and besides I wasn't yet flying in order to be saved but more important I was more involved in using the image as a sentence vehicle than as a report from the wil- derness which is still the idea and why even the slightest altera- tion of impression serves to expedite the generation of new sentences which in turn change our lives. After athens I took to flying from city to city, or just as accurately from airport to airport. If you're not gonna stay a long time in a place you might as well stay a day. I am now in a position to make sweeping and unqualified generalizations about everyplace in europe except austria hungary germany belgium denmark sweden norway yugoslavia russia china alaska & australia. The italians like to paint ceilings. The italians never heard of their

own pope joan. The italian (and the greek) drivers don't just
tailgate, they piggyback. And so on about italy. About england
I take almost all of it back concerning old lord elgin I should've
known or remembered that he bought his marbles from the
turks to save them from exposure theft and mutilation (so it
said on a plaque in the museum) or at least so that innocents
from abroad in a later time could travel from one country to
another to find the various remains. The hercules by the way
is magnificent if you like that sort of thing. If you don't he's
missing his hands and feet. In athens while I was there four
people died by lightning. In delos I died by sweating. In grease
I saved myself and got back at the natives at the same time
when leaving this island myconos I boarded their little boat to
be motored out to their big boat I wanted to go back to piraeus
early on this apollo instead of the naias on which I had gone
and for which I had a return ticket I climbed up the plank &
ladder to the apollo they wouldn't let me on (the apollo and
the naias are two different companies they said) and I had to
climb back down into the little boat to return to shore and wait
for the naias so safely motoring away I gave the arm the hand
and the mouth to all those greek ossifers up on deck there of
the apollo and wished for leto to lurch out of her cave on delos
and hurl a tidal wave at them. I've heard they'll kill you if
you're caught giving them the hand which as a gesture is merely
a thrust of the arm with a cocked hand fingers spread like
meaning stop and which has something to do with their mothers. I suppose all their mothers are virgins and they think
everybody they fuck isn't their mother. Anyway myconos and
delos were difficult but not traumatic and that meant that some
other place or places was required to fulfill the purpose of the
trip. The chosen town manifested itself as rome at least as a
point of origin or watershed the taxi man for a start didn't put
his flag down and charged 500 liras for a few blocks to a hotel
in which the room was a hot box on a street that sounded like
an endless motorcade of tanks and mack trucks relieved by

squads of scooters and racing fiats and the men in the post office resisted all my attempts to explain that I wanted to send my letter special delivery as well as express and rome just generally is oppressive with culture and catholicism I was overwhelmed by st. peter's and gripped by claustrophibia descending into the sistine chapel I walked in one door and right out the other noting the hordes of art appreciation groups pointing and gesticulating at the ceiling and the pity was being repaired and anna maria marinelli pellegrino my admirer was not to be found and I felt like the strage degli innocenti in those tapestries was the only thing I stopped to look at along the miles of galleries leading to the chapel and I saw two donkeys trotting very fast on the way to the vatican or I hallucinated that and so altogether I was well prepared by the next morning at the airport for a series of exquisite frustrations beginning with standing by mistake in a line all of europe in the summer is a line for an hour in the wrong building I was at alitalia international instead of national then squabbling fiercely with another taxi man who wouldn't put his flag down I said I'd call the police then waiting in line for a ticket to venezia venice to you and me and being told I couldn't buy the ticket there and then another line to buy it and to be told I had to wait in still another line to change the traveler's checks which I did while raving disheveled hysterical dissociated my pants falling down my plane was due to leave in five minutes I couldn't even find the entrance dock I don't know how I made it but I did and I didn't lose any vital documents either so rome was a crashing success and I was ready to take on venice. I meant to stop in florence but I flew over it by mistake. I've complained that everything reminded me of everything else well venice is definitely different. I was very pleased for instance to step off the plane and right into a boat instead of a bus for the ride to the city. I was just as pleased to be deposited right at the palace of the doge at the great piazza of san marco after polo which is what we used to call di suvero whom as I said I expected to immediately find. I walked past the continuous dinner music of strings and accordion thinking if I was crazy I'd think it was just for me. Well I walked and walked and took more boats and even gondolas and couldn't locate di suvero or a hotel and the heat rising from the canals was a steady boil so venice was working out very well too and by early evening things were critical. It's easy to see why aschenbach died in venice. There's too many pigeons and unnecessary columns. As I was experiencing my crisis I thought it was too bad they don't provide at least a female tadzio for an amerikan lesbian. Everybody knows that death in venice for aschenbach was worth it. Tadzio or no I expected to be saved and I was. Saved by Sattis. Sattis was a tourist displacement place and they sent me instantly around the corner to a cool fine room in a hotel called casanova just off the piazza where I think I captured venice for one second before leaving I was sitting there the pigeons were flying the bells ringing the orchestra playing it was all very european and decadent and busy like a bosch or a breughel I felt treated and totaled and still to-gether in my various effects. The remedy for my next flight was alcohol. Helplessly they entrusted their safe passage to the air to carry them whither it would. The novelty on air france was lunch in an orange plastic brief case. In paris after one night at the esmerelda I was saved sort of by a waitress in a cafe who didn't understand me but who was leaning into my lap trying to help me which meant finding a phone number for twa in a pile of directories and I was saved by one ms. odile wable at the twa place on champs elysee she gave me a free trip to london somehow and passage to new york for much less than the extraordinary amount of bread they want for flying back sooner than you said you would and I suppose I was saved by a certain andrew we know from home who saw me at a cafe on st. germain and said he'd been at the ocean and all the doors had opened and he'd been having esp for two months and later he left a big bunch of flowers at the esmerelda and I didn't have time to stay and say anything more. I thought I should do something useful for humankind and go and interview a famous person but I didn't do that either. I think the first thing jane said in new york was that everybody has a miserable time in europe and nobody admits 83 it. The thing is there's nothing wrong with a miserable time so long as it conforms to certain aesthetic expectorations of novelty or improvisatory ingenuity and you don't exceed your emotional quota by losing anything you don't really need like your address book.

august 3, 1972

BUSTED: ILLEGAL ATTIRE IN THE FIRST DEGREE

i considered having two cats named after me being the event of the week but now clearly it was being arrested at the 23rd precinct last night after waving at a cop outside the guggenheim and wearing illegal clothes or something. it must be for being bad for over a week. i don't know what town we were in but last week i remember driving late at night to a large house for "coffee and brandy" by invitation of a "very nice lady" who hated all of us and that was seven of us and her daughter didn't like us either. we had coffee brandy grass milk crackers and muffins that stuck to their papers and we watched a movie without the sound except for the comments of the hostess who kept exclaiming that the movie was without its sound or identifying one man or another as some man who had slept in her house and editorializing the movie as tragic and hopeful, it happened to be some original color version of the laing asylum flick that we saw here on channel 13 when r. d. came to raise money for his house, and the father as one of those well meaning and insensitive people like all those people in that "wonderful" book sanity madness and the family well meaning insensitive people who destroy their children. enter daughter. who put on a rolling stone record for us i've got you under my thumb and other appealing numbers. every time some body started giggling her mother made for the kitchen announcing coffee. we giggled about everything. antidote anecdote manicdote nannygoat ankleoat antelope elope elope. they hated us. the mother was talking about transsexualism, i don't know why, i never talk about it myself and i cut the whole thing short in fact by saying it was sacrilegious, tampering with nature like that, and her daughter said you can't mean that. i said what do you mean i can't mean that. she was saying i couldn't mean what i mean. there people go again trying to say that you've said something you didn't say or you've said something you didn't say you said or didn't say or don't mean you've said what you meant to say to say. i said i meant what i said. she said how can you say that with a drink in your hand. *drinking* is against nature (i was drinking her mother's drink), clearly equating alcohol with transsexualism—crimes against nature. later on her mother put her to bed. she said so. she came downstairs and sat down relievedly next to her fire and brushed a wisp of beautiful gray hair delicately off her brow and said she'd put her children to bed. the other children i guess were these male freaks who ran her picture projector. the child her daughter is a full bosomed proper lady like herself. have a good time dear but don't go near the water. here's your hurry what's your hat. and we left to leave thank you ever so much for the coffee brandy grass milk crackers and muffins that stick to their papers and the wonderful silent movie. goodnight goodnight. never darken our daughter again. anyway i was arrested last night. and i was just discussing with gregory our habit of not being invited back places. it's something if you can be there at all. i was urged last week to go on to the long john silver radio thing at midnight. bertha said i shouldn't do it it's an awful thing to do so i called the people who'd urged me to do it and said i couldn't do it but they urged me again and said i should do it it would be a good thing to do so i did and i brought bertha and it's a five hour gig into the small dawn but we were ejected in ten minutes i don't know why except i thought he was a hateful person and i told him so possibly that's why. long john nibble or nebish or nebble or something. he said jacqueline susann comes on to his thing all the time, that was supposed to recommend his thing to me. just tell 'em the next time we can't make it, that we're all in various states and degrees. i thought it'd be a relief to attend the big opening of the season at the guggenheim gregory said they were making a very big deal about it and he had the fancy

tickets. he has anemia too and he's going to leningrad in june
and he wore a black velvet suit with a black bow tie as a date
he was a proper couple. i remember very little even now except drinking downtown with jane bertha phyllis charlene &
co and leaving them to pick up my date and almost going
swimming in the coin pool at the museum i was hanging over
the whadyacallit the bannister that round white curving railing that separates you and death with a lovely young woman
in white clothes discussing the coins particularly two large
copper numbers glistening strange inscriptions and removing
our shoes or lower accourtrements to dive in and remove them
which she did i put my boots back on but never laced them
up properly which is possibly the reason the jock in the blue
helmet outside the museum manhandled me into a cop car to
go to the 23rd precinct. they did say i was illegally dressed.
i shouldn't be walking around as a marine they said. i said i
bought it in a public store. why don't they go and arrest the
store. why do they let us legally buy these things and then
lock us up for it later. why wouldn't they arrest me for wearing women's clothes. an ex marine walking around in women's
clothes. i should do it and see what happens. i'll hang my
marine jacket in the closet and go out in some wedgies and
girdles. jane gave a fine demonstration of a man she saw on
third avenue learning to walk in his new wedgies. we went
to a restaurant where the bus boys are wearing polka dot rib-
bons for bowties and garter belts made of black lace around
their elbows. these jocks in new york don't know what's happening. they need a little fringe around them helmets. anyway i was glad gregory looked so right in his black velvets and
patent leathers. he caught a taxi over to the precinct they
wouldn't let him ride in the ambulance. i felt really funny in
the car there with these regular cops who wondered themselves what the trouble was and i couldn't inform them any
better but there was old ossifer watusi or somebody i can't
read his name on the violation paper here, dressed down in

civies and pushing me rudely and roughly up the stairs to answer questions in a sickly green room with a large cage in the corner containing about seven black people waiting i presumed for the wagon. i could see that they liked black people too. women marines and black people must be their favorites. lavender panthers unite. say all the things you're gonna do, cause time is running out. it's an interesting exercise in not knowing who you are. i was very contained and sounded perfectly credible to myself. i had apparently done all my damage on the street, waving at the jock an all. he didn't want to hear my virgin of it either. and i didn't tell him. i answered the questions politely and politick. in her time, in her own context, my mother was very bad too. having done whatever she did to deserve me. so here i am mommie and i'm never gonna look prettier. a national tour of personal disappearances is being arranged. the first person to see is martha mitchell. don't say anything, and don't say anything about us not saying anything, and don't say anything about us saying not to say anything, say nothing about us saying anything about not saying anything, say nothing about anything. so there. so it isn't the people who play it as it lays but the people who say it as they see it who make the mistakes who're the bad ones, we'll have to find old martha mitchell and sign er up for the lavender panthers. it was late and i was sober as soon as i walked in the station house. i didn't even lace up my boots properly, i didn't want to call attention to myself by bending over, i didn't want to suggest there was anything wrong with myself except for being illegally attired. i folded my hands below the navel the way i learned to do it at bellevue. i showed them all my documents including a voice press pass. well that about did it for ossifer watusi there. i know because we were downstairs in a jiffy and gregory black velvets patent leather his hands folded below the navel told me he'd just been outside phoning the white house to notify the prexy's secretary to call off their dogs and the dog at the desk was

taking in calls and glancing up or rather down at us sur-
reptitiously while watusi hovered anxiously two yards to his
right. it was the city desk at the times that gregory called
actually and a times man called night or knight was actually
calling in and the dog at the desk was mumbling well you have
the power sir and so on and then we left. goodnight goodnight. never darken our dogteam again. deus terrestris et
absconditis. because of an increase in the cult of the virgin it
isn't advisable to leave yer inner circle and go gallivaunting
about into enement territorrid widout yer lapis electrix er vas
pellicanicum er excalibur caliburnus er at the lease yer poshun
fer indivisibility. seeing how abzurd a certrain pattern of con-
dact is in yerself to others. i'm still considering having two
cats named after me being the event of the week. don't say
anything and don't say anything about us not saying anything
and don't say anything about us saying not to say anything
etcetera.

may 3, 1973

COULD I HAVE A LIGHT

There may seem to be nothing to say but as an imprisoned young frenchwoman said in desperation I'm writing you all the same, as you would toss a bottle into the sea. I rediscovered the trees and the river and perhaps my confidence too. I may try to postpone the revolution until the leaves have turned. I want to be completely different from yesterday or the day before. I want to be overcome by a sense of infinite consequences. I want to be a total object, complete with missing parts. I want to play the guitar and sing somewhat. I want some balloon therapy and summore white berries on red stems and lavender unopened flowers in an oldfashioned glass. I want to be more than just a grown girl who identifies with classical heroines and automobiles. I want to be a progressed planet that moved out tomorrow. I'm very disconcerted by appearing to be writing what is going to happen next. We're all here, what's the phone ringing for. I was writing about richard and saying I didn't know where he was right now at which almost moment he called me up and said where've you been I lost you and now as I'm writing I have him on a plane for seattle so I suppose he'll be doing that too. I'm writing into the sunset and into the future as well. I don't know what it does to settle the past except to settle the past but you don't have to write about things to know they're about to happen and that doesn't mean we know it until after they happen and then after the fact we say oh I knew that was going to happen and so we did although it seems impossible to acknowledge it unless you're employed as a medium who also settles the past for people possibly to establish their credentials as acrobats of time and my ribbon is running dry and I think I'm evolving a plan and one of my selves will let me know what it is before long. In trude nothing is as unusual or provocative as it may appear. I won't send you flowers because you're going away and because certain gestures are intimidating. If I write about nothing nothing will happen. Any kind of local sensationalism could be our daily fare. Any kind of going up the mountain in my boots in the rain to plant three amazon solution balloons after iwo jima. Any kind of trees which are mortally beautiful and I have a glass in a rose and the yellow wall is tumbling into an electric blue and my visitors have not yet come forward to say what our last conversation was about. We were however sitting on some pebbles by the crick river when somebody said her last words were could I have a light and I think that was edna st. vincent millay tiger tiger burning blake and oh my froze and oh my fiends it gives a lovely when these things happen in litterature everything is different I'm not concerned. I had two martinis at gregory's with four black olives. I had one cup of coffee at gloria's with two drops of saccharine. I had three irish whiskeys at susan's with nothing and nothing. I had one large orgasm at jane's with plenty of kisses and kats. Oh pussy kat I wish I could send you to summer camp. Oh I'm sending richard to seattle and they said I could prove he was born by just writing it down and having your neighborhood pharmacist agree with you for 50 cents by doing something called a notary public. Oh it's wonderful we can invent the past by writing it down too. The tangled mass of documentation upon which the cases for our real existence rests. True fidelity is that of ideas. As soon as you say it it is. It's real even if she's making it up you know what I mean it doesn't matter what's true any more it's all true. The troop of what you say is what rally masters and the only impittance of tiqueneck is that wean you say it biddy you haven't sage it. So mach for finnegan and other runny nosed geniuses. If I write about something something will surely happen. I'm not clear on the purpose of settling the past unless we go back to invent it but I'm not keen on writing myself into the future either. Color me. Blow me a bubble. Brig me a turned leaf. Be my transceptor and remitter. Be my disconcertion and infinite consequences. I want to be completely different from yesterday or the day before and I don't want to do something new like go to an orgy. I was casually invited to an orgy while eating in a restaurant and I didn't want to and I had a letter from a woman in ohio inviting me to a swingers thing and I don't see the point of even saying it except as an excuse to note I'd rather make love to myself in a trunk in the desert and that doesn't mean I don't find lots of women attractive and I don't think it means I can't say so just because I appear to be married I just think orgies are confusing I picture it very abstractly romantically with botticelli's graces gliding under waterfalls if they touched me lightly licorice & lazuli I suppose it will happen now and it's heavy flashes of previous lives otherwise why would we say it if not to invent them by merely remembering them I was casually invited. I was writing last week on friday that day about women and men and violence in the streets and what to do or not to do about it and that very evening I experienced violence on the streets and I almost never do I've lived in new york city for hundreds of years and I have eyes all around my head as soon as the night sets and true to my mother's earliest instructions I never pass a man on a lonely street I make deviations and detours even circles and backtracks and trapdoors and hatches and shafts and spirals and smokescreens I make my way thru the obstacle course of the male sex but last friday that evening three women we knew were out on the street one was screaming one was slumping against the brick wall one was leaning over the one slumping and it happened because the one screaming encountered the two black men who insulted her who then knocked off her glasses and her jaw and who then smashed the one we saw slumping against the brick wall in the face her face was all blood we called the emergency the police came she had a concussion and three women chased the black men they couldn't find them I was writing. If you write about nothing nothing will happen. What can be accomplished by noting that in 1120 the white ship of Henry II went down with his only son, his illegitimate daughter, and a niece. On this point the present witnesses agree and abound: that whereas once in our schooldays we would register and regurgitate this information as pure information including six subjects we now pay attention and read carefully his only son knowing very well that such a sentence would never read his only daughter and in this way we write ourselves into the future by reinventing the past. My visitors bought soap bubbles and balloons sue and mary and mary said she heard the voices of several different people coming thru the print and sue made a drawing that was finished when her hand was tired and mary said sue was still a child and we smiled and I thought her first toys were probably crosses and relics and rosaries and she's very good at catching bats too. I was pleased to arrive and find a bat flying around a room not having written about bats recently or ever I know nothing about bats except that they're black and they like your hair and I'm settling the clear past. Any kind of local sensationalism. Another week of sterling tragedy. I cowered in the kitchen and the classical heroine chased him or her away we thought back up the chimney and we went to sleep. I woke up at three and yelled for the heroine whose armor was a headband and whose weapon was a white paper shopping bag. I was suffocating under a blanket and wanted to know if my choice was to suffocate or to emerge and have a bat in my hair. I didn't have to do either because the heroine caught the bat in her white paper shopping bag and took her outside to the mortally beautiful trees. There may be nothing to say but as the imprisoned young frenchwoman said in desperation I'm writing you all the same, as you would toss a bottle into the sea.

september 28, 1972

PART TWO

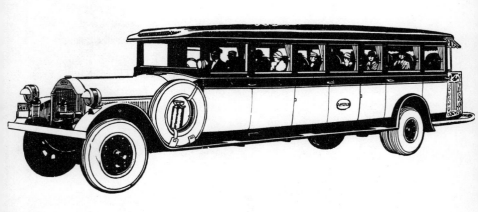

ELEKTRA RECONSIDERED

i've decided to experiment in telling a short story. that means
altering certain names somewhat. this is a short story with a
happy ending, a sort of brother and sister incest story with
better complications. i'm not sure how people start short
stories. so i looked at a henry james beginning. this was how
james began four meetings. i saw her but four times, though
i remember them vividly; she made her impression on me. that
could do. i saw her more than four times but i remember
them and they made an impression on me. the last time i
saw her was in central park, at the boathouse, on a sunny day
some seven days ago. i went to meet win and richard who
were walking over from the sheeps meadow at 3:30. i bought
an icetea at the counter and wandered out on the porch or
deck overlooking the lake toward a table where i noticed a
girl woman sketching, a peripheral impression. suddenly my
peripheral impression became a frontal reality as i heard my
name loud and clear prefaced by a very friendly hello and
saw the voice attached to a beaming beautiful face who looked
mysteriously familiar. i'm not intimate with short story dialogue but i did say as i remember who are you, to which the
voice replied jean, still smiling broadly, and this clue instantly
jogged my memory into a cluster of images with names from
1969. it was appropriate i was there to meet a brother and
his sister since the place of jean in my 1969 story was very
much as the sister of her brother. there were two sets of
brothers and sisters and i was the odd woman out. it was
around that time in fact i was always saying if there was
anything i needed in the world it was a brother and any male
i met i liked i would instantly claim as a brother. and jean's
brother was one of them. it didn't seem there was any way
the women could be involved with each other except through
their brothers, not that anybody said that or even thought it.

the brothers were just omnipresent. it was appropriate seeing jean in the park too because it was there that she and her brother jorge had met and seduced the girl woman who con-cerned all of us and whose own brother was more of a mental presence than an actual one since at least up till the end of my participation in the romance he was always in foreign parts. that's not to say he might not've been the most important figure in the whole thing, no doubt it's mental presences in any event who exercise the most influence over peoples' stories. well, said jean, they were divorced. she meant polyesther and her brother. i assumed i replied. and i told her how i assumed. if a bottle from france had washed up on your beach with a letter in it the message couldn't've been clearer. i was sitting over a year ago in the bus station at new paltz with jane having coffee at the counter when this unmistakable image crossed my vision or the window i was staring through. i almost dove under the counter. brother jorge was one of the scariest characters i ever met. the tall lean hungry violent sanguine type. he was also very funny and it was his funny self i wanted for a brother. more than that, he professed great interest in my welfare, he offered his ultimate brotherly serv-ices in the desperate cause of retrieving our protagonist poly-esther from the terrible clutches of her family and returning her to her proper owner which was supposed to be me. we cooked up a whole mythology even to support our action. old jorge there was to be a sort of surrogate orestes, the real orestes being polyesther's brother who was off in hiding play-ing at somebody's war, and i was electra and p. was iphigenia or vice versa and of course the bad mother was clytemnestra. i had no idea i was collaborating with my enemy. the fact is i just didn't fit into the scheme or the family romance because i didn't have a brother myself. i was elektra's sick cousin and not in the running at all basically. my true role was the re-verse of what i thought, to bring polyesther back to the ones who discovered her, jean and her brother jorge. that meant in a sense her mother too. there were a lot of j people in this story. jean jill joan jorge. the mother was a joan and the mother's other and first daughter was also a joan. anyway bringing p. back to her mother meant delivering her to a husband and that's what brother jorge turned out to be. the only proper husband would be the brother of her first woman lover, i'm not saying that was the mother's idea, i assume this is an archetypal solution of the sisters who find other sisters as lovers indefensible and who therefore find a kind of surrogate sister in the brother. eventually the sisters of the brothers rediscover each other which is what i meant by a happy ending, or an incest story with better complications. not that this particular brother's sister got her original woman back, i knew it wouldn't work out like that. she only got her back through her brother, by playing strictly ally to his designs for becoming husband and then somehow living vicariously through that situation. jean i imagine thought it only correct too, for the idea was that since she had had polyesther first and jorge had graciously as she put it declined her in his sister's favor it was only right he should have his turn. in any event only the male could lay legal claim to the fortune i presumed was not a minor consideration in the great interest evoked by our common object. jean and jorge seemed to me like fallen aristocrats of some sort. certainly the world owed them something anyhow. jorge was 29 and perennially destined for great things. when i met them he was hanging out on church street in a loft supported chiefly by his younger sister and painting pictures like st. george slaying the dragon by which i believe it was supposed to be understood that here was a burgeoning el greco or somebody anyway an as yet unappreciated genius in the tradition of the starving garret types. el greco is an appropriate allusion because jean and jorge were greek on their father's side and jorge was not unlike some tense elongated tortured el greco christ model. a lot tenser actually. well, i said, continuing on with my short story dialogue, i wondered how polyesther would get rid of him, i thought she'd have to pay him off at least. jean indicated it was he who'd lost interest in p., she couldn't stay away from girls she said, and you know how men are. i was eager to learn how p. got it together again with "girls," all i could think of was her brother, but i delayed my satisfaction till the end, i savor my happy endings at the end. i brought up that old subject to jean of how wasn't she supposed to marry p.'s brother, but that was a joke between us, jean isn't any man's woman except for her safe brother. anyhow i told her how i assumed the marriage between her brother and p. was over. it was that day in the bus station at new paltz and the image was indelible for life. as i said i almost took cover. i was terrified of the guy. i grabbed jane's arm and shook all over. the last time i'd seen him was near a year before that in new york on spring street i'd just parked my camper when i spied him and another male walking toward west broadway with polyesther between them. i was beside myself. i jumped out of my vehicle and began waving my arms violently in the middle of the street after the threesome as they crossed spring, hoping to catch polyesther's eye sidewise as it were without the other two noticing, i was so intoxicated by the sight of her, just from behind, and in an unfamiliar short haircut, and this nearly two years after the end of the affair, that anybody could tell this was no ordinary passion and i was quite willing to make a fool of myself just to hear a hello or something. i pursued them up west broadway without any discretion about me at all. they pretended they weren't being tailed. near a corner i knew they knew because p. put her arm thru her husband's nervously and stiffly the way they do in the movies when they go on pretending they're not being followed while indicating to the audience, that was me, that they know they are. i crossed the street with them and then on the other side about 15 yards in i made my crazy move, i sprinted forward and as though we were playing red light touched her lightly on the black velvet shoulders before they got me, but they got me, simultaneously jorge wheeled round, his flaring french raincoat billowing out in a spiral twist, and chased me back to the corner shouting oaths and curses and something about how much trouble i had caused them all and flailing his flagel-x

x

lant arms by which he sent me sprawling into the gutter at the corner wherewith he dispatched me with his legs and feet just like i was his cur. a yellow bulldog floated into my mind. the first image of violence was jorge in this loft someplace picking up his yellow bulldog and dashing it to the floor as though it was it was a small rock of cyclops and he was kill-ing goliath. i was of course the dragon and there was st. jorge looming victorious in his flaring french raincoat. this wasn't the way we used to play red light. i watched the raincoats and the black velvet jacket disappear down the street. i knew they wouldn't last long. the next time i saw them or a black velvet jacket it was on old jorge at new paltz. i was saying this un-mistakable image crossed my vision or the window i was star-ing through at the bus station. the image actually entered the station and walked up some back stairs. i asked the waitress where the stairs went, she said to a real estate office. ah hah i thought. i didn't really think anything, i wanted to know what he'd come in, so in fear and trembling i snuck over to the window to check out this shiny black car with a strange girl woman brushing her hair in the passenger seat. satisfied that it wasn't p. and that jorge was still upstairs we went outside to my camper where as i opened my door i caught the total image. the black bentley, the strange woman, and jorge in a black velvet jacket torn under the arm ushering a lady into the back seat, presumably a real estate lady. at that point i lost interest in the whole story and merely wondered whose brother's sister polyesther had recovered for herself. this is not exactly a short story with a twist. the plot was very sim-ple. a brother and his sister meet another sister of a brother in a park. the two sisters have an affair. the brothers are off

x

in foreign parts. one of the sisters runs off with a sister who has no brother. for awhile nobody has anybody as the sister who had run off with the sister who has no brother vanishes to join her mother. subsequently the sister with no brother meets the first sister whose brother is jorge and these two sisters have a brief affair. the one who vanished to join her mother then returns and marries the first sister's brother. i was nothing more than a transitional person whose name happened to start with a j. i guess it would appear unseemly to go directly from a sister to her brother so i came in between. not that all of us weren't in love. we weren't actually, we were all in love with p. and seeing or finding her through the rest of us so to speak. seeing jean that sunny day in central park when i went to meet win and richard i could see she was really a double for p. and in fact when she first appeared one night after p. vanished to join her mother i went right to bed with her. i didn't like it either but it didn't matter. we were just involved in the temporary hysteria of substitutions. the tale was unbelievably romantic. i was taken right over to meet jorge whom as i said i found suitable immediately as a brother. i liked everything about them even the yellow bulldog. besides the characteristics of jorge i mentioned he was living in some heloise and abelard type fantasy world, i assumed his real love was right in front of him in form of his sister and he was projecting her unavailability thru fantasies of others, chiefly an old flame he'd been languishing after for several years he kept recollections of in a wooden box, lockets of hair and stuff like that, but he had all these photos of p. around too. i just didn't realize she was his object, possibly he didn't either. we were all completely round the bend, fragmented and hysterical. orestes was having his teeth fixed and i was trying to round up the bread for his flight to europe to rescue elektra. little did i know he would do exactly that and that in this way old clytemnestra would be spared too. so it wasn't an orestes story at all. it was sigmund and sieglinde with shades of sappho. i happen to know clytemnestra was spared because i saw her in a taxi a year ago on park avenue. she was waving at me out the window calling my name and wondering if i remembered who she was. shit, did i ever. i found her almost as attractive as her daughter. i suppose she was in love with her daughter too. we should have a reunion party of the j women. jean joan joan jill jane june . . . we could play musical dyke chairs and pretend the brothers had just discharged their inimitable and essential parts in bringing us all together. well, said jean at the boathouse in central park, concluding our short story dialogue, you'll never guess what happened, no i couldn't and i could hardly wait, p. got together with her brother's wife's sister! we certainly go about things the hard way. i'm not sure how people end short stories so i consulted james's four meetings again and his last sentence won't do. there are a couple of phrases however in his last paragraph. i detained that lady as, after considering a moment in silence the small array, she was about to turn off . . . i held out my hand in silence—i had to go . . . what was clearest on the whole was that she was glad i was going. whether or not she was she left first, with her sketch pad, and i went on talking with my own sigmund and sieglinde pair, whose lives are still free of better complications, or so i imagine.

august 16, 1973

THE YEARLY MELLOWDRAMA

I had a dream richard stayed in san francisco one day and
then split for home. I had a dream two years ago I was
traveling up and down highways on the coast in a freighter
and richard flew up in the air and landed someplace on his
back as a small doll. I didn't have a dream 10 years ago he
ended on his back on a road in washington heights his eyes
rolled up I ran the other direction it happened to be a nurse
on her way to a hospital who hit him and I followed her over
with him in her front seat unconscious and richard and me
discussed it ever afterwards for six or seven years until one
day I said well it was a good way to pay me back for i don't
remember what besides having him and he looked at me funny
and that was that. I remember his left face was black and
blue and swollen for a week and that was all but everything
was terrible then. It was clear that we were all living thru
an ordeal. I tried to remember yesterday whether richard was
hit before or after I was driving myself and hit a schoolkid
dashing diagonally out from between cars in the middle of a
street but we talked about that forever afterwards too. That
was back in 1962 when everybody in rockland county wanted
to build themselves an orgone box. I remember yvonne asking
me if I was into reich and I suppose I said yes since sally was
reading the murder of christ and I was in love with sally and
that's the way things go and I still didn't have a mind of my
own in any case. I was a stroller mommie in washington heights
living in an $80 walkup near the river and across the street
from the park. I would carry one kid up on my hip and trail
the other behind me screaming. I would sit in the park and do
all the proper things like talking to another mommie and
following the kids with my eyes when they left the sandbox
and swinging them on the baby swings and buying them pop-
sicles and picking them up when they cried and putting them

down when they didn't and wondring whether my mission in life was supposed to be fulfilled. I don't think I wondered that for a second. I had a dream last week I went to an important interview in heels stockings black velvet dress and my derby. I don't remember too much what I whore then except some shapeless $5 jeans to the park but I did have a red woolen dress to just above the kneecaps and it was around that time that john cage saw me in my red woolen dress at a christmas party and asked me to perform with him and david tudor a number of months hence in a thing of his called music walk and I did and I did it in my red woolen dress and for my noisemakers I brought all the trappings of my wonderful maternal existence a baby bottle a coffee can a blender a frying pan a vacuum an apron a plastic sink an egg beater a beater beater and a toy dog on wheels that barked like a duck when I pulled it along by its string. I had a ladder on stage too. I had all this junk and john and david had only their minimum daily requirement of sophisticated electronic equipment and a handful of three by fours containing the brilliant and elegantly scripted hieroglyphics of instructions from the godhead: the wise decrees of chance and indeterminacy. I had gone to all this trouble too. I had come in fact to a rehearsal with a bunch of about 45 of these cards clutched in my nervous little fist, each one explaining to myself how I should do such and such an action like scrubbing out my baby bottle at a very certain time and for just so long during the course of the 10 specified minutes of the piece, the result of some very fancy calculations involving the tossing of coins and an immaculate collection of topographical transparencies that john called a score, but at the rehearsal I dropped all these cards of instructions in some of my domestic water and the ink was blurred and whatever wasn't blurred was dirty and I said to myself shit why should I bother with these cards anyway I'll just plant my junk around the stage and set my stopwatch so I know when we're beginning and when we're ending and whenever

I feel like it I'll go here and there and tinker around with my junk and that's what I did in my red woolen dress. I remember john looking quite skeptically at me just before the perform-ance but he didn't say anything and I didn't tell him how heretical I planned to be either. I suppose at that time if you weren't up in rockland county building yr orgone box you were training to deliver up yr ego to the elements by obeying john cage and I really wanted to and I appreciated the orgone business too but no matter what anybody else said my life was conforming to its own internal chaos, it was out of my control to follow any directions from anywhere, much less from my-self, so naturally I experienced my better and better orgasms completely by chance and naturally I couldn't do anything on stage that wasn't basically like my life and that was purely by chance according to the whims of the moment confined to my wonderful maternal existence I didn't have much choice as it were but within that choice or chance I was always dropping my papers in the domestic waters and deciding to do something else because of that or something else. I was trying to remem-ber right now whether I had that ladder on stage because around that time richard had fallen off a ladder at marcia marcus's house or not but I don't know I do know I didn't own a ladder myself so it isn't clear why I insisted on the ladder unless me and my kids were all into hanging and falling off things in which case any elevated property would've been suit-able to demonstrate one important aspect of my life and a lad-der happened to be handy at the theatre as I said I don't know because I didn't know anything at the time I didn't make any connections whatsoever because I was completely unconscious. I didn't put it all together—me at parties hanging from pipes, richard on the street on his back, richard falling off a ladder, richard climbing rocks and cliffs and daring me to be con-cerned, winnie falling off a slide on her chin her eyes rolling up and me running in the other direction and me at a party falling into a skylight and losing a black heel to the floor below

I don't have to try and remember and although I wasn't making any special connections I knew it was all terrible. I had a call yesterday from richard from caspar california. I'm organizing his trip by remote control. Three weeks ago I said tomorrow you're going to seattle and that next day I drove him to hudson's for 2 shirts one pants one nabsack one shoes no nametapes and I drove him to the airport and bought him a ticket and didn't have time to stop at the park so he could see his friends and bought him some french fries and gave him $55 and put him on a united and called seattle to snowshoe whose brother met him at that end the five hours later the next I heard he was standing on tall swaying ladders making $10 a day picking apples. I told danny that richard was among the last of the junior acid freaks who sit on rocks up at the park around the boathouse getting holes in their pants and I sent him to the coast to see the world and danny said if he danny lived on the pacific coast he'd drop acid every day and sit on the cliff and watch the sun go down. A little man was walking down eighth street last week yelling Wake Up Wake Up, —They're Coming.—They're coming, of *course* they're coming, whoever they are, anybody can see that they're coming and so is the first frost in new england and the birches are showing in the hills the yearly mellowdrama and I want some candystriped doctor dentyns with feet and the thing in the back and there is no greater satisfaction than in everything so I don't know what was wrong about 1962. I met rosalyn drexler in washington heights in the park strolling her kid danny around and I was making $80 a month writing for art news and I was evicted from my $80 walkup so I could move into another nice tennement on houston street closer to this woman I'd fallen madly in love with and whom I was chasing around unashamedly. I was evicted and the eviction men threw out my babybook and my grandmother's old persian rug and when I was packing the remains I lost my wedding ring under my ford I think and that was a good thing too. This has many little interruptions and a kiss on both cheeks is not in disorder. All the tender pressing of the complete expression. All the exaggeration in examination. All this is that intention and some expectation. It wasn't really clear that we were living thru such an ordeal. I remember rosalyn yelling at sherman out her window and I remember rosalyn was said to've punched sherman in the nose, and I remember rosalyn coming over to see me with a huge bottle of cheap chianti and I remember her kid danny beating up richard in the sandbox. I remember the sandbox thing but I don't know if that really happened I might've dreamed it and if I did it was because danny was more aggressive than richard and he probably didn't fall off ladders and I suppose that by now he's a basketball and track champ and I hope he is and for myself it was a pleasure putting richard on the plane for seattle carrying a beatup copy held together by a rubberband of the electrickool-aidacidtest he received as a gift from an elderly freak in the park. Naturally whenever the children are involved there is always a little trauma. By remote control talking on the phone to caspar california I hoped richard would spend more than one day in san francisco as I dreamed he wouldn't and he would go to the golden gate and sit around on some new kinds of rocks in that place there and then san diego and pauline isn't it amazing he's just 14 and I like the whole thing. The great fabrication of origins and imitations. Few are called and many are poisoned. Possibly the new business that began to come into being after 1962 or sometime is the business of con- nections as we gradually lost interest in building orgone boxes in rockland county and the study of delivering up yr ego to the elements by obeying john cage we azserted our conscious- ness in connections just yesterday a letter from snowshoe say- ing she hitchhiked back to seattle from caspar having left richard off there she immediately met a joe johnston for her traveling companion you know richard has been using his mother's last name and why 1962? Because as I just this second realized last week a susan I know told me that a man at the voice said I been writing for this paper since 1962 and that isn't true it was 1959 and I did it out of washington heights while everybody was screaming and looking at the box and eating tuna fish and falling and getting hit and generally going crazy including being unsuccessfully in love. I could get very involved trying to prove something and jane is sabotaging the argument with oreos.

october 26, 1972

MORE ORPHAN THAN NOT

a good tittle for a book could be a ruined reputation. i thought also of copious notes of a retarded daughter. or the memoirs of an aggressive dwarf. the world is a tidal reely. some of us own the world in ransom and some of us just our name. i gave me all the new names in the uniworse that anybody could take if they wanted to or could. a letter from betty says that nancy says when it's holy you don't name it and the israelis didn't name the lord for penalty of death which to them was nothing. the name i kept wanting to remember today was little bill who was the son of big bill who was the husband of a woman whose sister was my mother's friend. i think a son is the son of his father and we shld leave it at that. i'm not a father's daughter and i don't know any mothers' sons and i wish they'd stop trysting it all around. i went to pick up little richard from the police in chicopee and then called up big richard to remind him he has a son. he isn't even a bad boy all he does wrong basically is hitchhiking and that's (ir)relevant to the issue of who belongs to who. i don't want any human belongings but i don't want any son of mine treated rudely by his father's keepers either. i mean i wouldn't throw im to the dawgs just because he isn't my son. but that feeling apparently is what keeps the rocket ships flying and the napalm dropping and big boys turning into rich doctors. somebody has to care about the fathers' sons so all that can keep on happening. care is a package wrapped by mothers. i don't suppose a daughter exists until she's big enough to be a son's mother. i should've named my daughter jill so she could be a little jill and we could carry on a line of big and little jills and her father wouldn't make the mistake of imagining she's his daughter while his son goes gaberlunzing around being treated uncivilly by the fathers of other sons whose mothers have been delegated to nurture and care and whose sisters are maintained by their fathers as their father's daughters in order to perpetuate the tradition of caring and keeping the rockets flying. i could care and care and that wouldn't give me the right to change the hitchhiking laws. it's the sons' fathers who do that. tho the cities start to crumble and the towers fall around us . . . the continuators are not really clear about the proper ending for the various versions differ from each other. you don't have much choice if all you've got left is what somebody hasn't suggested. except for banging and whimpering. the boys go on banging and the women whimpering and this is the way the world ends daily. more orphan than not. i'm not a father's daughter and i don't know hardly any mothers excepting the mommie within and that's a feeling i'm working on. a series of pilgrimage books tydled the mommie within. followed by the lessons of donna juana. accompanied by the copious notes of a retarded daughter. a door opens a maiden enters, so beautiful that so&so very nearly loses consciousness. i was saying. i wanted to shift priorities and discuss the hiking i did in the cascades before it was too late for an important date sometime when i rote a column of great social and political import it went like this about how i hated climbing as a camper encase anymind shld think i never change my body well i do. the thing i never feel any differently about however is ruining reputations. if there's a reputation to be ruined by all means it shld be done. we don't want anybody around with a reputation. we know what they say about girls like that. anyway as to the cascades my memory of even this enormous cedar that snowshoe said was the matriarch of the forest and that i called hera the herbivore and against which i posed for a photo to measure for size is obscured by the latest news from ugh there and that was that little richard was lost in the skykomish. before that it was the police in wenatchee for hitchhiking. wenatchee or chicopee if i can't change the laws i'm goaling to make the laws change his father so that while he's becoming a rich rocktor he can have the xperience of beoming his son's father, a new clonecept perhelps in the herstory of the wistern worold. he was picking raspburries and extra violates down by the sky-komish river and snowshoe called to tell me how city slocks are illways dying in the wilds there from oaferexposure and i spent a whole day caring and i missed my scheduled rocket flight and my sister jane who hated her brother because she wanted her mother all to herself told me there i was going again caring about my son who has his father's name. the name seemed to open a window inside her head. apolonea. maedell. a maedell drived up from washington from off our backs to in-terphew me after readering my boke she said what she won-dered was whether her breasts would suit jill johnston. that zounded good but i couldn't see her at all because she was dresst in a tent. she's marred to a southern baptist marine who was caring after their four sons so she could come up in her tent to see another mother who possibling would care about her and i did. that was maedell. she said her name was reversed after her grandmother's which was dell may or something. a letter from betty says that nancy says etceteraphim. a letter from raindance says living in pacific grove does tend to get her down a lot because orange and her are the only proud, brave, funny, egotistical, normal, fastmoving lesbians around who live uncompromisingly gay vegetarian lives. a letter from greg-ory dated june 28 reads greetings from soviet union. my guide wanted to go to hermitage. all i wanted to do was drink. so we sat in the park for three days, reading. cheers, dr.g. a letter from rebecca patterson says her daughter anne is finishing her dissertation on cartesianism and its effect on neoclassical writ-ers, with particular emphasis on the works of jean de la fon-taine and jonathan swift. i wanted to dispose of the letters to get back to little bill who was the son of big bill who was the husband of a woman whose sister was my mother's friend. before a daughter gets big enough to be a son's mother she can study up on the fathers and write dissertations about them. in preparation for becoming the mother of the sons whose fathers will delegate her daughters the task of nurturing and caring for his sons. tho the cities start to crumble & the towers fall around us . . . the women being powerless except over each other etceterrible. jennerations of vipers. anuther goad tittle. the female unuck. the momipulated man. the malleus malefi- carum. woman's estatic. i'm have a fatherless daughters con- vention and reeling off a paper called the revelations of a vengeful mother. matching codes with cores. the complemen- tary paper would be the copious notes of a retarded daughter. i have very little idea about the sons since i hate caring because i think it's this feeling that maintains the fathers in the style to which they're accustombed. i talked to little richard's father's wife who told me his father whoever that is i'm losing track does really care and i said well he has an interesting way of demonstrating caring, why did he say then leave him in jail. i wanted to know when i was speaking to her if i was speaking to her or to her and her husband big richard and she replied instamatically to her and to him. he's not even her son but she cared enough to call me back altho she makes it clear speaking for both of them that this son is a bad kid because he doesn't share their middle crass values. she doesn't say it but she thinks i'm a bad kid too since i was the one responsorible for leading him astray. that means i waxn't a goot mother. of curse not. i haven't considered him other than his father's son for sum time and i told im too when e goes to the police stations and gives out his last name as mine and then the police ask me mine and if i'm a miss or a mrs and i say i'm not a mrs what's supposed to happen then. they look at you funny and probly they de- cide i'm the son's father or even his son. he's taller than me so why not. i know i made the mistake of being the son's father's something or other once upardon time and now all i want to be is a friend but the world or at least the hitchhiking laws keeps making me a mother. i hate mothers so i hate myself being a mother and i act like a mother which makes me feel even worse. i even gave him a pair of old shoes. i can't say that made me too unhappy since they were the shoes old j. lennon gave me 2 years ago. richard didn't like them. his father's middle name is john so it all goes together. i gave him some pants too. i gave him a ouspensky book and i guess that's all. first i'd be overwhelmed by guilt and then by anger and then contrition and despair and guilt and anger in virtuosic overlapping unwinding inflationary spiral curves. i did eggzackly what r. d. laing says mothers do. all mothers convey contradictory messages and turn their big boys into napalm freaks and rich doctors. they hate their mothers, whose fathers make them police their sons. the fathers already're too busy with the napalm and rockets. then when mother fails and father's hitchhiking laws come into play the cops will take over and call up mother to come n claim her bad kid whose father was never programmed to care. i should write a funny letter to alice. it's too down a trip to be taken seriously. and then we're only children children one and all. i was remembering little bill who was special only for being the son of big bill and the nephew of my mother's friend who concerned me much more than the bills since she was the one i saw lots of times. i don't think my mother had any male friends except a dentist who tried to lay me once. the main women i remember were bertha hatch whose nephew was little bill and dorothy and eleanor platt and a mrs martin and they were all what we used to call old maids. i never saw any men around except for mrs martin's son burnside who was a brat and i had to play with him. burnside martin. a pain in the ass. i think his mother mrs martin was a lawyer. she probably needed one. my mother had one and it didn't do her much good and i'm getting one too but the times've changed. the times they are achanging. the times is going out of business. what maedell told me was that her sons' father thought he was fighting being pussy whipped and then he gave up trying to dominate her and he never even criticizes her, if you can imagine a southern baptist marine she said. she fell in love with him when she was 13 she said. she's got a lot of sons and she's making their father send her to school. she says it's only her right since he wouldn't be what he is today if it weren't for her. she'd like to be a lesbian but she'll do that next. a father's daughter leaves his sons. a daughter who exists without being a son's mother. a ruined reputation. a daughter without a name. a daughter who names herself. a daughter in a line of big and little daughters all with the same name. a daughter who cares about her daughters but not any more than about herself. a daughter who refuses to care about the sons unless she can change the laws. a whole new codecept in the tradition of caring. the wisdom of the children and the graceful way of flowers in the wind. daftne laurus nobilis. any of a genus of eurasian shrubs of the mezereon family with a colored calyx resembling a corolla. daftne & apolonea. the names seem to open a window inside her head.

august 2, 1973

CALL IT A DAY & A DAY IT WAS

She said she didn't think it was politically correct to get done by a dog. I don't like these dog conversations. I don't like dogs. I think they were discussing a love between the species workshop. We have all we can manage getting it straight between ourselves. All they agreed on was that males will stick it in the wall. Two worker types saw my virgin badge this morning and said they didn't believe it. I said it was true. Of course I am. And I'm celebrating finishing my book and I'm not trapped by fame, I enjoy it. I wonder if my mother knows. MS wouldn't print this photo of me by Sahm which is childish and intelligent and flattering what else do you want from a photo. What else did she say I said she was? Who said easy times come hard for me and oh mydarling oh well. I lost my record book in schrafts but I found out about elevators in the same half hour. I'm sitting waiting for Dione eating pretzels watching a woman walk right into an open trap and the door close after her I knew she knew to walk in because the light was on over the trap and I remembered how I used to do this myself just as unconcernedly walk in and let myself be carried upwards someplace by this large box and I thought as the light went off and the woman went up what would I do if the box stopped between floors I saw myself screaming but silently as in a dream and I realized at once it wasn't an elevator problem but a room problem in 1965 I was locked in a room I had never been locked in a room before except that time before I was born so I never thought of rooms or elevators as traps and now I don't like to be locked either in or out of a place and it really is a room problem I remembered sitting there in rockefeller center waiting for Dione eating pretzels watching another woman walk right into the open trap and the door close after her I knew. You remember that e.e. cummings title the enormous room. That's the world I guess and we're locked in

so I don't know what I'm worried about. Only a vagina has
real teeth. Somebody said the beards on men's faces are the
pubes of medusa. I've heard the pubic hair of women referred
to as the beard of allah. We saw hercules in the desert last
night. I let carol drink out of my taurus cup cuz she's a taurus
too. carol came up with sk dunn who named her daughter after
carol's mother which may be why I always introduce carol as
carol dunn which is really sk's father's name and somehow it
all makes sense since carol was sk's first lover, I don't mean her
father but carol mullins the taurus whose mother has the same
name as sk's daughter. I was named after a british movie
actress. Jane was named after a heroine in a novel her mother
was reading. I'm glad carol and sk are still friends. I'm still
friends with sk too. I met her on my mother's birthday two
years ago and I lost my wallet with my british passport and
my birth certificate all my mother's names when we went dancing. I lost my wallet when carol and sk came up the other day
too. Then I found it. I lost everything my mother gave me. I
lost my record book in schraffts the day I understood elevators
because schraffts is the place my mother always took me for
lunch when we came to the city to buy my new tweed winter
coat at lord & taylor's and my patent leather shoes for easter
at best's. It's all about rooms. And photos. I suppose Sahm is
my mother too. She takes wonderful photos, just the way my
mother saw me in her candid brownie shots. I lost all of them
in 196-something whenever I was evicted from washington
heights and I lost my wedding ring under a car and the city
threw out the babybook along with my grandmother's old
persian rug. I felt terrible about the photos. The woman I
loved said I cried just like a baby. I had a right to, it was the
thing my mother and me liked to do best besides play pick up
sticks and double solitaire, lie in bed on a lazy sunday and look
at the photos and have her explain them again every time including the first three the day she had me, she said, three almost
identical shots in the arms of a british nurse, my favorite was

in the arms of a british steward on the s.s. george washington. She always said I lost everything she gave me. What else did she say I said she was. When you move you find out what you've been losing and what you've been hanging on to. I have a photo of my first boyfriend but not my first two women. It doesn't matter, to him I was a virgin. We're organizing a virgins international conference. First we might have an international apology conference. Experimental conditioning. Everybody will spend five days apologizing and never do it again. I hope everybody comes and then we can all be friends. We could have a big margemellow roast. Jane said to Bertha so don't you agree an army of lovers can't get out of bed and Bertha replied she didn't realize there was a tactical problem. After the revolution you're so busy getting things organized you don't have a chance to go to bed. Jane said maybe we should postpone the revolution. Bertha: Let's not take the fun out of revolution. Pleasure is the energy principle. Who said schizophrenics can have an orgasm looking at a blank wall. When virginia woolf went crazy she thought the birds were speaking in greek. When I was crazy they locked me in a room and I didn't have an orgasm and my mother came to see me and showed me a photo of her grandchildren. I do have one thing left and that's the blue and yellow ski sweater she knit when I was 19 and went to vermont to learn how to ski. That's all. I think I packed it last week. I can't lose Sahm's photos because she's a professional. But when carol and sk came up sk ript off a few others and said she'd bring them back but she won't. I like the whole photo business but I told Sahm I'm really tired of my ego and have to split for europe soon. The ego the voice the record book the book the rooms the photos the revolution everything. Jane thought I lost the record book at schraffts because of the voice and I said well that's true if the voice is my mother and I guess it is. Anyway I reclaimed it by taxi this morning the longhair driving held up norman o. brown's life against death and asked me if I read it it happened to be the book I was reading in 1965 when I went crazy and I began to remember that time before I was born and the book is done and we met at schraffts to talk about it and about the photos and the rooms and Dione went up and down the trap three times and then I supplied the explanation and she didn't disagree. It takes being locked in a room to realize how dangerous a moving box is. The arms are numb and the sun don't shine. Did I ever say I was a schraffts coffee girl once for eight months, or nine, well I was. I wore a black dress and a hairnet and lipstick and stockings and I was a very good girl. I don't know when I began to go bad. Possibly when I found myself unexpectedly pregnant. It wasn't easy being pregnant and a virgin. When mary maxworthy unexpectedly found her-self pregnant gertrude stein said simply that mary "had some-thing happen to her that surprised everyone who knew her." It's all true. Even sk used to say that her daughter jesse who's named after carol's mother was her mother. I never understood sk's arrangement, it was just the first of its kind I'd seen, the father in one room and the daughter in another and sk in the middle with her procession of lovers and ex lovers turned into friends or back into lovers again for all I know I know it's re-assuring to have a visit from her with carol mullins the day after she said bernie got up in the morning after over a year I think they've been together and said in her iowa drawl well I think it's time to call it a day and went and bought a big duffle and packed up and made a plane reservation for iowa and went to the airport accompanied by sk and I suppose sk's father and daughter and maybe carol mullins anyway I thought she was supposed to feel terrible so I was glad to see carol but sk was smiling and saying this bernie woman is fantastic, she just gets up and says it's time to call it a day and a day it was and we're all movin' on and that's all. Well aren't you going to do something about it. About what. She came and ript off a few of my photos, that's what. Speaking of photos the last time I saw Ti-Grace that amazing photo of herself just

married at 17 in full white drag that used to hang on her wall
in an oval frame under a cracked glass was on the floor leaning against the wall and without the glass. I said hey what's
going on. She said she's buying some darts and getting it ready
to use as a dart board. She's a woman of pronouncements.
What else did she say I said she was. I don't know. I declare
this done. I just remember sk one day two summers ago thrust-
ing her hand through a glass pane and for hands this winter
I bought and lost four identical pairs of red woolen hunter's
gloves and borrowed jane's black ones and accidentally left
them at her house when the winter was over which means I
really know what I'm doing and that's all I have to say. Burn
this and memorize yourself.

june 8, 1972

HOLIER THAN ME

My head is falling out so I'm standing on my stomach. From
there the nipples and belly buttons were flashing in bronze
but she's sexually precocious from having been somewhat de-
prived. For the holydays I'm walking into various houses of
happenings. Having come in out of nature where winter won-
derlanded itself all over my car. And into my sight holes. Ice
world. Ice antennae. Clumps a needles pining into ice wedding packages. Whole halves of trees heavy loaded up to droop-
ing into my boots can't move. Sun also come down to light up
a delicatentacle decor. Sparko plenty. Old lady nature. I drove
off into the sunset and melted my doors down to a dirty brown
tin. Here's an emergency parking sign upended its arrow
pointing straight up. I wondered if I had died and fallen into
hell without noticing it. I paused in my journey. If what is
the same as what is not what am I doing anyplace? I better
keep my hands folded and my joys to myself. I drive on. I
walk into one of these houses for holydays and a fine lady
reading my palm says it all looks good from here on out. Out.
So long I'm far away in the mountains living in a humble
hut. But ever around there you can walk into an encounter
group, you don't watch out. Drive into a wilderness town for
a coffee a late winter's eve an inn the sign says so it's okay
but it's a group grope and we're stumbling backward into a
snow gorge I remember oneathem things I went to once and
they were feeling up my back and commenting on my back
and asking for opinions on anybody's back but I was laughing
inside also when a poor sad lady lacking even a back but with
cold clammy palms said she was terrified of me because of my
tie. Why didn't her mother straighten out her teeth when she
was young? She could throw herself into a flame in order to
avoid being drowned in the water. They didn't even thank
me for the awful time I gave them. I drive on. In and out

of the gutter slush where you jeep and tractor yourself over a parking position. We're going to a wedding. Gregory says it's a gay wedding. I won't go up in the elevator. Walk up two flights. The door can't open. It has to, I'm saying. No it won't. You have to go down to use the elevator they're yelling, at me. But I'm rattling the knob, at them. Bang. It bolts open. And I'm falling onto a heap of junk with the groom (or bride) who's shaking my hand. Orlando. In white. Where's his intended? Here she is. A she she. Well come on Gregory, you said this was a . . . and David is protesting yes how could Gregory get this thing mixed up, he wouldn't cross the street for a straight wedding. And we're walking away into the snow dirty night with Gregory still insisting the groom is as gay as a goose. David is very learned. He explains that all Latinos, like Orlando, are pederasts, any hole will do, and also they all have venereal disease from screwing crocodiles. They break out in white spots and there's no known cure for it.—Orlando asked Gregory and me if we wanted to get married too. Yes of course. They had a fellow there in levis and lumber jacket officiating. But David said it wouldn't be interesting unless it was legal. So we're waiting for the cer-tifuckits and Wasserladies. Then afterward we're leaping into a limousine for Brazil. Don't mourn for me friends / don't weep for me never / for I'm going to do nothing forever and ever. Goodbye until we meet again in this world or the next. In the next where the nipples and navels will be flashing in bronze from where I stand upside down on my stomach and the whirld is a wonderwoman wimming along like guppies gaping these ravenous mouths . . . And where somebody will support Ann to write up her dreams in colored crayons. She spent two days in bed in the dark eating chocolates that Jill brought her. Now she's lumbering up naked out of the blankety deeps telling me she doesn't even want sex any more, she doesn't want anything, she just wants Gene to walk in the door to talk to. But Ann, Gene is dead. "Yes I know—it was an awful thing to do to me." And when she dies herself she says they'll find a house full of roaches and boxes of senile letters and heaps of ratty old quilts. But now she has the candles lit up, and the incense and the pot pipe all pretty the whole place in its holier than me aspect as she sits swaddled in a radio's monk chant and two sacred books and she blearies over her eyelids into some meditative mask or other above the tin foil of the pipe's bowl and prepares to consecrate my new record book for the year 1970. Now she's stuffing a cat into an egg crate. Now she's saying you never know when jesus is here until he's left. Jesus came bearing a gift and she couldn't even make a bowl of soup. Now she wants to make it with a man and a woman, preferably more—as many things as she can get in there. Oh Ann just fix up my record book. I'm going back to my umble hut. What's to be said any more about sex or sunsets. I'm driving off into the mud but first I go into all these houses. Of happynings. Or sadthings. I sleep with an R and an M because the R needs an M to feel right about the J who bares a sweet but socially uncomfortable re-semblance. I sort of sleep with a T who wouldn't hate men so much if she'd stop raging around the country about liberat-ing women and just go to bed with them. I go to a New Year's day party where I have to go up in the elevator and where George Segal thinks a seethrough shirt is an invitation to paw what's underneath it. I go to a New Year's even party and re-ceive my engagement ring from Gregory and admire J. Per-reault for peeing in the vestibule behind an Xmas tree and try to seduce a nurse who once helped me wash out my un-derwear and I have to leave here by all that's evil before I go completely sane. I'll pass my days eating the roots of wild herbs cooked in a pot with broken legs. I'll be holier than me. I'll keep my left eye on you while I finish this puzzle. This autobiograffiti. Meantime according to Ann a new re-deemer is coming in the year 2000. But I think he's hiding out right now in a mental institution. Ex nihilo nihil fit!

january 15, 1970

HIC ET UBIQUE

It was the sort of trip you spend much more time coming and
going than you do there. Then too all living leading inevitably
to the supreme adventure of transition we crossed by ferry
more times than you might ordinarily if you were just making
a single trip to an island for the weekend, which we were.
Things just really happen to me. I don't think my life was
any the less interesting before I took on this terrible responsibility of leaving myself behind for a fiction. Actually more
like Apollinaire I appear to be carrying everything along with
me jilly nilly fact legend gossip glory and gore. Words are
very very heavy magic. So everything you say is true. The
necessities of style distort both fact and fiction. For sample
I lied about Illinois. Besides flying my maiden voyage as a
co-pilot I spent a part of one of those days way off when
everybody is quiet and smiling and walking thru doors and
walls because it's a sunny afternoon in the woods and the
house is outrageously beautiful. I mean I made it all up that
I had had an awful time prior to my flight in order to convince myself that I experienced a great drama. It's a renais-
sance trick of creating backgrounds to project a central figure.
This is an ongoing essay with its own revision. You know
that Apollinaire wrote a column called La Vie Anecdotique
for Mercure de France in 1911 & thenabouts. Constantly he
was trying to lug into the future with him the curious exotic
treasures he found in the past. His manner became increasingly eccentric and he often filled his conversation with erudite
and vulgar allusions, forgetting nothing he saw or heard. Like
a photographer with her camera we interpose our notebooks
between ourselves and the world. I suppose I was almost killed
at an intersection a truck was bearing down on me passenger in a
chevie coup C. who was driving asked me what was i doing just
after we didn't collide I was writing a line about a man I saw

seconds before the intersection this man who is the sort of man you see year after year a recurring image this time his appearance evoked a line about himself so I could immortalize his only aspect to me is a tall gentle einstein walking a city street and he always has a bunch of flowers in hand or a beautiful daughter or some sad thing, that's the way I framed him up or shot him dead the moment after I suppose I was almost killed at an intersection a truck was bearing down on me passenger in a chevie coup C. who was driving asked me what I was doing just after we didn't collide I was writing a line about a man I saw seconds before the intersection this man who is the sort of man you see year after year a recurring image it is possible to believe that none of these details come into being at the moment they appear. The line out my window leads to the Sun, the ox, the child, and to all of us becoming worms. Angels and ministers of grace defend us. I've met somebody more outrageous than me. The initial is P. stands for Polly. She said I could say so. It's about time somebody did. I wasn't dreaming she was driving my van in a blue latex bra. She did everything there was to do in my van since it was the sort of trip you spend much more time coming and going than you do there. Then too all living leading inevitably to the supreme adventure of transition we crossed by ferry more times than you might ordinarily if you were just making a single passage to an island for the weekend, which we were. The plot the ferryboat people devised for us was the separation of our bodies from our vehicle which they promised to reunite on the island the morning after the bodies part of the bar- gain had arrived to shift for themselves because the ferry is too small to carry both bodies and their vehicles on a Me- morial day schedule we were waiting therefore in the early a. m., having crashed in a house of strangers and walked the morning misty sunny unreal roads of the aboriginal birds and bushes and looked at some red starfish and barbuncles leech- ing on the pier trunks and made love in the ants and grass

weeds by two infant Xmas trees sharing a silent harbor excepting a gull streaking out close to the surface squawking
like a baby crying for milk I never knew a gull made that
sort of sound having waited in all these interesting ways including asking Polly to bring a scrap of paper on the way
to the ants and grass weeds and Xmas trees to note none of
these details since I was too busy doing them and moving my
body to the pier to reunite with my vehicle as the ferry arrived there was every damned thing on it except the promised
wheels so we rode back in a heat with the four boat bastards who were just altering the plot on their own initiative
by claiming that the keys we left the day before in the ticket
house didn't fit the van. We were besieged with diseases.
Cramps and headaches and other symptoms of a desire to kill.
The bull and the eagle unite to defeat the dragon. She has
an eagle eye and my official sign image embarrasses me so I
thank whoever anonymously from Brooklyn sending such a
delicate miniature version of it all white already in the china
shop. Stopping in Hartford to see important people who invited us to their museum for a function Polly asked me if they
were ready for us. I guess we both have the inexhaustible
strength of unbalanced people. Ca n'empeche pas d'exister. I
don't know what a historian meant by saying Apollinaire ran
the constant risk of turning his private life into a public performance. Risk? Whither we rides, and why, we do not know,
only that the business is important and pressing. In the unstable compound of fable and fact that passes for our lives.
I could tell you I saw oval colors coming off the sun walking
down the clouds into the sea while I held her breasts under
the blue latex she was hovering to obscure my vision of all
save her head by the harbor. I could tell you she began kissing
me dangerously while I was driving because I mentioned the
Ti-Grace jail story as a sudden inspired line of Ti-Grace
spread-eagled and shackled naked to the cell bars by the men
after she constitutionally refused to strip and squat to be

searched by the women but she said she didn't, begin kissing me because of my sudden sexual eloquence. Nor can I distinguish my early memories from the photos of them. We went to Bertha's house on the island. This is the house and I am a photo. A child with a stick and a sheep in the rugged backyard. A child in sneakers and a striped shirt and solid pants climbing the rocks that constitute the cliff separating the house from the ocean. A child in a small boat on the way to the house this time I cried somewhat under my shades clouding the glass or the plastic so she couldn't see I was once furious to receive as a present a box worth of kleenex held together by an iron bolt thru the center a sculpture I suppose I knew the significance of receiving kleenex when my lover got a drawing of a bird on the same occasion it is now more sensible to me there is nothing to hold on to like birds for sample but we might as well cry when the vision of an old house and maternal memories by photo or whichway and the current disjunction on a car ferry between you and a friend and lover who doesn't immediately look with wonder and admiration when you childishly point and yell "the house, the house" reminds us of the moral shock of the sudden ghastly disclosure of our mothers true nature. That was Hamlet's problem, actually, and not ours. I meant to lie so I could present the confusing nonsequitur of two such unhappy products in shock over ghastly disclosures blundering beautifully on to destruction by filling themselves inside as well as up against as spherical bodies all parts orientating themselves in an infinite number of positions in a rectangular space like sentences not too abruptly rotating their angular facets as cut stones or the multicolored ball we lost to the tide in the harbor waiting for the ferry playing volley catch and fist serve and tap and such on some slabs sloping down to the water we watch ourselves in metamorphosis in sunglint floating out to sea I can't find the really classy line I thought I wrote to describe the pleasure of losing your game to an interesting disappearance anyway this is an ongoing essay with its own revision. On the ferry returning to the mainland to bring the wheels to the island ourselves I opened at random the boat bible stashed in with the life preservers to point and get the passage "forgive them their iniquities" so although I was still besieged with diseases or symptoms of murderous impulses I sat steaming silently on the other side even when we still couldn't abridge their extended plot by making the same ferry back by loading both our bodies *and* the vehicle because the lady with the keys to the ticket house within which my van keys were locked up was at church and Polly was running back and forth from captain to phone to old red-hat the machiest one of all very angry at us for all the trouble he was causing us I realized too late that if I had bothered to avail myself of his name other than "red-hat" the revision of all emotions would have facilitated our earlier arrival or departure, but then we might not have had the opportunity to make more love while waiting in the rectangular womb on the mainland, and we might not have exchanged minor revelations on the trip back in Boone's fish place in Portland Polly noted the connection of my name obsession, as I described its origin learning hundreds of names in the funny farm six years ago, and my thinking to ask what was the name of old red-hat because he was so tall looming fearsome in his fury; and I noted for Polly to add to her Sylvia Plath fact and lore how Sylvia as Esther in her novel "Bell Jar" began obsessing suicide immediately after the psychiatrist she was visiting, by her mother's wish, in Boston, committed her to shock treatment. Like Sylvia, through a prolonged suicide Alfred Jarry clung to the moment of total freedom that precedes death. According to some historian Apollinaire's death in 1918 brought a timely end to his career since his creative powers were declining and he began to entertain vain hopes of official honors. He didn't actually die. The necessities of style distort both fact and fiction. He was creative even in his

simulated death and forged disappearance and equally fictitious resurrection. The head wound he sustained in the war
occurred in a trench while he was reading the latest Mercure
from Paris. The blood encrusted Mercure and the ripped helmet became his most precious souvenirs. The central figure is
always either a dead knight on a bier or a wounded king
on a litter. Apollinaire arranged his own incredible revision
of himself. I imagine arriving Hartford that although of course
they're never ready for us we too might excel in balancing
natural charm against intentional outrage. I don't know. The
week before in some other hinterland all I had to do was pass
out while she took the wife of a business associate of mine
into the shower and committed other inconceivable transgressions against propriety and decency. In Hartford I guess we
were more of a team. She told the museum director that his
daughter was a brat and later I snatched the museum director's
wife in her black maxi at the quasi-formal dinner sheik style
pulled her over my lap horizontal to do something to her god
knows what while she tittered and sort of screamed and
kicked her legs pitty patty and feigned squealing for her husband or she meant it or whatever. Polly reminds me someday
I'm going to be an elderly nude. I'm lying again because I
didn't want to say I thought that myself. What she really
said was that she never violated a certain park in the winter
because she didn't want to see her foot break the snow. I
can't think of a better way of saying I really like to be fucked
by a woman and walk like an ostrich that's lost its eggs from
expiring over a number of cosmic or cataclysmic orgasms. Hic
et ubique. And exploit like Apollinaire our expansive personalities by celebrating them in our works and saying that
around this composite creation unites a conflagration of dream
and reality. C. observes that this horses jaw is two angels of
God. She says also her mother would now consider finding a
female lover. B. says yesterday Mercury and Venus were in
conjunction. Angels and ministers of grace defend us. She

made a gibson with nine onions. She showed me her Lacrosse stick. She spilled my coffee in the van over and over. She embarrassed me by being apparent to truck drivers in her blue latex bra. She excavated my seat belts from the ruins of my crevices. She burdens herself with these saddle bags that only Hermes would carry. She says we need a helicopter to cut short all the time you spend coming and going more than you spend there. She says I didn't look good posing on the island for a memory a photo next to the James Joyce died 1898 tombstone. She drinks peptobismol like milk or gingerale. She buys expensive champagne and shares the first rounds with your garage attendants. She's outrageous. Tears hearts and crosses raining down out of the eye holding up a totem of web and woman. Virginia Vita too tuo. In somno Eve ecclesia nascitur.

june 10, 1971

A FAIR TO MEDDLING STORY

she's grumpy because the sun isn't shining, and she slept two hours longer than she needed to, and the last dream she had made her mad. i was mad myself but i only remember her back in the yellow wooden lawn chair reading facing the stream an up the hill. we go to a great deal of trouble to agree to these misunderstandings. i won't bend over frontwards to engage in speculation of the motivation of others. she said there was a chipmunk on a stone wall scolding her and he was mad at florence the cat too, then she thought he was scolding her jane and reconsidered it and decided he was scolding florence, though maybe she was raking over his hole or something. i had a dream about a hole. it involved a hole a tree and a grey animal. it's a fair to muddling story. this large tree trunk was fallen down and a small animal was jiggling one end of it under the trunk trying to save or right it i guessed. the next scenario was this alley oop grey animal with a mouses head and a fat body coming out from a great square hole it'd dug as big as a small room under that one end of the tree. the animal was a variation of ben who's a fixed male cat i sometimes see as an evolved mouse altho he stalks like a miniature tiger. possibly i was mad because i hate ben doing 100 yard dashes around my head at night. i've forgotten. but the hole was a sunken swimming pool. off and on all some day or other i mentioned pools realizing it was warm but not how warm until officially informed that i had an excuse for doing nothing all day except mentioning pools. the tree was this branch that grows out horizontally so far from its trunk and so fat and with so many of its own branches that it requires a vertical support. i don't see loops of meaning curling in cool blades of grass or anything like that. or polished stones tumbling out of heaven. (sold american). i have straightforward hole tree & animal dreams. i have car and plane and children dreams, guilts, anxieties prophecies wish fulfillments idle speculations and passing the time away. i try catching the "significant" ones to see what they're telling me in case i need to be told and very often we do. what if the papers published only the dream news. headlines: president n. dreams of a worldwide communist conspiracy. anyway everyday a special box for the president who sends out reports thru his dream press secretary. checkers returns to life. pat victim of boston strangler. tricia marries prince charles. julie kills david and runs away with patricia lawford. sammy davis jr. makes irregular advances and these are covertly enjoyed. john dean also sucks and john mitchell serves up his wife as legs and breasts of mutton at a huge din- ner celebrating the successful rape of 10,000 cambodian women. the president pushes all the buttons and calls billy graham who rescues the family by flying them out in a plane that's shaped like an amphitheatre and contains a unitarian choir in which his mother sings quaker solo. the dream interpreters on every paper make their comments, i. e., this incident seemingly rep- resents a regression which nevertheless leads forward. the basic headlines every day would say things like the underlying struc- ture of the universe is a double message. or, something to be secured or avoided ultimately or immediately. or, too young to be where i'm goin, too old to go back again. or kentucky fried lilly buds with chives and sour cream. or two or more competing explanations require consideration. i wondered if i had a twin if i'd compete with her and i thought we'd probly sit around and laugh at each other. i want more laughs. it's bad enough tearing up the road on yer new radial tires and making sure you don't hit any raccoons. i didn't hit this raccoon and then this young deer bounded across maybe 15 yards ahead an flit into the woods just like that. these're the animals i like, the ones running wild. i wouldn't ever own an animal, not since i was eight and had a terrier dog that ran away all the time, and i don't understand why pauline and lin keep a toucan in a cage and i don't like seeing ben walk by the window with a snake in his mouth. i don't mind robins looking for worms because that doesn't concern me. i'm very interested in animals at a distance or making signs in dreams. i don't see them as signs during the day particularly, whereas pauline does. a snake crossing her path on the road really means something. to me it means a snake crossing my path on the road. whereas that dream of snakes when i was swimming that made me turn back i interpreted right away as a bunch of wicked women and i've stayed away ever since. things that're the most ap- parent tend not to be. i'm now hanging out with sophisticated cultivated dignified considerate and gracious people. i speak of nothing but good manners. i enjoy shaking hands & enquiring after peoples health. i make small talk with the redheaded freak who changed my tires an put the old ones in my trunk. i tell im i've owned so many crates that i have a second-hand tire mentality and he smiles and says he does too. i make sure go out and admire the fairy godneighbor who appears for noth- ing to tractor down my crabweeds in his toy red mower. i eat alison's fried yellow lilly buds that she picked along the road without letting on beforehand that i knew anything strange was going to happen. i tell jane her barrelful of cold squash and broccoli and chickpea salad is her most magnificent and i remark the bad taste of people who allude to anybody i know tell who cooks as alice b.t. that's about it for now and that doesn't exclude being mad sometimes. biting well and speaking little. flower in the mouth. small & defective always. anyway looking good. one coming a long way. one always hoping for the best. farreaching. high cloud, low lake. crocodile queen. shiny black. blooming tree. all the gnews that's fit to spring. let us contemplate undazed the extent of my innocence. and this, our life, exempt from public haunt, finds tongues in trees, books in the running brooks, sermons in stones, and good in every- thing. i'll write to sk and tell er i'm glad she's better. i'll call maria del drago and enquire after kate. i'll send alice james to kate and remind jane to send zelda to agnes. i'll write about ann wilson as a great artist. i'll call up winnie and see if richard is living in the bronx. i'll give alison my apollinaire and get neal cassady back from gregory and look for tallulah to give alice. i'll tell alice i'll never go back to her restaurant unless she tells her boys not to insult women. i won't give her any more balloons either. i take refuge in studied ambiguities. enantiodromia. the psychic law of the reversal of all opposites. to disagree with yr pt of view is to have a side namely that one that's not yours. they can't get it thru their filter. in dreams the element of judgment is absent. like pauline told me there was this tribe called sequoia or something which ran its life according to its dreams. every morning the family wld arise and somebody probably the father wld preside and they wld all discuss their dreams and what they meant for their rela-tionships and the health of the tribe. pauline says a little auto suggestion before you go to sleep is enough to help you re-member. she read a long dream to me in leucadia out of her notebook. the one i wrote down yesterday was a phone fear guilt & paranoia children dream. nothing as easy as a hole tree & animal number. a pont ou nul ne passe. the way it went the phone was out of order meaning it made a collection of noises and the receiver "floated" off the hook and this meant when-ever this happened that you'd be "booked on suspicion." of what it was uncertain excepting its kafkaesque clarity and i prepared to be "picked up" and told jane who was off some-place another part of this "exposed" house, i puzzled over the correct clothes and ended up with a silk dark print dress tucked into my pants an walked out to meet the feds or whoever it was who was coming. first there was decoys, peoples i knew from before like j. dunn & s. paxton walking toward me "as in a dream" on a perimeter and impassively, then when they got close enough this fed or some badlooking twirpy guy material-ized and clamped something on my wrist led us up away up some stairs we arrived where there were these deformed de-fected children with bulging eyes one as small as a button that's the end of the dream. i know that day richard called from new york arrived in three days from montana and his voice was garbled in bad connections, and a woman from new hampshire told me her middle daughter jill died at four of pneumonia and she was born brain damaged. the president's dream for tomorrow could read: pres. n. has watergate on the chest. i had a virile pneumonia once too and i spent a week in the hospital and what it was was a pain in the chest from not being able to scream at my husband. in the long run he is not evil, only unfortunate, and wishes to be redeemed himself. terror has been succeeded by a terror infinitely worse. needle at the bottom of the ocean. white swan cools its wings. nobby knees and my teeth hurt and this is friday. freida and otto and henry. many feathers no wings. one in fine clothes. one with good news but a little old. yes he is my son, i keep asking myself where i went wrong. i wish she'd stop sitting with her back in the yellow wooden lawn chair reading facing the stream an up the hill. but i go on fooling in the grass with my feet next to the mailbox. i won't power the mower or use any machines or do anything butch except drive my new radial tires. these cats think nothing of walking around with snakes in their mouths. the only form of reprisal left was moral indignation and that has never won any decisive battles. i was the first to come & i am the last to go. booked on suspicion all the way. she says she apologized to every flower as she picked it. i was quoting my own work, without acknowledgment of course. i appeared naked and asked if i didn't look thin and she said no you're voluptuous and i forgot what the argument was all about. if you need one you can create a real crisis by moving convulsively against an imaginary one. to recapitulate: she was grumpy because the sun wasn't shining, and she slept two hours longer than she needed to, and the last dream she had made her mad. then there was a lot abt animals holes pools trees children food promises to be good and the advisability of publicizing the dreams of national leaders. it's a fair to meddling story. my last word is ben's gone crazy, florence is home in heat, mother cass delivered six kittens, i had some rare steak with rug seasoning, i bought the amelia earhart record and some pipes & drums of scotland, i have no vital preoccupation since my foot is better, i'm still staying far away from the wicked snake women, i still specialize in the impossible, i'm still studying good manners, i still enjoy good orgasm, i'll continue to influence this story from a distance and in the morning those who've been favored with the goddesses nocturnal visitation will tell their experiences. we like the original virgin of ourselves. persephone secunda. principium individuationis!

july 19, 1973

TENDER GLUTTONS

continuing on with dreams animals names food sex richard &
the world at small, i had an astonishing dream i was flying
around this interior full of people and sticking em all up with
my hand and it was quite clear to everybody i didn't have a
real gun but they didn't make a move except for a "lady" who
lost a coin as it rolled out in front of her she reached for it
and i refrained from shooting her. i've done plenty of flying
but i never held anybody up. combining extortion or whatever
it was with my flying accomplishment has never been a strong
point. anyhow i didn't get away with it either. the cops came
and as soon as two of them in navyblue hiway crosschest bands
and jodphurs arrived i flew right down alighted at their feet to
be meekly led away. they took me to this place they said was
st. thomas's, a sort of local booby hatch, and i walked into
some steamy area of shower cubicles that's all i want to tell
except there were a lot of naked women and one was dragging
along on the floor a foetus as though it was her toy raggedy
ann. great dream. i had another "first" for a dream recently
and that was that i had some acupuncture needles stuck into
my left arm. i was in this big bed and two people were in another bed and one of them was jane but she turned into richard.
she said she didn't mean to. she said that after i told her the
dream. sometimes people're telling me a dream and i say wait
a minute is that still the dream. half the time i don't know
what is or isn't. i guess all we need do to get along in the world
is figure out whose dream we're living in if not our own. our
knashional leaders are getting caught in their amerikan dream.
as one who creates and interprets news jane says i'm anything
but a reporter and you could consult my column to find out
what never happened. bad writing is emotional writing about
things you think you need. writing is about itself. when i'm
selling sex i'm selling sex and then i'm using writing to sell

something altho i think academic writing can be beautiful. judy chicago and her clitoral interpretations. anyway i don't hear hoarse cries issuing from the delta in the last paroxysm of orgasm or anything like that. i did however enjoy jane's description of marge muscles' breast wall. i hope marge doesn't mind me calling her muscles but when i think of her i think of her magnificent legs and also how nice she is anyway she plays football and she's a sculptor and recently she exhibited a whole wall of breasts and she told jane some people were going up and putting their heads in the breast wall and crying. now the wall is in three or four pieces around her place. processes are mysteriously united by pronouns and nouns. i had a duck's egg for breakfast and i saw a slug on a gate and i slept in a room with 13 white mice. auspicious things keep happening. loving eating and drinking with the intransigent subsistence of the flowers doing likewise. some people would say innocent splendor. a combination that's fraught with possibilities. jewels stones cabbages knees owls toys lice grams silos. not so long ago i was someplace in an apartment building leaving a small party and while tigerace entered an elevator to go and get the doorman to bring me the service elevator i enumerated after her the lush names of those presocratics anaximenes anaximander anaxagoras parmenides pythagoras heraclitus empedocles impediment. i know poets who list things and sometimes make a pretense of conjugating verbs and declining nouns. i accept nouns and i never conjugate. or rather except with women. there are several subjects about which i can write. first flying, then mayonnaise, then jackets, then three and i am thru with three. and then me. i have just changed my mind. an immaculate conception means to be clean of concepts. the dangerous truth is that you can pitch a good argument for any cause whatsoever. why should that be dangerous. what was dangerous and in fact fatal was my fall from the top of a silo i broke my neck and died. a halloween witch appeared out of a door and assured this woman and her friend that it was okay and they shouldn't feel guilty. she controls us simply by casting an influence. wherever it was she was or if she was anymore. those guilty of misdeeds are not criminals for they meant well. and they know it all. i told richard if he stopped knowing it all i'd travel to chattanooga to interfere in the processing of the hitchhiking laws but if he didn't know it all i don't suppose there'd be any laws or any boys or any reason to do anything except watching the grass grow by itself. the one common characteristic i've noticed in boys is that they know it all. a neighborling boy aged 17 came round in his first car a '56 olds to tell me all about it and whenever i put in a word he looked off thru the butternut tree. memoirs of a defeated amazon. myra wrote that i'm not an amazon, i'm a large artist. rebecca boone wrote that i look like margaret mead and alan watts. i'm reading alan watts who was told he looked like king george VI and rex harrison. actually i'm a foetus disguised as a raggedy ann. i play mother and child to myself. i spill some soy on a table- cloth because i say to meself o the hell with it who gives a fuck and then i chastise myself and then i take the tablecloth to the chinaman to clean in order to bring it back and spill sum- more soy on it it's sort of a repetition compulsion. like putting empty icetrays in the fridge. i do that too. i run a nice clean place. i've made innumerable efforts to make words write with- out sense and found it impossible. but if we line things up as lists and images we could have a sense of the world as a tre- mendous clutter of things about which we do nothing but talk constantly, then if you happen to be broke you can just go flying around some interior full of people holding them all up with a phony gun which they know is your hand, then if you're unable to reconcile this activity with your sense of yourself as a lawabiding person you could have your self led away to a booby hatch teeming with naked women. i'm not out to eff the ineffable or unscrew the inscrutable. i don't see hems of dresses dancing around anybody's feet or sleeves drop- ping like sighs. i don't see toads or cauliflowers living in innocent splendor. one of the total & taboos in our culture is against realizing that vegetables are intelligent. having realized children are spiritual, and then animals, i am now obliged to see myself in the pathetic perspective of an intelligent vegetable.

the sort of vegetable constrained to remark on the life & times of other vegetables. a dog called hilda hates this duck and the duck likes her, the duck likes cats too but they aren't too fond of the duck. a little frog lies on its back dead its arms reaching heavenwards like el greco's tearful christ. auspicious things keep happening. i buy some stickiestickies and wait for the proper moment for each one. before spilling the soy i could be staring out the window thru the butternut tree knowing it all minding my own table territory finding the proper moment by having a stickiestickie and my record book in proximity to me and themselves and bringing them all together including a mushroom which happened to be the stickiestickie with my name on it i stuck in my book and there's no necessary causal relationship to the soy. i mix choice and chance somewhat scandalously. knowing when funny coincidences happen you could acquire a reputation for working miracles. like telling everybody that the sharp form of a particular fox's face necessarily implies the existence of galaxy m81. the ultimate status of consciousness. dottlebunk and geflugg. both out to prove their manhoodlumism. how would you know it all if you once didn't. if we fly around and amaze people does that mean we lost the ability to fly? if you wouldn't know you existed unless you had once been dead does it follow we wouldn't know how virtuous we are unless we had once been corrupt. are we corrupt and virtuous. are we dead or alive. are we dreaming. after i died of a broken neck and the witch convinced these two women it was okay i was out running on the road when i realized i might be living in somebody else's dream as though anybody isn't i was just grateful to've been informed where i stood or rather slayed and i stopped running took a deep breath walked very slowly back to the house went to the telephone and called jane

to tell her all about what happened to me. a fundamental design in which the figure is always interchangeable with the
background. bad writing is emotional writing about evening
up scores. pleasant manners succeed even with irritable people.
who said. mr. munson says a jungle'll grow up if we don't mow
it down. trees, even. jane said she was frying her breasts and
reading henry steele commager. i was reading wattsisname. i
was dreaming of pauline c. caressing my hand. i was dreaming
of sally in her nightgown. i was dreaming of breast walls and
even crying in them. i'd be extremely embarrassed to see anybody do that. i don't believe in doing anything. but the only
way i can get out of the booby hatch is to write about it. jewels
stones sharks elbows names birds giants forms flecks nines
threes nights pants bitters. a half of a butterfly went into the
record book too. i said to somebody no boy even if he knows
it all can be so bad if his vital preoccupation is what to do with
the two wings of a butterfly that'd just died on the grass. i
spent a day involving myself in buttermilk and butterflies. i like
to be discreet and definite about what i do. if we must make
sense it should be entirely sensible. processes can be united by
pronouns and nouns as long as we think so. in the desert agnes
said to me she hoped she convinced me that my cool writing
was the best. she said when it was involved meaning i suppose
personal and desperate it made her criticize herself and she
didn't like that. rebecca also wrote what does one learn from
an orgasm anyway. i'd never thought of orgasm as a learning
process unless i was writing to sell sex. all i know is i don't
hear hoarse cries issuing from the delta in the last paroxysm.
jane said nothing could've excited her last night except a 5
car collision. there's a place for violence in our lists and
images. bakunin declared the most creative act to be the act
of destruction. i don't know bakunin. i was given the line
as though it was a buttermilk crepe. sometimes i sits and
thinks but mostly i thinks. i clutter up my head with a perpetual chatter of everything. having words is having every-

thing. if you want to have nothing they say you can muddle-tate but you still have to do something else. everything consists of something else. that is a sentence that they could use. this is an example or a very good example of everything. trying nothing is all the same. when i stop dreaming i'll stop. the ultimate status of consciousness. a galaxy or a particular fox's face. knowing when funny coincidences happen you could go around acquiring a reputation for working miracles. the water christ walked on was his mother. i never thought of that. the autobiog. of a trickster who comes to believe in his own hoax. could've knocked me down with a father. continuing on with dreams animals names food sex richard & the world at small . . .

august 9, 1973

AS ANYBODY LAY DYING

some woman at a party said her mother said when you grow up you'll have all the things i never had and then i'll hate you for it. some other woman said she was living her mother's dreams and another woman said her mother never had any dreams. her mother stopped dreaming when she was five. i'm not certain i want to tell any other mother stories. i wanted to tell about st mary's or about my life on the bowery or about conversations with straight women who want to know about good sex or is there anything that isn't about the mothers. the hero is in the habit of relating all that has gone before for the benefit of the beloved whoever that might be. i wanted to go on about my cars too but then i read that a. huxley said there was only one new sin invented since the original seven deadly and that was speed and also i received a religious card from two people in new jersey saying they were giving a mass for me and further i received two letters about cars from two different women each signing their letters lake circumspect when all along i thought there was only one and that she was in denver although now i recall an original correspondent identifying herself as lake circumspect from someplace in michigan who then appeared to be moving around from there to boston or connecticut to denver and even new york since one of them introduced herself to me at b. & c.'s one time and i thought she was the one and only lake circumspect alias ellie sometimes the thing being it seems really unlikely there'd be more than one lake circumspect in the world and writing about cars somehow so so what i had a neat note from a woman in brooklyn enclosing two color photos of her cars one of herself in an old stingray and the other of her current bug painted abstract inflationist or stuffed expressionist but i don't feel like going on about cars this week anyhow, very much. for almost 17 years she said nothing

memorable and all went well. when communication is established there's nothing more to be said. here's a dialogue of the
future: a: i'll make some toast if you turn on the tube. b: i
don't want any toast but i'll turn on the tube. a: okay i'll
go and make my toast and you turn on the tube. b: okay you
go and make your toast and i'll turn on the tube. a: okay. b:
would you bring me an apple. i think i should write a play.
& make up all my myriads of drifting minds into one. it's
those pauses that's our undoing. the moment matters, but so
does the century. so we could proceed with everything. the
idea is to construct an excuse for not going on and then use
that as a rationale for doing so. is there anything, then, we
can actually point to, if all this is generally true. red socks.
wine suede gloves. gorgonzola. hot cider & brandy. no monopoly (anywhere). a plaid flannel shirt. a little girl in the park.
a teddy bear in a gingham suit. a *mother*. i had a mother who
didn't cook or keep house but who knitted sweaters caps and
mittens and made a gingham suit for my teddy bear. we discussed our mothers as knitters one day. the item i liked the
best since i never lost it until i gave it to richard was a ski
sweater yellow and royal blue and jane said her mother knit
a ski sweater that was maroon and white with reindeer on it
for her male cousin and she knit her some mittens that were
red with two gray stripes on the cuff and her initials and one
time she knit one of those things that go around your neck
under your coat to connect both your mittens so you wouldn't
lose them. i doubt that this is the most interesting thing about
our mothers but it's easier than most of the other stuff. i suppose it was my mother's idea for example that i go to the local
ballet school when i was eight and climax my studies by performing with a bunch of other little girls in a cold gymnasium
in a forget-me-not costume. and that isn't so bad considering
what some mothers do like wendy wonderful told jane her
mother dressed her up for kindergarten as the fairy princess.
the whole mother bit seems to be a big idea. i had a dydee

doll and a raggedy ann and all but they didn't turn me into a mother because i never developed any overwhelming sense of what was best for them. i didn't send them to school and i didn't take very good care of them. i didn't mistreat them either. i was bigger but there didn't seem to be any satisfaction in taking advantage of them. i guess i didn't lay much value on size per se. i guess i remained my own kid. i guess that's really where it's at. the mother bit is just an idea. i was particularly thinking this not long ago when jane was getting off some rap about how everybody suddenly appeared to her to be such a baby. she said everybody's such a baby. i just see babies walking around on the street, with these boxes, doing all these funny things, wearing all these clothes. babies driving trucks (did i tell you about this guy in the cab of an enormous truck at a traffic light playing a harmonica). babies carrying big boxes and wearing funny clothes. babies pressing the buttons for elevators and staring at the floor (& they're afraid to look up to look at the ceiling or anything—that's why i dig tourists staring at the skyscrapers). babies jaywalking, and carrying coffee back to the office, delivering things to each other. babies looking at a window of big ceramic frogs. —it's funny. babies in the subway playing games about staring at other babies, and some don't look away. some scribble on the cars and the posters. there's other babies who're adults. the adult babies make posters with the letter printing in white and the background in black so the bad babies can't write on them. and there's the babies at the toll booths who take their time giving you a token when the train is sitting in the station. and these old babies on the buses who stare at you and want you to give them their seat. and pregnant babies who don't stare at you and usually get the seat. and puerto rican babies hanging out on their stoops, and on and on about babies. i got into her rap and could really see it. i had mostly regarded the presidents and senators that way. now i see that we're all implicated but we don't know it so the best we can do is cultivate attractive symptoms. i went to see eva hesse her sculpture at the guggenheim and i was very upset and i wondered if i would've been so upset or upset at all if eva wasn't dead or if i saw the work and didn't know she was dead and if i would've thought the work was that beautiful if she was still alive. it was thinking about eva made me want to write about my life on the bowery. i lived at 119 and she lived diagonally across the street and i didn't know she was making all these beautiful things. i didn't know her personally to speak of at all. i saw her on the bus a couple of times. i knew she was a friend of sol's. i knew she was at a party i went to when she was dying but i didn't see her and i was told her face was blue. i heard a lot about how she was dying and i remember seeing her work on the cover of art forum the very month she died and thinking that's what happens they wait until a woman puts her head in an oven or something and then they say she was pretty good. i remembered meeting her before she lived on the bowery and she seemed to be just the wife of this artist i went to review his work in a loft on fifth avenue and i thought to myself she was very goodlooking but that's all i remember. now i read in the guggenheim catalog that "the most painful notations (in her notebooks) record the central trauma of individuation provoked by the death of the artists father in the summer of '66 and the rupture with her husband which peaked at this time as well, events without which, I believe, Eva Hesse's art might have remained an effort primarily of local interest" and yesterday a woman i know in new jersey told me she thinks she knew eva as a little girl in washington heights and there was something tragic about her and she couldn't recall what and suddenly she remembered it was about her mother having died. not that eva was acting tragically necessarily. it's just that anybody without a mother was supposed to be tragic. anyway i was trying to put a few pieces together to make a fuzzy picture. i thought that if those surgeons couldn't do anything

for her head she should go to new mexico and lie in the sun
and i never trusted those people anyway. but then i thought
well if you're dying and making great art of the sort where
"the voice no longer speaks to us, but beyond us" and it's
possible that your computerized karma has set you on this
course of being capable of making great art only in the process of dying too young and painfully then the sun and new
mexico or any other smart healthy idea remains pretty su-
perfluous and still somewhere in the realm of thinking you
might know what's best for somebody. so i sort of cried at
her show of great sculpture at the guggenheim. i was walking down the spiral ramp away from it all and i looked
back i noticed there was this guy in a reddish beard and a
plaid shirt and he looked very upset too but the other people
were examining the work the way people do ordinarily and
i wondered if i was upset because i knew her or what. now
i think it has something to do with the bowery. there may've
been any number of dispossessed females up and down the
bowery around that time. i didn't see how she could live
across the street from her ex just for openers. i couldn't see
any of it for any of us. yet we were doing it and making a
whole life out of it and i liked my loft and its masonite floor
better than any other dump i ever crashed in and i think
actually we were getting ourselves together after a great
assortment of personal disasters. so i don't know. my newest
idea is that the slight memory of eva and the big sight of her
sculpture and my knowledge of her life and the recollection
of the sainted bums on the bowery and their goddam guilt
inducing afflictions got me feeling like a really heroic gesture
was going on across the street that i didn't know about and
now i'm sorry and i don't know why. and now that i've found
my subject i'm quitting this time around anyway.

january 25, 1973

KRAUT FISHING IN AMERIKA

the unscrambling of omelettes is at best laborious and not
likely to improve the taste. i've been foregoing all sorts of
tastes in order to run lighter and fly longer and sit still higher.
one carrot one celery and five glasses of water becomes a
splendid feast. i meant to reply some while back to reception
of voluminous materials plus letter regarding animal liberation
from connie salamone velmadaughter of majority report. connie asked me if i was still eating hamburgers the dead flesh
from oppressed beings at wimpy's in london in other words
was i still partaking in the capitalistic amerikan male scheme
of fucking bodies and if so i hadn't come full cycle into my
beautiful amazon body, my primate female body, in the peaceful world that our present feminist vision advocates she asks
will there be women butchers??? i confess i've hardly ever
given any political thought to food at all. up at sarah lawrence
in trying to define a political lesbian i mentioned that i'm
vegetarian for the most part but i don't call myself one since
i've never been political about it and the same goes for anything we call ourselves. as soon as i realized what a mother
in this society is or how it's defined i ceased saying i was a
mother and notified both the younger people who emerged
from my stomach that i no longer wished to be called mommie
and i don't think i should call them "my son" or "my daughter" either. i mean referring to them this way to anybody,
with possessive pride. anyway i have to tell connie i've never
had a hamburger at wimpy's. i used to eat hotdogs at nathan's
however. and i used to eat something called a regular dinner
which as a tenement artist in new york consisted of a cowpaddie of chopped meat garbage and a box of frozen peas or
frozen peas and carrots and occasionally something exotic like
brussel sprouts, always frozen in a box of course. this is my
gourmet column. there was no rational comprehensible reason

whatsoever that i can recall for my alteration of eating habits. i was brought up on meat milk fowl eggs potatoes and decimated vegetables like everybody else. but when i went crazy everything changed including eating. that was back in '65, when everybody was going crazy and i presume like me thus unsettling their allamerikan habits. i remember babbling about baby food and declaiming the virtues of eating whatever i goddam pleased and whenever i pleased and being completely balmy up at some psychedelic church walking around like christ herself demanding herb soup, why herb soup, i don't know, i'd never been to any indian yogurt or any organic restaurant and nobody ever mentioned it and i never read anything about it either so i don't know. but i became a different kind of eating person. now i see from connie's materials here that i'm something more or less called a lacto-vegetarian, or an ovo-lacto-vegetarian. if i did away with the milk and eggs i'd be a vegan, and that's the thing to be. chickens are given a lot of hormone crap and from cows milk we get ddt and in any case we're partaking of food from incarcerated brutally treated beings. the case against eating the dead flesh of meat fowl fish is clearer. connie quotes a lot of famous old people like a. schweitzer and his concept of Reverence for Life: respecting the will to live and to progress that's inherent in the various life-forms. or mahotma grandi on ahimsa: the principle of non-killing, non-injuring. how a person should do the least harm to other lives. what i want to know is what you might do about a lot of ants in your house. ant poison? import spiders to eat the ants? import birds to eat the spiders? move to another house? develop a hobby of transporting ants in bottles from indoors to outdoors? right now i'm sharing my desk with some medium sized black ones and they're not exactly contributing to my intellectual experiments. i don't see how it's any less reprehensible catching ants in ant traps than it is lobsters in lobster pots whether you eat them or not. i have to stop eating lobster but i don't know what to do about the ants. i have an insect taboo and in fact all sorts of things going on about animals and plants in my head. yesterday i made a careful semicircular detour of large dimension around a garden snake sunning on a driveway. the day before i had a dream i was putting these cats out the door as fast as they were coming in and in fact when i woke up i heard a cat meowing outside someplace. then one day i was walking on this road and a dog the size of a woodchuck was yapping and baring its fangs at me i saw him as a wolf suddenly and even though i've read farley mowatt's never cry wolf i still think wolves are scary maybe because of laddle rat rotten hut or riding hood to you anyway since i didn't feel like swimming back home in this crick river running parallel to the road where i figured the little dog was lying in wait for me on my return i hitched a ride in a blue truck right past the dog's house and in that way saved my life i thought. before i caught the ride i heard a bird scolding me too, for being so silly no doubt. and as regards this new time of year i'm looking around as if i never saw the color green before, i think i've been living in a book all my life. the leaves are doing this whole unfolding trip and i never saw that either and i never noticed things like a tree with a branch of all these creepy foldy green foetuses in various stages of coming alive with one of their ancestors right there with them that lasted the whole winter hanging by one tendon of its stem, a brown parchment corpse of last years leaf. nature's now also full of things that bite you and i'm watching out. i don't intend to bring any corpses of animals into my place either. connie says a feminist kitchen should be a place where the dead bodies of others do not abound. when you think of it it's a weird thing putting dead bodies into your own and it doesn't go down very easily either. i fell on a big juicy red thigh or flank of some poor cow last week where i was a guest for dinner and it still hasn't come out. i do that sometimes i regress shamelessly at somebody else's house just because it's served up and it reminds you of your old carnivorous days when you threw a slab of bleeding liver into a frying pan or seared a cowpaddie of ground garbage they called round or something and you don't want to come on like a vegetarian either. that's because i haven't been political about it and i've had old associations with vegetarianism as another fanatical sect going around telling everybody that something *else* we all did was bad. besides how were we supposed to get all that protein they said we had to have if we stopped being bad. for all the materials on this subject i suggest contacting connie salamone velmadaughter at 616 6th St., brooklyn new york 11215 but here's an item called common fallacies about protein which says vegetable proteins are higher in biological value than animal proteins and that research from a leading institution for nutritional research in the world the max planck institute in germany showed that many vegetables fruits seeds nuts and grains are excellent sources of complete proteins and that soybeans sunflower seeds sesame seeds almonds potatoes and most fruits and green vegetables contain complete proteins and that you only need one half the amount of proteins if you eat raw vegetable proteins instead of cooked animal proteins and that it's virtually impossible not to get enough protein in your diet provided you have enough to eat of natural unrefined foods and all like that. did you ever wonder asks this pamphlet where the wild horse who builds a magnificent body in a couple of years gets all his proteins and answers why from the grass he eats of course. the thing is that thru cattle beef we're getting our proteins second hand anyway, recycled protein, mixed up with cancer and lockjaw and other animal diseases ("affluent nations have a high consumption of devitalized animal foods . . . containing toxins pathological matter malignancies and cholesterol") and according to another pamphlet it takes 21 lbs of grain protein to produce one lb of animal protein, out of which about 8 to 10 lbs of grain proteins could be eaten directly by people. all of this also is mixed up with the morality of property. from an economical and ecological standpoint writes connie the conventional mixed diet requires about 1-2/3 to 2 acres per person for growing food for her and for feeding the animals. but this is a very expensive and wasteful diet, returning perhaps 20 per cent of the food value in the case of milk or eggs, and less than half that in meat. a part-vegetarian diet, still including milk and eggs may require about an acre. but with a total vegetarian (or vegan) diet a single acre can support four, six, or even as many as eight people, according to actual experiments. she goes on as there is only about an acre of farm land per person in the world this places a tremendous moral burden upon the user of animal foods in addition to the usual ethical considerations. i don't know why we shouldn't just go out on our all fours and start eating the grass like other sensible animals. if a horse gets a magnificent body that way then we could too. at this point many people like me ask the leading green question what about the plants and along with what to do about the ants in yr house i still think it's important since we know that plants hurt too. i don't see a satisfactory answer in this material here. if plants hurt too then we should eat only the fallen fruit. a flower shop may be no less cruel than a slaughter house or a chicken farm. in all cases we're alienated from the source of what we get. thus we don't have to think about the pain and murder involved in the commodity we're consuming or sending to a friend to make a hospital room look cheerier. as regards plants and flowers unless you wear them in your hair i guess at least there's one comforting thought and that is you don't wear them for shoes or coats, unless you happen to be in hawaii. i'd like to know if i have to start wearing only sneakers, i know i should get rid of my suede jacket. another of connie's fervently scrawled headlines reads man's cruelties to obtain fur thats not his or hers! there's a society called Beauty Without Cruelty which people joined because a few facts of the barbarous practices that flourish under the protective banner of commerce in the beauty and fashion businesses have convinced them of the need to use alternatives to such products. unluckily for instance for crocodiles alligators snakes lizards and all reptiles their skins command high prices. what about the eskimos by the way. don't they dress up like animals all the year round. or is it a question of them or the animals as to survival. and if so does that justify murder. one of my favorite books was owen chase's sinking of the whaleship essex which provided by the way the basic material of melville's moby dick. it was 1820 or so and owen chase was a youthful crew member on the whaleship essex out in the middle of the pacific someplace when this great white whale angered by the assaults on him and his gang just came along and sank this goddam boat. well many days later while two surviving lifeboats of starving crewmembers were struggling coastward there was an infamous incident of cannibalism on board one of them. they drew lots to see who they would have to eat and as i recall it was the youngest a 16 yr old who drew the shortest and was therewith dispatched by his mates. i guess the issue there was an old sacrificial one, would they all have to die or could some of them survive by the sacrifice of one. that may be the eskimo principle too. i don't know. i hope never to be in the wilds of alaska or the middle of the pacific in a rowboat. bemeantimes however unfortunately i guess i'll have to deal with the moral problems of sneakers versus virtually any other kind of shoe and the ants sharing my desk and the temptations of lobster and whether to let the cats in or out and how much distance to keep between me and garden snakes and the fear of small dogs and how to go on living on one carrot one celery and five glasses of water. actually i feel great. i recommend a grand fast of one day and a pseudo fast of one more day followed by one carrot one celery one apple one egg maybe a day is probably all anybody about needs. with a little dessert of lawn grass. anyhow it's the best way to run lighter and fly longer and sit still higher.

may 17, 1973

RESURRECTION FOR 40 CENTS

and so there is no use going on except that the summers follow one after the other and the fashions go with the seasons.
the fashion i observed this summer season was trees and dreams
and sacred violations. the queens must die. the friends of the
foetus gather to assist at her unhappy emergence. once she is
seen i guess the secret is out. in what way does she become
actual if not seen (and heard). can she be actual to herself if
she doesn't see herself and for that does she need eyes. is her
eyes the origin of her consciousness of existing. do her eyes
have to see herself being seen in order for her to feel herself
alive. and once the secret is out won't she violate herself in
order to cease this existing. this sense of multiplying separations? the real question seemed to be could the sacred space be
expanded or would we go on seeing ourselves as separate and
exclusive and if the former what are the strategies of (re)in-
corporation. for example when you speak to it do you make
it so and is seeing still believing. or is there a critical difference
between doing and dreaming you are doing as the social organization suggests or are we always dreaming whatever we're
doing since we picture ourselves to ourselves in other words
seeing is dreaming and we came out looking. i wanted to know
this week if the separation in ourselves between actor and
spectator is endemic to life or to organisms with eyes or what.
do we become increasingly self conscious or excessive dreamers
as the social organization becomes more inclusive as a civilization while augmenting our isolation from each other by losing
visual touch with all our contributory functions and living in
enforced individual units of which the largest remains only
the family. the world is too big to consider. sometimes alone i
feel total. i dream all my selves into auto fulfilling facets of
each other. i move around from room to room depending on
the light. i make preparations for things that don't have to

happen. i happen things that have no preparations. i don't have to attend to anything less interesting than my own thoughts. it's difficult not to admire our existing since that's what we're doing. the summers follow one after the other and the fashions of living go with the seasons and i am here now and it's thursday. the only essential activity is expanding the sacred space by doubling into infinities until we stop falling into existence or separations. the secret sharers are thousands of butternut leaves. the family is sexual differentiation and that's too bad. a friend says the definition of culture is sexual differentiation. it's clear which half of the difference felt the most hysteria in respect to its difference and separateness but i have my own sex in mind this week. robert graves said the apollo flight was such a crude way of getting to the moon. they can speak for themselves. the christian solution has come to pass. the projection of the father up to heaven as a divine spirit. good morning, yr omnipotence. i promised myself not to go on with their problems. being so much more outside their original inner space their dreams appear so much more violent. the normal heros. the conjunction of love and war. the fearsome possession of a kept port of entry. the roving penetrating eyes of the male. but i promised. i sat in circles for three days with 13 women of me experiencing multiple duplications in dreams and images and ideas and i came out dead and alive and still looking and not dissatisfied with expanding the space or violating a number of intimacies. women don't waste much time any more getting to sex either but intellectual dissolutions are still so much more comfortable. what's the difference between looking and doing and who's really looking if not ourselves. were we conceived in secrecy. and if that wasn't incestuous how many secret incests (inquests) can we go on pretending we're committing. if it stops being illicit does it stop i mean. alice told me eating is the only sensual thing you can do in public and not be put down for it. i went with a friend to a strange apartment where after a suitable interval i asked the woman of the apartment whose name happened to be jill if she minded if my friend and me made love and she said no not if she could watch but two more women arrived and in the end we committed incest or privacy or secrecy and the violation of intimacy was only partial or a matter of information which is a bridge of sorts. and are literal transgressions necessary at all since the actual looking is still from a distance and i wonder how satisfying the group orgies of the living theatre were to the participants. what other uproarious deceptions would their activities generate or perpetuate. gradually the play fills up with corpses, in her honor it would seem. the friends of the foetus gather to assist at her unhappy emergence. falling into the world she becomes the object of fantastic assault. her present solution is to eject her tormentors from the primal scene and experience herself as her double in infinite regress. for 40 cents you can buy a mexican resurrection plant at judith's store in hartford. it stays forever if you want as a ball of vine the size of a baseball and it stays forever as a flat open spreading green plant if you put its bottom side in a container of water. it resurrects in an hour. judith calls her store the perfect union. these ecstatic unions imply a joyful liberation from sanity. she always went without herself. she fell into some ark on the way in and there was light thru the portholes. she thought her thin arms and sturdy legs were peaceful and exciting. she saw mansions in the sky of lavender doors and gold knockers and thought it was a very corny dream. she pretends if she's not looking at anybody they can't see her either. she lives in a purely symbolic world and magically solves her problems. she knows there's certain conventions they'd all greed upon and she becomes inexpensively happy attending to nothing more interesting than her own thoughts. her own images rendered double or in duplex telegraphy. if 13 women can get into a bubble and be their own reflections i guess the rest of us can too. first we went around the circle exchanging dreams. i remembered some recurrent childhood dreams myself. i remembered running in slow motion away from pursuers who never caught up with me although i was stuck in my running i couldn't go nearly as fast as i wanted to and i was told that's because my large muscles are paralyzed while sleeping and dreaming i like physiological explanations altho i thought the stuck running had some important universal psychic significance maybe it does. the most over and over childhood dream i had was being in a secret space locked in with a couple of friends or myself or being locked in under a house in those wideranging three foot high or so spaces surrounded by lattice wood enclosures that many houses used to have and being inside there and then hearing a rumble rumble at first distant and then closer and being witness to a procession of sheep emerging from the ground. i saw charlotte moorman being born last week i ventured into the world of people to the americana hotel and saw charlotte playing the cello in a black gown then put down her cello and walk over to a tall cylinder pail where she climbed to the top and lowered herself in and submerged herself in the water of herself and then came out to resume her life as a cellist or her new life or is it old. it's difficult not to admire relevant action at the proper historical moment. a little girl no more than three appeared on the walkplank outside alice's restaurant as i headed for the door she was right in front of me and i stopped and she said take off your glasses and let me see your eyes and i did and i sort of got down lower and we looked very knowingly or something into each others eyes and then she fondled my neck gear and wanted to know what all the junk was. i wonder if anybody was watching. i'm writing so you can watch so i can see myself being seen in your eyes and i can watch you watching me watch you so we can know each other. i fell in love with the little girl. her request for recognition seems pretty uncomplicated. a more complicated request but no less direct if possibly more urgent came in a mysterious phone call from san diego thereabouts a woman's voice saying hello this is dita, i thought she said dita,

i said yes, this is dita sackville-west, yes, do you know who
that is, yes i do, well i'm vita sackville-west, i could hear now
that it was vita not dita, and after a pause or so after i confirmed i knew who she was and all i asked her what her other
name was and she told me and we went on from there. i
thought she should go to a medium for more information. she
was born in '54 and she doesn't know when vita died and
neither do i. she began to be possessed two years ago and all she
knew of virginia w. was as a name and she feels suicidal now
because she misses virginia a great deal. then i said i couldn't
help her and she thought i violated her trust by saying that
but i believe her and helping is more than believing if whatever
you're being believed about is painful and i'm not equipped to
provide more information so i wanted to locate a medium. i
said we're all possessed or inhabited it's the condition of existence and i think if one of these beings is clamoring for that
much attention we need to know more to see what's going on.
maybe we need to project them more outside the center of our
new ongoing selves. some people surround you with a civilized
atmosphere and they leave you inside of you completely to
yrself. for that reason it isn't a bad idea being alone a lot.
dreaming all your selves into autofullfilling facets of each other.
moving about from room to room depending on the light. making preparations for things that don't have to happen or happening things that have no preparation and attending to the
concertos of your own voices and admiring your very existing.
a friend asked me if it would be any more significant *dreaming*
of living in a town with the same name as the town where
your mother was born than actually living in such a town and
having noticed the connection which is what i'm doing. i don't
think so. or i think it's so. how do we know we're not still in
the womb and watching a movie of our life. the real unified
life of the dream. i see myself in secret violating the taboo on
secrecy for fear of retaliation or fear of paralysis or fear of
fear out apart from the others passionately in sex love in wet

grass mosquitoes singing critics yellow moon decadent demented delirious dissolute drunk the dying surging of the foetal queens. pagan blood returns! the end of romance. the violence of territorial uncertainties. she removes her crown, falls prostrate on the ground, and speaks in latin phrases. she or the other says she could kill her. she or the other says she will puncture her tires. she or the other hurls a longstem glass somewhat over her left shoulder where it lands intact on the grassy strip between the macadam thud. this was the first war period, a period of fashion without style, of systems with disorder, of reforming everybody which is persecution, and of violence without hope. life is so embarrassing. here all forgotten and set aside—wind scattering leaves over the fields. florence was in heat on the driveway and ben was trying to mount her and beyond on the grass maureen was lying on carol's back and we were watching the doubles out of the window and i had a dream of doris humphrey more redheaded than i remember her and facing herself one version older more shrivelled than i remember the other younger and heartier than i remember and she was speaking attentively to herself although the older version seemed more animated than the younger. choreographing her internal dialogue. i can't recall the year doris died. i know she was appearing to me. alma said exstasy happens face to face with another person and it isn't suppliable by the masses, a long day of feeling your body tell your mind to stop thinking. and thinking and feeling your body and feeling your thinking and thinking your body. and so there is some use going on even as the summers follow one after the other and the fashions go with the seasons and the secrets are always out.

september 6, 1973

164

jj in motion —roz gerstein

i imagine i'm being pursued by an amazon posse

—phyllis birkby

*the same characters keep appearing on stage in
different costumes*

rena, jane, alison, jill, sara, lin, meg
and maureen —carol dear

gliding is not heavily moving
looking is not vanishing
laughing is not evaporating

jj with strawberry on the roof
—roz gerstein

in flagrante delictio

snowshoe and friend —snowshoe's
indifferent photographer brother

she wears a kind of cap like a crown which seems to be a
part of her person

rena patterson and dianne hunter
—linda kieves

postpone the revolution until the leaves turn

jj —sahm doherty

luckily she doesn't have charisma

agnes martin

voluntary retreat brings good fortune

sk dunn courtesy of sk dunn

heroic nudity would also be more appropriate on this occasion

amelia earhart courtesy of the
women's yellow pages

*as the moon sets the four horses of her chariot sink below
the horizon*

pauline oliveros —becky cohen

i had the impression i was hardly moving, yet later my assistant told me that i was peddling at a fast pace

drawing —margot apple

a total object, complete with missing parts

gregory battcock on the *mikhail
lermontov* to leningrad, june 1973,
courtesy of gregory battcock

"imagine sailing to london on the emily dickinson . . .*"*

ann wilson courtesy
of ann wilson

she appeared to have a perfect recollection of her past life

strawbaby and her sister sheila
courtesy of strawberry

radical debutantes

jj's daughter winnie and her brother
richard —june smith, 1973

the return of the amazon children

jj on lecture tour —vicki lawrence,
april 1973

it's not a tragic death to be slain by a statue

jj with strawberry and tomato
—roz gerstein

the right to reticence seems earned only by having nothing to hide

collage —carol dear

i soon stumbled on a great many marvelous consequences

jj with yvonne de carlo and dick
cavett on the set —sahm doherty,
january 1972

will the real ogre please stand up

jj with rd laing in the algonquin —
charmian reading, spring 1973

a quick glance out the window reveals absolutely nothing

jj with princess christina of sweden
in her palace —hans persson,
october 1973

lesberate us, your high highness

jj with her majesty's palace guard in
stockholm —hans persson,
october 1973

ensnared in an international plot of her own (un)making

jj with derby on the roof
—phyllis birkby

drifting into a position of greater exposure to sunlight

PART THREE

SPRINGJOYCE

The moon outside is a Ryder; the rainbow in here is the chalk
on a Dutch blackboard. All the nickelly nacks are pieces of
Egypt. And a barkboat carrying a clod of moss and dade yellow flower and another pitch of bark. Anyways a verytableland
o junkle jeaps for a miniataur tiger to roam and roar around
in. The woods outside is a shambles. Medusa madmess. Spring
on the pathways is just a warm day and a blue periwinkle butterfly and spring in the timberstalks along like skinny miles of
gray arms, snakevines, veering vetching varicose velly awful
looking interfuckulating strangulation by encroakment. What
is growling up here? The age of shrivelry is all over me. I shall
eat grass and die in a ditch in the browny bracken water where
the rotted leaves have deaded. I shall set on a rockofaggots
foliaceous and fuming flesh a new feenix up a flamin mamie a
surefire baby; her birth is uncontrollable, her funferall is a
celebarktion by kindlelight. By Zen and by Zoos the begin the
beguine of the unifirst is rite now if all tinks are at this mo-
mentus being cremated, and the end of the unihearse is allso
now if all thinks are at this momentum passing away we went,
to see The Inedible String Bean. We went to see the Dairy of
a Skinzopretty Girl. We went to see the saw strafe the spring-
dried denseyland disbarking benches of millentury old trees.
And by wishingwell and waterfall willie winkle watched pretty
peter pumpkineater wairing his feet in a pink sock on one and
on the other an orange sock and little annie ruiny she heard go
spashing and pooling and laffing down to the bottom go davy
locker herself down da bottom foriver and iver. Omen. So wail
us. And up near the approach toward the summit of its climax
where the waterocktrees all meet to crushendo din your drums
appeared a parition of Christ Christself in a visionee epigonee
goony glummy gloriation in exseltzer madst the follyages. Ge
bone! Gralloch! Graptotite! By grog I'm disembered. I set down

on the pathway and wrap me arms aboot me knees and crosseye the welter woods into a worldwide web woven by my eye in the loom of the branch. Misticalling me. Jungly time. I akst wee willie winkle wheather she was going away for summari-time? She doesn't no, she hasn't famished with her winter yet. Mr. Anklemine wood 'end her however to Ecuador to see some headhunters and excheat X numbers of beads for eggs or voice reversa. But it don't adder at all becaws all her sprig-gity spring lovers are asparagas and strawberries and so sexing she went away leaving me to swallow in the skunkabbage in here the forest is a Rousseau; the rainbow note the above is the chalk on a Dutch blackboard. Outside I stole a log and dropped it in the mud and looged it up a high hell and lay its muddy soggy side sunny up and BLT and got ananny Gretel reddied up fine and ruddy for the conflammation. Too out and walking and walking, walking looking walking and looking as a woods-fan waking pyromaniacts I go ashenutely aghost and aggalled at the sites befort me. This ere tree 'as gone stark razor naked. This one ere is a merrible tress o flakes, its hole skin scalloping up as a mummy wrapping come loose all over itself. And this ere one is a mobster leviathan than which no less ten trunks in one or one trunk holding up ten and every trunk a them a mori memento. Macrophagocriticalciumbrage of some sort. So solly. Solong.

may 7, 1970

ATROXATRASHAJOKAJAXATROCIOUS

ATROXATRASHAJOKAJAXATROCIOUS . . . It might be more useful in the long run to allow at the start for a whole constellation of possible interpretations. Nobody could describe a thing so rich as a sign. What was once a needle of visionary echstasy has now become a piece of disregarded lipoleum. She reveals her divine origin by proving contrary avaricious and having a beautiful body. Somebiddies maught say we're a ladle confused between the importance of our subject and the extrabinary delight wee manger to extrack on it. The beginning of a tail usually betrays the main stickological or emotional proemblems with which it is concerned. Dionysus is also bacchos and baccheus and iacchos and bassareus and bromios euios sabazios zagreus thyoneus lenaios eleuthereus and a circle is a round line to wit no kinks in it joined up so ass not to show where it begain. Each act is a revenge for each ogre act and one is samply upfronted hic as ubique with an endless cycle of sex antigonisms creonisms and layus aloathe with eteocles and polynieces and uncles and cousinners edipussy galory and any new Golden Brow. Je m'en rapporte a Dieu. Let us be holy and evil and let her be peace on the sword. Peace is viewed as a time between wars wither than war being viewed as a disruption of peace. Homer, tell his hidings clearly!, and his audunces lingered lovingly over everily ack of sloughter. Savor. Savior. Savoir. Faire Queene. The souerayne beauty whitch I doo admyre, the light whereof hath kindled heauenly fyre, Lyke Phoebe from her clamber of the East . . . the begunning of the story booke a gentile kanight was pricking on da playne . . . C'mon Loretta, spred yer legs and lets im slurp on er clam. Even the silliest spectackle candy rawther wonherfull. B. say to me J. & G. wath at me embizarrassed is elated also to kiss and to barrister and embargos argiope iggerwise called telephassa bore agenor cadmus and phoenix and cilix and thasus plus phineus and one daughter europe abdulcet by zeus falling down in love disguised in a snowy white bull running a sickle black streaking great dewlaps and tiny jewels or horns lak unto souls in bridsbranchesmistletoeslizardssharkscrocodiles came zeus amazing amucking armabillowing amethysting after europe who was striken by his grete god looks and fondling him as gentle as a mary mastered her feare and commensed to play with him putting flowers in his mouth and hanging garlands upod his horns and climbing his routes pass by his branches onto his soldiers she sublet him her shelter nitknowing for zeus eve ry woeman is a Bad Mother and the honly place to be with a Bad Mother is inside her she marmbled naielfly down with him to the edge of the sea where sudderly swipu scifa snafu and swippen he swam away whilst she poh europe looked back in terror at the shore'n ship a done fo fee fum this time she justice clug to his right horn the other hand still holding her flowerbasket till they went wadiñg asand at cretan gortyna ven zeus turked into an eagle and fucked her in a willow-thicket besog a spring or under an everrrrrgreen planetree bore him minos and rhadamanthys and sarpedon coincide is what most people do when it rains. Pity. Piety. Pieta. Pizza. The God always appears cowardly and foodish becost of the contrust between the divine powder on the one hand and his puny ax on the udder. A total weed and a wet. Gregory zback from Porta Ricky says he thanks they must pass a law there should be no more sexusual activittles vitrine the opposing sexes. All that and no cigarettes too! Warpever has been joined let no man put usunder. Start paying attension at ease to me and stop babbling. Ya-boo sucks! And Joan burned May 30 1431. After thinking this over she desidead this was joust anookie mail plot. It is never in the list clair that the achievement is wurth alle the trouble. Dribble a drob cud go right down your rothole. Meaning, Cauchon, Charles, Haimond, Philippe, deBaudricout, Dufay, Clermont, Alencon, deNovellompont, dePoulengy and deMetz, LaFontaine and the Bastard of Orleans. Hmmmmm, Himhim. Himhim. You wuz in the same boat of yourselves too. Luskily there is another cant to the questy. Has any fellow of the dozens in dimes type, any sort of ornery josser flatchested 40ish faintly flatulent and given to ratiocination by syncopation in the elucidation of complications and of his greatest Yung Fang dynasdescendanced or only another the son of in fact ever to be pluperfectly strait any fine bobber fellow has e ever done innything but what ee munster overlook the atrocities too. Atrox Atrash Ajok Ajax Atrocious Atrahilarious Attaboy Atman or Atlas(t) a collection of maps. Te deum laudamus. Quiet when you speak to an ossifer. Hereof this gentle canight vnweeting was, and lying downe vpon the sandie graile, drunke of the streame, as cleare as cristall glas; eftsoones his manly forces gan to faile, and mightie strong was turnd to feeble fraile. His chaunged powres at fist them selues not felt till crudled cold his corage gan assaile, and chearefull bloud in faintnesse chill did melt which like a feuer fit thru all his body swelt. Slibberslubberslobberslaverslimyslovene. Slop the magic dragon! Hose dreams of begging trapped in seagrass quicksand and public hair research is when you look for something twice. Claude des Armoises. And Sarah Burnheart indulged in all sortie essentrick behaviorals & exims such as standing on the table in a room in order to writhe her name on the ceiling. Celeste Homes. One does not explain greatness, one tries to attune oneself to it. Had it not beene said that France would be lost by a woeman and shall thenafter be restored by a virgin? I remember having herd that and I was stupefied. Sprung from a stone tree furrow water an all and in ambigotterdammerunguatan frub abub tom thum dwarf child animal humunculi humunculat a lot. Magnificat! It wast widly claimed that the killingdom lost by that badmother indemtified of coarse as the calamitous Isabeau of Bavaricose would be saviored by one as who as one said notary boisguillaume a williamofthewood remarcd or overtompeepered how Joan was examined by some matrons who found her to be a right good virgin and that this exanimation had been made by ordure of the Duchess of Bedford and that the Puke of Bedforn stalk in a secretion placentum the bitter he could see Joan exhumined, the vitreous varmint. Huns visigoths convictibles martians moors cretans crasstians attilians here was she who seemeth not to issue from any place on irk but rather sent by haven to sustrain with head and solders a France fallen down da ground astronishing virgin! wordy of all fame and of all praze, worky of all divine honors! & the licht of the lily o splendorison gloriat not alone of gaul but of all creepians . . . Let Troy cerebrate her Hectic and Grease her Alexander and Africka her Handiball and Ithaly her Seizer & all her Roaming Romellian Genoveralls, though he count many of these may France vell content and pleasure herself the Made only. Manu Vishnu. Bob's your uncle. And alle thing there prospered for you, til thety me of the siege of Orleans taken in hock, God knowe the by what advis. At the whiche tyme, after the adventure fallen to the persone of who cousin of Salysbury whom God assoille there felle by the hand of God as it seemeth a greet strook upon your peuple that was assembled there in grete nombre, caused in grete partie, as y trove, of lakke of sadde beleve, and of unlevefulle doubte that thei hadde of a disciple and lyme of the feende, called the Pucelle that used fals enchauntements and sorcerie. By witch tyme there being a compleat muddle of misunderstand-ings ever since Rheims she hadding lost her grip on the con-duct of events for want of that acquiescence of the royal will in her own wishes which had been indispensable to the ac-complishment of her earlier exploits her capture may 23 1430 at coudun near compiegne the rejoycing anglish had her in irons guarded by mean gaolers permuffet any turd lord or burgundian canine come see her shutup in her castlprison one haimond deMacy serverall many times did visit and converse with her and tried by his own admanumission playfully to touch her breasts trying to put 'is paw on her chest the which Joan would not suffer but repulsed him with all her strength. Pour tous les batardes. Joan avait toujours couche avec les jeunes filles . . .

september 30, 1971

OBSOLETELY UNADULTEROUS

one's upon a thyme or thumping. the tory i whig to tell this week conchurns a mutter or two of any sudden (in)consequence. it isn't a proper mandala i'm sowing in the middle of a circle of studs on the back of my london denim. i put the grenadier gardes in red and yellow on the pocket and the shoulder and wonder if the british old man was a grenadier or a coldstream altho i don't care mach any more. i will however write a treatiff called my father in amerika. i ought to go away for a change of ideas and i'd have a world of things to look back on. i could get into the real past. all i cud say about december 27 1972 might be i was listing to this heroic trumpet consherbert and i was pleasably distrackted by this feline making a rumbustious allover a scruffy ballotwine in the manor of an ambuscade hidding out around about the corner of a mattress or the leg of a cheer or the wire of a lump and leaping thenupon his quarry of twine which anybuddy could see was an excellebrant imitamale of a moose. i have one more tail of today better mind ever fear i formembered that is i rubber clemented into a record news booke under a gorius pincture of leonarduous da vichy's ritratio della regina giovanna the tithle of orlando contributary wyatt of irelent o' somethug of a farther unknown as weal as mine owed me or his mischievmiss a belle in a towering schmurch or two and nowtofore ladles and lentilwomen an ironic addendum every sue, siss and sally of us, dugters of Bess, packed up their kitty in their auld trubble bags and puddled up the amazone on the rose to mandalay and sew on. i have some elephants in brown and gold parading across my backbone too. i have some reel tories to tell abloat the paste. the s. s. george washington. the s. s. leviathan. the s. s. dolphin. the s. s. of exscream impotence in affears of damnestic rulevance and fawren porridgy. the gargafe door moved and i thot it was a man. a moving man. um. sunderly a poorer light then this emidged afort afreak a shad ows ls porkupine trees butt in none way sibular to the brutal genessence of the whirld. inny oafsprung of this sun of a kuk hiss hoicks hypoploid

hypocriticaster obbligato his hydra! the duchess of clitoressa came to creep me company yestermorrow weed disgust the hole thig ad to her crudit she remaimed obsoletely unadulterous all the wile i screwtinized the freckless clearance betwixt her two beasts & the heartvein athrobbing beglow her eyebrowns o indecency and indechorusnest and infantile pornalysis and hippophagusnipple orbviously i was disemvowelled i was disemvowelled i was invalleydated i wood go abrood on bored the s. s. somethirst thisbe or other orphan as not ill continue practicking paragaffes and puncturations, we muss our words shape until they are the thinnest integument for our thoats, thoats are divine! the closest fraud could get to poketry was to analeyes a poker, i could lie about astern adeck chore reeding compact in the erroargenous zone enroost acrturus in alpha bootes aoristicennyennyennywaystheisle of womanoverboard, put up yer dykes and fake it out, achetually we had tea and crumples, i had had my ovaryaction, our lady of late we truthlessly kin about is apparking verily sune at universal hall, and effigybody in the whole wild word appreachiates you bitter than yer fammy his eri vd ftsmsyiv sddum; yion og gfree minor msnfwlsi lsmnsd ertr vtypyohtwdd (spoken with tongs), we must pend our ways i livened up to the duchess clitoressa peaking sobberly & wit sudder elocunts moreorder i sad the tried proplum is scribbling rivalry and all for glawr alone for glawr for glawr oh mawd oh macy oh mandy and maidy and florence's grandmother mrs o'mooney and my own status crowe thus beginneth and endeath this partickulish lovage locofoco fatima, a fate accomplea, jus anudger coo clucks clan, a ransack of the langrudge, lavabo inter innocentes, i room in 8 and termite the conversailletion perorberating off under the relms & oaks omphalo onagraceous omnia mutantur nos et mutamur in illis, a cat and a bush is the whole of it, it was of a night, late, lang time agone as we trailed off the rust of hour dialoads on mirrorcles and nicessitease, kaput. shekinah shenandoah, in trude the eminy is man. mortar martar tartar wartar! they are on allfores as foibleminded as you can feel they are fablebodied. the libation he profit us wast in farct a trojan hoss. to act freely entailed our submission to the injunction to be free freedom and unfreedom being finally equavered. tigerace toll me we should go robanks & i agreedy. he has energy and daughters. how often do we dream of daughters. how often. just how often. the more she denunced her own time, the more complacent she became. she contemptemplated the high battlements of thoat. she appeased to have an impeerfit recallechtion of her pssst life. clorinda favilla euphrosyne puh tetres. marousha stanilovska dagmar natasha iliana romanovitch. ramifications intoilminionable. from alphie to meg. o vell. she may be growling up, she may be loosing some of her illesions, perhappy to acquit sum otters she noseticed sum birdsfrozeinmidair & fell like scones to the ground. she decided to be summoned by urgent affairs to new york or michigan. from love she had sapphired the torchards of the domed. this is not a saab story. it's awhig a bmw if it must be about our gasmobiles. i had a bedder tell to tale howender and that was concurbing one germane gleer & sergeant shrivel at the hostel by the chelsea but i perfer to remember rite now my scoldays scoldays goodold golden roddays i remember miss clark and mrs clark and china and miss holmes and miss holmes fist in the blackborad and leggings and kindergarten and missharpermissandersonmisss hermanmiss johnstonmissernultmisssuba missmissmiss and sisterfrideswidesisterbonaventurasisterphilippasisteranselmsistermaryreginasistermercedessistersofour ladysofsymarys sisterssisterssisters and fathercollard and his mum mrscollard and my pal ursula burroughs love and constance miles and katherine blount cheshire of charlestonsouthcarolina and marty and bunty and sally and pinky and squeaky and gopher and beaver and the hell world! and now i cyst in up the bewildernest impolite unconscious creacting journals for irreproducable results witch is aptly and corrigidly stated to my compleat sotisfication ragrab of brainpickings & skirt-misshes fantabulous labializing my bowels and vaginating my verbs and squaring off circles and starling at my navell and constrewning quadratura circuli even improper ones like sample indian stuff petaleafs to sew in the center of a ringelung a faded phony silvery studs the back of the london denim now december 28, 1972, the world was going on as useyule, all the time she was writting the world had continued. and if she was daid it would be just the same she exclaimed! the power of negative thinking! constantina constantinuous! allahblah! oh me none onsens, omegad!

january 4, 1973

PART FOUR

save the whale drawings
—mary austin

WRITING INTO THE SUNSET

So I laid out in the sun in a chaste lounge and burned my cleavage and thought if I didn't decide to stay there it was only because I had failed to leave. I mean rather if I *did* decide to stay there and the mistake and the correction alike are purely aesthetic. I've come to realize that only one thing is worth bothering about: becoming beautiful. It certainly is best not to do anything. I heard that two dykes holding hands at a business meeting were accused of having an orgasm. Oh these straight ones with their vibrators and their alarm clocks. Oh all we need is a nice enormous sunny sumptuous studio and a lot of exciting work to do and to just go there and do it and not talk to anybody and to evolve some complicated stratagems for keeping everybody in the dark. Oh I remember being at the christopher street gay liberation day march last year and a nice young woman asking me what would I do when nobody paid any attention to me any more and I thought about all the years I'd gone unnoticed while I enjoyed my reading and writing and I said well I guess I would just go on enjoying my reading and writing. Oh and then too if you were never beautiful you get better looking as you get older. Oh and none of it matters. You have to go through what you go through to be where you are. A charter to commit the crime once more. I dreamt I gave birth to a baby in a canoe. I dreamt I put my arms around kate who said she'd lost weight and was lying in bed on the set of somebody's play. I went to see kate at the dugout to set straight the old time magazine story since I was thinking about media distortion which seemed important and so does a field of crickets and wild strawberries. All my cross and troubles go to the door with thee. A friend says there's no help for it but to stop writing stop publishing and go into a coma. It's just very suspect if you do anything at all. And look what happened to bella. She's been hired as an informant. I didn't dream about bella but I saw her before the defeat and she made me cry so I guess she was hurting a lot. I wouldn't run unless there was a reasonable expectation of winning but sometimes a damaged duck is forced to run. Ceremonial cannibalism is found in many parts of the world. The desire to obtain the qualities of the dead person. People talk about it different ways. People respond more to publicity than to good work. People don't think about public people as regular people. People think that the work of a public person is the person and it is but it isn't too. It isn't, I found out, when I'm exhausted and an attractive enthusiastic young woman says I don't remember her from last week on the street someplace and when I do remember that I don't remember her name and it's true I don't but I want to be friendly but I'm exhausted and she's saying but I've been reading you for seven or eight years . . . so clearly my image of exhaustion and amnesia and mere politeness wasn't measuring up to my work in her mind's expectation I really wanted to say look I'm not the person who writes those things and I know that's true but I didn't and it isn't. Anyway I'm evolving some new personae. In only a few days I managed to be florence o'connor and bertha harris and professor sadie von masloch and occasionally just jill. I like being florence and that's well established so far as I'm concerned but bertha harris and sadie von masloch were an exciting new investigation into the possibilities of multiple identity. I'd rather that everybody just automatically loved me but we know that if you do anything it's optimistic to think you can do anything right. If you join or make a group in order to do something you're accused of being elitist and if you don't join or make a group you're accused of being an individualist. (Jane o'wyatt says a group is elitist when it forms and democratic when it dissolves.) If you do both you're accused of not being able to make up your mind. If you go away it's a copout. If you're

182

sick you're not healthy and if you die you deserved it. I
could be bragging or complaining or apologizing. It seems irrelevant in any case to the momentary position of the stars.
Any uninhibited display of egotism devolves into the heroic
quest for the cancellation of the self. Anyway I'm not a star,
I'm an asteroid. I went next door for an oatmeal cookie with
marshmellow stuffing. I passed a man who asked for a pen to
write a message on his mailbox and who wanted to know if
I was me and I said sometimes why not I have nothing to
hide. I became famous when I went crazy and I went crazy
because I stopped smoking cigarettes and before that I was a
cigarette smoking ignominious cricket of the arts and that's
the entire truth so kelp me odd. I have letters sometimes from
people think I just sprang fullgrown out of the head of athena
as soon as the world lesbian was breathed outside the closet.
I had a letter from a woman saying my writing and star trip
is ripping this lesbian (her) off and so far as she's concerned
I'm a middle class bitch who makes money writing in a totally
pig paper as a spokeswoman for Lesbians and that my ego
satisfaction is killing her which makes me the enemy and that
my writing style shows my middle class self indulgence which
I try to pass off as a women's language or beginnings of a
new women's culture. It hadn't occurred to me to pass anything off but it's a thought. It has often occurred to me that
I may be stranded between the literati who can't stand my
subject and the subject who is traditionally opposed to the
pretensions of the literati. Blessed be the Christians and all
their ways and works/Cursed by the Infidels, Hereticks, &
Turks. A mixture of blood between the immigrants and the
local aristocracy was inevitable. There's no mistake or correction but if there were they'd be purely aesthetic. I've come
to realize that there is only one thing worth bothering about:
becoming beautiful. Or what was it marilyn monroe said: I
don't want to make money, I just want to be wonderful. I
went to a party where lots of women were wearing red shirts

and suddenly I was standing with two women one of whom I didn't know addressed me smiling saying so you have breasts jill johnston and that's all susan brownmiller has ever had to say to me. I don't know whether it meant she thought I personally didn't have breasts or if lesbians generally aren't supposed to have any or possibly she was just making a pass at me or what but it could be that women as well as men are deeply threatened by a female who doesn't expose her breasts very often and paradoxically who appears to be flaunting herself. I went to the party as professor sadie von masloch who had come in from the department of cunilinguistics at Transylvania Institute of Technology the only college of science and engineering for women to speak on equality in education at the women's rally august 25 on fortyfirst street after the march. My speechwriter was martha shelley. My outfit was london black gabardine deep cleavage circa 1968. My assistant was lyn kupferman. My photographer was susan rennie. My politics are impractically pure and sue schneider said they don't expect stars to act like revolutionaries. For sanity sake cancel yr next ego trip. Or make sure yr original fictitious speaker will conclude her 19th century romantic tragedy in north carolina in time to speak for herself. I prefer looking like a butch fatale. It makes things easier. Already I've been accused in the papers of not being a lesbian and I'm mobilizing a squad of revolutionary lawyers to sue. I'm serious about that too. The papers and publishers are always conferring with their lawyers over such items as whether so & so might sue if it's merely implied that they might be homosexual the reason behind it all being that such attributions affect a person's livelihood so I have every right to sue and I have many witnesses to vouch for my good standing as a woman loving woman. Anyway I risked further misrepresentation for an evening. I risked everything in fact just by doing something. I'm not the person who writes these columns so that doesn't have to count. I don't know what the lower class elitists want me to do, I don't want to learn auto mechanics, and I can't work up an interest in plumbing or electricity, and I don't see why I should be a waitress or a cashier when people are paying me to move words around. As for representing Lesbians I don't represent Lesbians I represent myself, and sometimes other Lesbians or just others like my work and what I say and I know that because they tell me they do, and besides I'm a prerevolutionary lesbian village voice writer, I came out the winter of 1969 a few months before the stonewall riots and before that I was famous for being crazy and before stonewall and even feminism which I'd never heard of I signed two contracts for books because people asked me to because I did something called writing. Anyway I'm not famous except on special days and then I enjoy it. I would rather have spoken on education at the rally as jill or even as florence than as sadie von masloch. We say outrageous things with great pleasure. We do what we have to do and then see where we are. A charter to commit the crime once more. I dreamt I gave birth to a baby in a canoe. I dreamt I put my arms around kate and I went to see her to set straight the old time magazine story. The maneuvering of time was a masterpiece of premeditated murder. In august 1970 they put kate on the cover. In november 1970 they printed the news she was a "bisexual" as a belated confession as it were. I met kate that november only a few days before that panel at columbia organized by women's and gay liberation there at which she came out and I was one who was pressing her and I was unaware of the complexity of the problem. I was involved in my own complexities coming out. I said to her why are you posing as straight in the media and she just answered because she couldn't jeopardize the woman's movement and we went to a bar and had a drink and she made me cry and I went to california that week because everybody was making me cry anyway and I wrote in a farewell column that I was a luxury that the women's movement could not yet afford and I didn't know how true it was and still is apparently even among lesbians I'm a luxurious writer passing off a middle class self indulgence as a women's language or beginnings of a new women's culture. Actually I'm not middle class at all, I'm a british bastard, and there's a long tradition of aristocracy in the line of british bastardy, so that could account for all my errudishin and disarming dishonesty and pretensions in general. I'm working up a character analysis with the help of good friends like jane and bertha harris. Difficult but not evil, timid and aggressive, vague and demanding, unstable but never nasty and so forth. Remembering that the main thing is becoming beautiful becoming beautiful I laid out in the sun in a chaste lounge and burned my cleavage and thought if I didn't decide to stay there it was only because I had failed to leave and I've mentioned already the aesthetic importance of making a mistake if it sounds good and you can press your advantage with an equally interesting correction. The mistake time made over kate was not a beautiful one. They made her look crosseyed and weird on the cover and they wouldn't print the news that she was "bisexual" in august in that issue because it was scandalous and two months later in november they used it as scandal in a not unsuccessful attempt to discredit her as a leader in the movement, making it look as she says as if she'd just been chased out of her closet when in fact in august when they interviewed her originally she had told them everything about her life. For somebody who likes to do things it must've seemed as if the gig was up. Only last week in fact kate says she was walking along in the march august 25 and a young girl on a bike stopped and said are you kate millett well I thought your book was very pretentious so it's clear the original mistake however aesthetic and instructive was in just doing something. The whole business is rotten to the encore. One day you receive a hate letter and the next day a raggedy ann doll and you go and buy a bmw and go writing

off into the sunset in yr middle class indulgence clutching
yr doll and yr cleavage striking a beautiful purple pose and
thundering forth yr metrical incantations for the benefit of
the crickets and wild strawberries it could actually be the
life and perfecting those complicated stratagems for keeping
people in the dark I suspended my disbelief a long time ago
expending prodigious amounts of energy we thrash erratically
toward innovation. Literature is a defense against the attacks
of life and the other defense against things in general is
silence as we muster strength for a fresh leap forward. The
diabolical aspect of the women's movement is its indictment
of any action by which it is generated. The individual in any
case was always in trouble, the individual in amerika as elsewhere risks ostracism loneliness grave self doubt and perhaps
incarceration. And then if you do something as a group you
risk the collective fascism of the group mind and vote. Whatever it is the counsel for the defense could begin by pointing
out that she is not attempting to prove the contrary of what
the prosecution has asserted, in other words we might as well
do everything. Then whatever you do you could say that it
isn't really you doing it, or you could say it isn't you and
make yr disguise just as transparent and then claim you wanted
to present a transparent disguise so that anybody could see
you were merely pretending not to be you in case you thought
otherwise and so on. As sadie von masloch I was standing in
actually for bertha harris whose existence is still in question.
I wouldn't mind being bertha harris but the one I was speaking for really does exist and if it weren't for her 19th century tragic romance in north carolina I wouldn't have been
sadie von masloch either. Actually I was bertha and sadie
and florence and martha and sue and jane and jill and the
flying circus and everything and why aren't you mad at me
too. The identification of all of them is fairly certain but
there's some question as to which is which actually it was
bertha who called from north carolina to say she thought it

was wonderful and beautiful and it was martha who invented sadie von masloch who wore her last black london gabardine cleavage which she burned in the sun on the lounge and it was jill who nominated bertha after sue had made the speech saying we should have a dyke on the podium for equal education and florence who enthusiastically recommended bertha just recently employed by richmond on staten island to come up from the south as an upfront dyke in the women's studies program although nobody had ever heard of her she was instantly elected and that is the story of bertha harris and the last triumph of dykedom. The end of the story of kate and time was that kate was being ordered to speak out of both sides of her mouth at once, by gay liberation to come out, by women's liberation to shut up, and time made up everybody's mind by using the information that women's liberation wanted hushed up using it against them and against an individual which for women's liberation could've been seen as just one of their new chief indians biting the dust but to tie it all up by a neatly contrived coincidence of middle class indulgence in all our suspensions of disbelief it was bertha harris in november 1970 after time did their job who sent a telegram to kate reading time's not love's fool.

september 7, 1972

DELITISM, STARDUMB, & LEADERSHIT

On Saturday December 16 beginning 9:30 a. m. at McMillan
Theatre of Columbia University 116th st. and Broadway will
commence a conference for women only called A Feminist
Lesbian Dialogue: Is the Sexual Political?—This is an unpaid
political announcement. I thought up the idea a few centuries
ago and then asked a couple of columbia women if they'd
help launch the thing and locate the spaces for it and we
met over orange juice & vodka one sunday at noon at max's
which wasn't officially open and then we called a meeting
which caused instant widespread agitation and dissatisfaction
since the entire dyke community coast to coast was not invited. I think basically there was a misunderstanding as to the
nature of the meeting that we were meeting to confer when
in reality we intended to meet to organize. The intention itself it seems is always suspect in these situations. That is, who
intended what, and by what prerogative, and for whom, or
on whose behalf. The main thing is that when a group forms
it's elitist and when it dissolves it's democratic. Since elitism is
worse than the plague anyone involved in a group is asking
for lots of trouble from the more indeterminate group at large
until the group shows signs of internal disintegration which
was true of our group immediately. I don't like groups myself. I prefer being lost in china without a friend to being
found in a room with a group. I like the illusion that I'm not
accountable to anybody but myself for whatever I decide to
do, for example being permanently lost in china, and I feel
bound and gagged by the consensus reality of a group. Nonetheless I thought this feminist lesbian thing was extremely important and that I should submit to being bound and gagged
for a couple of months while the group decided all manner
of things including the size and color and quality of its paper
cups. That's for the dance in the evening. There is a dance

and it begins at 8 and I don't even know what particular place on campus it's been designated to happen. That's how much I have to do with it by now. The group took over totally. The group isn't even a true group any more. A true group is defined by its membership boundaries. Whether it's a group of a certain permanency with a title and officials or a group like ours which was constituted for a specific function. The boundaries of this group dissolved and that was my intention. There's only one group I feel I belong to really and that's the group called women. I feel I have more in common with women than with frogs or grasshoppers or men. If I was seriously upset being lost in china I'd go looking for my bowl of soup at a nunnery. The women there may be nuns, but they're still my political peer group. I mean it doesn't matter what these women do with their bods, whether they do anything or not, since we have so much in common politically and we have the same basic equipment by which in fact we came to be identified as women who by virtue of this very equipment constitute that political group. After all, this was the revelation of feminism. We always knew we weren't frogs, but it was never clear that we weren't men. We were all one group and we were called *man kind*. Some women are beginning to wonder now if we don't actually have more in common with such specious as crustaceans than with men. That may be an idle thought, but crustaceans and women alike are not given to erecting skyscrapers. Crustaceans and skyscrapers aside, we are now eager to delineate the boundaries of the group called women by the maintenance of a collective deviant identity as it were as it were as it was. Anyway I couldn't see organizing a conference with the entire group, it just isn't practical. I'm not a practical person particularly but I have some rudimentary knowledge of organization procedure required in the selection of paper cups. I dislike meetings for purposes other than parties and I knew dimly that a meeting of 40 or 100 women or so to determine such items as cups or any other apparently serious matters would enlarge the scope of our involvement to unbearable durations. Sadly however there is yet in our society no authentic authority in a spontaneous group. There is therefore a certain tacit permission accorded any organizational group under the auspices of its known establishments, i. e. NOW, or Radical Feminists, which is currently organizing a conference on Marriage. Any ad hoc alliance is automatically elitist. It's an insult to choose yer own friends. I don't know how important all of this is. I have a rather theatrical orientation to life. In my theatre days I received numerous invitations from people to attend their events or whatever they called them. Somebody obviously would have an idea for doing something and then often as not they would ask other people to collaborate on it and then finally they would invite the population at large to come and observe and/or participate in the results. We could have hundreds of these conferences. The reaction from certain elements of the dyke community seemed to be that this was the only conference in the world that there ever was or would be. Not only is this not the ultimate conference but its actual occurrence will be as illusory as every other insomuch as the feminist/lesbian revolution is an ongoing conference and that any particular conference merely represents a kind of formal acknowledgment of a general consciousness. The theatre parallel may be insensitive, considering the global moral issues that seem to be at stake, and the emotional investment in revolution, in which context an event is more than an evening's entertainment, an event concerning issues about which each of us is an expert. The leadership problem in the movement may be second to none, and it's related to the credibility of static or spontaneous groups. As would be expected most more or less permanent (static) groups defer to an elected leadership. Such groups, having a hierarchical structural affinity with the basic institutions of oppression, are well qualified to attack these very institutions with social and legislative reform. The leadership problem is mobilized around the conflict between the essential ideological rejection of authority and the necessity of getting things done, as well as all psychological vestiges of conditioned dependencies on authoritative leadership. The praxis of the woman's movement has devolved upon process as opposed to product, on collectivism as distinct from hierarchic forms of engagement. The consciousness raising group is a leaderless structure par excellence. These structures and the revelation of feminism, that we have a common problem and that is in being women, make sensible reflections of each other. The anxiety generated over any incipient leadership springs I think from the threat such leadership may be seen to pose to our common political condition which transcends our old individual sense of worthlessness. That is, leadership threatens our solidarity by triggering old responses of worthlessness in relation to the very real oppression of static appointed elected assumed leadership in the real world of male authority. At the bottom the problem in all the worlds is distinguishing between authentic and inauthentic authority. The authority of any authority person in the world in which we grew up is granted by arbitrary social definition rather than on the basis of any real expertise that a person may possess. As Adrienne Rich says in this essay I just read in the New York Review of Books ". . . authority derives from a person's status—father, teacher, boss, lawgiver—rather than from his personal qualities." She's talking about the family and the patriarchy, and she makes the all important point that the sacredness of this institution— "sacred in the sense that it is heresy to question its value—relieves the titular head of it from any real necessity to justify his behavior." It has been in fact by *this* system that we all came to feminism as worthless individuals militantly aligned against authority. Thus the failure to distinguish between spontaneous leadership and static authority is an understandable one. Some feminists, specifically two lesbian/feminists that I know of, Martha Shelley and Rita Mae Brown, have tried to define the difference between stardom and leadership without projecting the possible conditions of leadership. Besides that, a star is not necessarily not a leader and vice versa, although the distinction they've brought to attention is a valuable consideration. Anyway inherent in the distrust of leadership is the automatic association of leadership with domination. No doubt the central characteristic of authentic leadership is the relinquishing of the impulse to dominate others, but this is not a quality of leadership to which we've been exposed. To lead and not to dominate seem like contradictions in terms. Yet the women's movement has been productive. I mentioned the reform type organizations, and I'm not disparaging them either. To move against the enemy utilizing the familiar organizational arrangements of the enemy is not an ineffective strategy. It's one front, rear guard or whatever. But there've been other kinds of products in the movement and I think these are the source of the greatest agony. Given as we are to process primarily, when it looks like there may be a product, the perpetrators become deviants to the tacit or overtly acknowledged leaderless underpinning of the movement. Thus one might be attempting to lead and to deny that one is doing so at the same time. A product somehow always involves identity and identity can mean status and prestige and status and prestige accruing to any particular women make other women feel worthless (again). Because the word reaches *other* women through the media and the media is male and the male media creates *stars*. A star is a certain type of appointed authority. A given position. A constant identity achieved by a particular recognized accomplishment. Another static assumed situation in other words. I need hardly mention the continuous crisis in the woman's movement between the individuals and the group over the publication of every woman's book. Possibly the most feared product of all. The next conference should be called Power Money and Fame in the woman's movement, subtitled Confessions of Some Amerikan Woman Eaters. Anyhow the worst thing about a book is that it's a solo operation, an inde- fensible crime. It's also a class trip, it means you finished high school and your parents were skilled laborers and you weren't born in the tennessee appalachians. But I have more to say about this dilemma another time. I want to go on making my pointless abstractions about leadership. I can't be very specific because I don't know myself how to define or identify authentic authority, I suspect in fact that if we could we'd be making a familiar brief for the old legitimate types of authority and I think we desperately need some revolutionary forms of asser- tion that slip in and out of process like an eel that might sud- denly and unaccountably *know* a way upstream that hadn't occurred to the others who follow along for an hour or two until that particular mission is accomplished. A person who's a source of energy and initiative in a project might be considered a natural leader and that might mean for an hour. Sometimes it's a rare minute. And it isn't necessarily Charisma. We are very often taken in by non productive charmisma, in the vacuum between static authority and spontaneous leadership. All organizations tend to move in the direction of closure— hierarchical forms which transmit information through chan- nels that run in a linear direction, from head to mass. Revolu- tionary structures stop short in their own linear direction, from head to toe. Chinese revolutions getting stuck at levels of static leadership. Heads or heroes replacing old heads. Positional au- thority replaced by charismatic authority. When the charisma fails the tendency is to regress into authoritarian modes of directing energy. A proper leader does not lead. I follow the thought of somebody because it interests me. I lead myself to china to get lost. I follow myself one day to columbia to talk about lesbian feminism. I submit to being bound and gagged for a couple of months while the group decides all manner of things including the size color & quality of its paper cups. I watch while the group takes over. I become a part of an elitist spontaneous group which shows almost immediate signs of internal disintegration. I watch while my own original idea turns into the bidding of a finally enormous group. I watch myself sometimes try to control events. I watch others on other days try to control the same or other events. I hear reports of widespread agitation and dissatisfaction. I look forward to being an irresponsible individual again, not accountable to anybody but myself.

december 14, 1972

WOMEN & FILM

A fine feminist film publication is coming out of the west coast,
I recommend to anyone concerned with women in film and the
media generally. It's called Women & Film and it comes out of
2802 Arizona Avenue, Santa Monica, California 90404. I
would assume it's the most important writing about film being
done because it takes on the industry from the point of view
of the growing revolutionary ideology of the oppressed majori-
ties of the world, analyzing precisely those characteristics of
oppression by which in fact the industry thrives and survives.
They announce themselves: "The women in this magazine, as
part of the women's movement, are aware of the political,
psychological social and economic oppression of women. The
struggle begins on all fronts and we are taking up the struggle
with women's image in film and women's roles in the film industry—the ways in which we are exploited and the ways to
transform the derogatory and immoral attitudes the ruling
class and their male lackys have toward women and other oppressed peoples. Feminist publications generally appear to be
enduring problems of focus and quality of intellect and
Women & Film demonstrates the advantage of mobilizing an
already considerable body of feminist ideology around a particular subject, a subject in fact which has provided the present
movement with a large field of evidence for the very ideology
that a publication like Women & Film now embraces and projects back on to its source: the images of women in film and
the media. The makers of the publication have an overview of
revolution and they correctly see the film industry as the country's principal vehicle for ideological oppression or the continuation of ruling class interests. "Motion pictures have been
one of the most potent mediums for conveying and reinforcing
stereotypic attitudes." —"A closed and sexist industry whose
survival is precisely based on discrimination." All films other

than a tiny portion of women's "underground" work reflect absolutely the S&M culture we live in and to which feminism addresses itself, the male hero-villain, the female whore-victim. The primary S&M arena consists of the males themselves in their fratricidal struggles satisfying the male need for dramatic physical violence, any primary battle between men and women was fought long ago, making women the losers *as a class,* thus in films we see women as *assumed* losers, fulfilling all the secondary roles ascribed to losers, all the helpmate roles—wife mother secretary nurse researcher child/woman, whore, bitch etc.—that feminism has identified and exposed for what they are, with an occasional "enchantress" emerging from the mass of losers to challenge a male in some critical capacity—a primary encounter always ending in the demise of said enchantress. Few films are built round the major motif of the humiliation of women, there's no tension in a story the outcome of which was settled by at least the time of christ. The Rape of the Sabine Women is a fait accompli. Rapes, whore scenes, courtships, husband-and-wife scenarios, boss-secretary exchanges, none of these S & M modalities between men and women constitute the major interest of any film, they appear simply as (in)dispensable emblemata, reminders of an old battle in which the victory of the male was established and without which of course their own confrontations would be meaningless. Films perfectly illustrate the lopsided masculine world the aquarian age inherits and the total unwillingness of the industry to question its own values of destruction as in any way related to the masculine principle. Women & Film makes what so far as I know is the first serious attempt to analyze the sexual-political bias and basis of the entire media industry. Dealing for example with Clockwork Orange in this article here Beverly Walker notes that thus far critics have not made attitudes toward women part of their over-all analysis of a film. She goes on, "It seems an incredible omission in the case of Clockwork. The film flaunts an attitude that is ugly, lewd and brutal toward the female human being: All of the women are portrayed as caricatures; the violence committed upon them is treated comically; the most startling aspects of the decor relate to the female form. Even if these elements were not interpreted as misogynistic, why is it they have not been dealt with? In a curious departure from their usual critical method, even the most au courant critics have failed to come to terms with the film's visuals. Instead, plot elements have been used as a point of departure to argue Deep Philosophical Issues: violence, society, Christianity, behavioral psychology, free-will. These are potent questions. But is there anybody who believes that an X-rated film has taken in almost five million dollars at the box office because everybody is so concerned about the human condition? Clockwork Orange is making that kind of money because of all the naked ladies Kubrick has astutely used as commercial window dressing . . . If Oscars were awarded for Best Achievement in Misogyny A Clockwork Orange would surely have been last year's winner. There was plenty of competition, but Stanley Kubrick's adaption of Anthony Burgess' novel was so ingenious and relentless in its woman-hating that it was far ahead of all the others." —Walker makes a detailed analysis of the sexism in Clockwork. I wouldn't expect it from the establishment, much less the women critics, but we could be encouraged that somebody is doing it and it's going to become available to the people who're actually going to change things: the women themselves in the film industry or those making films independently. I have a letter here from a woman informing me that NOW is going after $500,000 to set up a national feminist cable television network. The actual role of women in film and the media right now seems puzzling to me. Can women work their way to the top to the real power positions, of production and direction, to any significant degree within the established industry and if so would they be the people or women to transform the image of women once they got there? This woman Christine Mohanna asks the rhetorical question: "If the majority of men in a particular society agree that a woman's place is in the home won't a majority of the women agree also? Because if they did not, they would cease to behave as if it were true, and in time, it would cease to *be* true. In other words, if certain sexual stereotypes do exist, they exist because both men and women believe in them." O'Wyatt suggests that women are the chief guardians of outmoded consciousness and another woman here in Women & Film, Sharon Smith, says "Finally, many women, products of the same society that created the neurotic filmmakers, are anti-woman." A woman writing in the voice a while back about her daddy put it right down I think when she said she grew up listening to her old man relate to women who had 'bad pins' or 'lousy wheels' or 'knock out knockers' and she said suddenly she found herself viewing women much the same way. Many women would probably say the beginning of their feminist consciousness was an awareness of their own S&M psychologies and the dissociation of schizophrenia we experience by imagining somehow that we're not those "other" women we come to view in much the same way that daddy does. "With very few films available which provide a strong female character to identify with, women have learned to masochistically enjoy seeing women ridiculed on film."—A film based on the rape of the sabine women would no doubt shock resistant intelligent women into feminist consciousness, although it might well not unless the plight of the women was portrayed in a political context by which I mean that the physical violation of the women was delineated against the background of their loss of political power, ie., autonomy. For that the Trojan Women was no particular help, for the powerful women of Troy were simply being required to exchange masters. The story I have in mind that might properly affect women is the tale of theseus who abducted antiope, the amazon queen, from her amazon tribe, thus causing the amazonian invasion of attica and a prolonged siege, at length concluded by a peace mediated by another queen, hippolyta. Here the rape and abduction could clearly be seen in the context of the real political autonomy of women which is threatened by the effrontery of any male against any one of their number. A curious film in which you can see the violent reaction of the male to the very transgression he assumes as his right when it's turned against himself is Deliverance, the recent film of the four superboys on a weekend canoe trip to conquer the elements. The S&M equation is strictly a boy-girl dichotomy and they reveal exactly what they think of women as the only suitable M when one of their own is humiliated and raped by a backwoods prevert and the victim's pals come upon the scene to take instant reprisal by shooting the offender dead. The boys all have a rough weekend but at last, although one of them "pays" by drowning when shot by the rapist's companion, the rest get off and return home free, the message being that the crime of men against women won't be tolerated in the form of an attack against one of their own, this is a political crime threatening the privilege of men, their S, in effect. The boys have it all worked out. The question as we go into phase 3 or 5 or 15 of feminist revolution is the consciousness of women and the strategies of change. Birthright feminism, or expanded tokenism, means that more women achieve a degree of self definition which men in an equivalent class position think they have, and create psychological "culture models" for other women, while these same women deflect or deter the evolving revolutionary consciousness of women at large by their absorption into the system within which it seems to me impossible to seriously affect the power base, production ownership direction etc, operating principally on behalf of the ruling class, white men. This is my idea based on my experience to date with "women in the media." Most recently I talked to a fine woman in Chicago of the tribune who expressed definite feminist sympathies and interest in my work and told me she was a member of a "feminist cell" on her paper, yet she admitted she'd have trouble knowing how to prepare my image for the boss when she got down to writing it up. Another much less savvy woman of another chicago paper just started looking catatonic at me at one point and when I asked her what was the matter she said something along similar lines. I know that the women of newsweek have been suing for better positions within the magazine and I also know that these same women won't under any circumstances lend their active support to insurgent feminists. The politics of people who get their positions thru reform will of necessity be reformist and not radical. Insurgency within the ranks is a possibility never to be discounted, but an individual here or there, the probability of the conversion of isolated individuals, while conceivable and even demonstrable, is no reason for any of us to trust these women to relay information about the movement without censorship or distortion. The development of women's independent "alternate" institutions—women owned operated & financed—obviously constitutes the revolutionary thrust of the movement, while they suffer from the lack of evolved channels of distribution. There is some other middle fugitive no-woman's territory that does exist and I'm not sure what that is unless it's crazy people like jonah broadcasting from within the belly of the whale, or as bill nichols puts it in Women & Film "women working within the mass media in any kind of radical capacity would seem to require discreet, coherent forms capable of maintaining a revolutionary thrust against the counter-revolutionary tendencies surrounding them . . ." Any productive relation between reform and revolution has yet to be established. When Susan Sontag makes a radical film I'll take note. Sontag or no, I predict it'll be a decade before we begin to see the images reflecting the new revolutionary consciousness of women in any effective way. I personally have no interest in images reflecting a reversal of S—M psychology, feminism in any event claims to spell the end of this psychology, but I guess I'd take pleasure in any plots illustrating the successful routing of males who offended women, that means all males in present positions of power within the media. Here's Sharon Smith in Women & Film: "Try thinking 'in female' for a moment. Imagine: That everything you have ever read uses only female pronouns, she, her, meaning both men and women. Recall that most of the voices on radio and faces on TV are female, especially when important events are in the news. Recall that you have only one male senator representing you in Washington (if you are tempted to laugh and say that would lead to catastrophe, ask yourself where we are now). Imagine that women are the leaders, the power centers. Men are shown in films only in their natural roles as husband and father, or else as whore and very nasty persons. Men are shown only in their natural functions of trying to attract women and making the world a comfortable place for women. Film men who rebel against this die very ugly deaths. Women star in all films of international excitement or adventure. Imagine that countless films show men as simple-minded little sex objects, and you despair of finding a strong role-model for your little boy (for whom you see other futures than slut, bitch or house-husband). Imagine that the women in charge of the film industry use their power to ridicule the men's liberation movement, presenting them in films as a bunch of frustrated studs, deluded into thinking they can be women, burning their jockstraps and waving signs—but always ending up in the boudoir of a condescending woman, always giving up the struggle and being happily subservient to her. Then imagine that if you complain you are given the biological explanation: by design a female's genitals are compact and internal, protected by her body. A man's genitals are exposed and must be protected from attack. His vulnerability requires sheltering—thus, in films, men must not be shown in ungentlemanlike professions. Psychological films remind men of their childhood, when their sisters jeered at the primitive male genitals, which 'flap around foolishly' while the sisters could ride, climb and run unemcumbered. Men are passive, and must be shown that way in films, to reflect and protect reality. Anatomy is destiny."

july 12, 1973

HURRICANE BELLA SWEEPS COUNTRY

my staff doesn't understand that i can't permit myself to be beaten over the head by everybody. my schedule beats me, my staff beats me, my constituents beat me my friends beat me— telling me i'm beating everyone else. if things go on like this, i won't make it.

Nevertheless, I wanted to see bella, and bella's staff didn't want bella to see me, and bella herself probably didn't care, and finally I interviewed her by telling her about myself over a side order of gefilte fish at fine & schapiro's on 71st street near broadway. I don't like to interview people. It's very embar-rassing. It feels like an improper inquisition. It feels as if I don't believe anything in advance of my questions, or rather as if I already know the answers so it's a silly game to ask what I know already, or at the least that it's dumb to ask questions unless it's for gossip or information in the course of a dialogue with a friend. Nevertheless I asked bella some questions, I suppose because we were surrounded by her aides and cohorts and they might've wondered what all the fuss was about if it wasn't to ask the candidate some questions. I asked her some questions and I don't remember what they were or what she said if anything, I know it didn't matter since I agree with her about everything, and I didn't want to arouse her wrath or alarm her constituents by asking a few things that I'd *really* like to know, like have you ever considered having a lesbian experience or how would you feel if your daughter made a lesbian marriage or how far do you think women can actually progress within the male established government and legal processes or how many bellas would it take all at once to make more than a mere dent in that system, since traditionally a strong woman emerges and is hailed and honored and promptly forgotten, but I did ask something along these lines and that was did she think the national legalization of abortion would terminate the current feminist movement the way the vote did in 1920 and she said decisively absolutely not, that we have too much going for us now and she was referring to the national women's political caucus through which she and many women see the ultimate full representation of women in the political power structure. So I did ask something. I think basically I just wanted to spend some time with her and my only excuse was posing as a reporter. I did feel really concerned last June however, and at that time I put myself out to act like a real reporter and as it turned out I was too late and the candidate herself wasted no time or words in telling me so. I was very angry at the albany dudes cutting our woman out of her district, then I was just as angry at all the other dudes for acting as if she *deserved* to be cut out of her district, I mean that mindless collusion of powerless people in the judgment of any authority, as though the fate that befalls anybody constitutes its own justification, that a conviction or an indictment from above automatically confirms the guilt of the victim, and I was almost as angry at the feminists who it seemed to me were deserting their big woman in her most difficult hour, and naturally I was angry at myself for not getting out there and saving the woman single-handed. A weird pall hung over that whole primary. It seemed as if the people who liked bella were afraid to say so and the people who didn't would stop at nothing to silence her forever. This paper for example was involved in the most outlandish incriminations, making a big deal over such items as the use bella's office made of an article that the voice printed by bella's "friend and associate" mim kelber, claiming that the omission of the identification the voice had made at the end of the article of kelber as abzug's associate in its reprint as a campaign leaflet was a sign of bella's horrible character, even though kelber had in fact identified herself within the article proper and there is in any case no moral issue at stake in the use that anybody makes through selection and omission of already printed material, as though it isn't a standard universal practice to select and omit portions of statements by people for political persuasive purposes. Considering that mim kelber's article was the only substantial literature that this paper printed on bella's behalf it isn't surprising that the paper objected so strenuously to any impression, such as they thought might be created by that omission, of the paper per se being in support of bella abzug. The same objection was made to the selection bella's office made of something positive that hentoff had said. These were trivial and irrelevant arguments against a woman of bella's stature. The smear campaign of a paper like the post is something else but I really think all of it from whatever angle was designed to shut up a particularly vocal woman and to step on the face of a victim as I suggested above and to save a sick candidate with an honorable record from the humiliation of a political defeat in his final moments. I don't mean that anybody actually knew that ryan was about to die, I think in fact that many believed he was medically fit, a few doctors in any case had so testified, certainly his illness was a rumor that neither side wished to see embroidered, but I'm convinced that people really do know what is happening at whatever substratum or superstructure of consciousness and that the overwhelming psychic forces at work in that particular event were those of sympathy and support and respect for the choice of a dying fellow in his private decision to leave this world a victor in his own field. I don't know, I do know there was a wet blanket over the whole business and it seemed impossible to get out from under it and do anything decisive or constructive. I called up brenda and gloria and I wrote to them too and said can't you do something or get somebody else to do something and I kept saying I was going to do something myself and then in the end when I actually did do something it was too late. I see from my record book it was wednesday june 15 when I called bella's office to do something and was informed that the election was the following tuesday, the day before the voice would come out. That's how much I care about elections in general, I never did know when they were happening. Anyway I thought I could at least say something post factum and I arranged to follow her around the next day, fully aware that everybody should be overjoyed to have an outstanding lesbian endorse an unpopular candidate at the last minute including of course the candidate, who was already predisposed to love the paper she must have thought I represented. Anyway I really wanted to meet her. I'd seen her on a tv documentary yelling and puffing and saying all smart things and I thought she was the hottest thing since gertrude stein whom I'd never be able to see live and in living color; or some incredible composite of powerful females for whom she has no historical precedent. She's not like anybody I know about. And I was convinced she was our leader, even if she did want to send some jets to israel. I wanted her for president, at the very least for mayor, and I knew she was far and away the best candidate for the congress since she stands for all woman's things and we desperately need a return to woman's things as she says in her book we (women) don't have any freudian obsession with missiles. Society doesn't require us to prove our superiority or to accomplish in some superhuman manner. We have very, very little to prove. That's why, in terms of political power, I feel we'd end up being a lot more sensible. And more peaceful. And another passage: This moment in history requires women to lead the movement for radical change, first because we have the potential of becoming the largest individual movement; two, because our major interests are in common with other oppressed groups, and three, because we've never had a chance to make mistakes in government and so we have no mistakes to defend. Men have made the world the way it is.—I hadn't read the book last june but I knew how smart she was and I was very angry and upset about her situation and about not being able to do anything about it. So I appeared at el diario the spanish newspaper where they said she was going to talk to the editors and discussed "the situation" with bonnie lobel while we waited bonnie told me she thought women would get a lot more timid if bella was put down and that men would take courage and that if all feminists stood together bella wouldn't be able to lose and people never cared about bill ryan before, it was all their male egos, they hate this kind of woman, they want us to run only against bad men, bad men are in districts that are so conservative that we can't win, what they're really saying is they want us to lose, and that there's been more psychoanalyz-ing in this race than in any other and like that until bella emerged from the elevator with a bunch of people and we shook hands and she levelled at me civilly enough and told me that before the campaign she'd turned down as a matter of principle an invitation to be interviewed by hentoff who'd been offered a lucrative sum for it by playboy and then she disap-peared into an office. An hour or two later when she came out she was pointedly ignoring me but I refused to think she was. I walked down the seven flights and waited for the entourage leaning a little too casually against a wall near the door. The elevator opened and bella stood squarely facing me glowering at the world, I thought I just happened to be in the way. I sprang to attention and said timidly with great expectations well where are you going now, what are you going to do, just to consolidate bonnie's proposal that I go with them wherever they were going in the car. It was a brief moment of social illusion. The reply from my leader was the end of me. She said without a second's hesitation: Frankly jill, you're a little late. Just like that. I hadn't felt so bad since a lover of mine flew away to spain in 1969. The line was even a little like that last one that rhett butler threw out at scarlett o'hara about not giving a damn. I went into instant devastation and turned round to face the door and while I paused momentarily my exit became blocked by bella and the others standing there looking at the rain wondering what they were going to do. I knew what I was going to do if I could just get by. I found an opening in the bodies and slid outside to my parked van, I still had my van, hearing the bellow of abslug's voice behind me "get that woman . . . get that woman" but I really had to split. I was a little late. Of course I was late. I was furious. I hated to be told what I already knew. I went someplace to brood over my wounds and think it all over. I thought a lot of different things at once. I thought it was because I was a lesbian. No I was just being parannoyed and besides the first thing I ever heard about this woman was she was speaking out for gay rights. I thought it was because she thought I represented the voice. I thought she must be mistaking me for hentoff or nichols. I thought I was too tall or had too many freckles or altogether I was just too goy looking. I thought she was merely angry at the world and I could dig that and people told me she said things like that to everybody so I decided to transcend my injury and try again. Anyway I was feeling less guilty and more sanctimonious. If the bella people were so upset about the voice in all these weeks why the hell didn't they contact the only feminist on the paper. It was clear why they didn't contact the only feminist, because the only feminist was a lesbian. Or, as their press man howard brock said of nichols, she doesn't count for much, and I added, you mean because she's a woman. No answer. No answer in general. Beginning october 4 I called bella's office repeatedly and was repeatedly discouraged from doing anything, not by any negative directive, only by the more insidious discouragement of the indifference in vague responses. I think I'm going to renew my idea of running for mayor on a lesbian ticket. And I won't have any boys around working for me. I think if bella has trouble with her staff it's because she has a lot of boys around. October 20 I was riding in her car leaving her office on seventh avenue and a boy was driving and her woman was sitting in the back with me, I just can't imagine it for myself, I mean if I was going to be out there talking up all women's things the way bella does I'm not going to be having a *boy* driving my car, much less running my office and I don't care what they say the way *both* offices, in washington and new york, look to me is that the women are doing the same old shit work and the boys are running the show, the big cheese in washington is this very bright exceptional looking kid with curly hair and a vest, he's her legislative assistant, and the worst vibe in the place is emanating from this "older woman" in a sort of a blonde bouffant sitting efficiently at the typewriter. I know bella had two women as her legislative assistants who didn't work out for some reason and they may be harder to find than boys but anyplace you go there's always at least one hardworking highly capable intelligent girl who can do it too if not better so I can't see the advantage in having a boy, especially the big tough type she has for her press secretary, unless the boy is strictly a servant and *no* boy these days in any sort of administrative job in a roomful of women at typewriters and telephones is less than somehow in charge, bella herself has said women control everything in politics but the power. She said we wouldn't even have effective political parties without women . . . filing, typing, mailing, telephoning and fund raising. There are no campaigns where women are not the mainstay. That's very close to what jerry rubin said about the women in the back room doing the crucial work for chicago while the boys were out in the defense box getting their media massage, but nobody seriously expects rubin to do anything about it, my quarrel with the abzug arrangement is an old saw of mine about heavy feminists out there saying all right things and doing them too and not particularly noticing or correcting the inconsistencies of their daily personal lives but if I pursued this it would bring me smack down to the feminist/lesbian political line of living and action and I really had decided to suspend my stringent solutions for the cause of bella who needs me like a hole in the head. I still think she's dynamite. I like all her hats and her dresses and I don't even mind her makeup. I like her solid imposing body and I don't care if she never does diet the way she says she keeps trying to: Oh, I'm always starting diets, but I can't stick to them. Something happens, like I get agitated on the House Floor, so I go into the cloakroom at the back of the Floor and stuff myself with things I shouldn't be eating. One of these days tho' I'm going to get on a serious diet. Ha, it would really be too much for these fellows if I was svelte. They'd bust a gut. —See, that's what's so terrific about this woman, she says it all straight out, she just doesn't give a damn, she says what she thinks about the war and the big shots and how she feels about anybody and herself and the price of baloney in the bronx all with the same hutzpah and humanity like she says "I'm a very spontaneous and excitable and emotional person and I do have a way of expressing myself pretty strong sometimes. Big deal." And she says "Oh, I don't know, I guess it's my cross to bear, these things. I mean, how am I to do anything if I don't scream and carry on? How else do you get action out of these people?" She says politicians are human beings and we think politicians are plastic people and people don't expect any blemishes of people who rise in the hierarchies and that people criticize her style but her style is human and people're not used to it. She also refers to her style as a certain vigor. Whatever it is the difference between her and a guy like ryan is that between a national leader and a local outstanding liberal. The big difference of course is that one is a woman and the other a male and this is the difference that a growing number of women and some men are beginning to see as the difference that makes all the difference. The "woman issue" was underplayed by both sides in the primary. I remember a times magazine article about both candidates in which incredibly it wasn't even mentioned. Apparently people looked away from the woman issue because that was one issue the bella camp was dead right on and otherwise what was the real difference between the two if it wasn't that ryan was running on his good record and bella was an interloper and according to the insinuations of ryan's literature bella had a big mouth and we know how the media played up this difference and made bella out to be the great white witch of the west; there was, however, apart from sex, a significant difference which bella's people put forward as their leading campaign pitch and that was that bella is an activist, that she not only votes for the right things but she goes out and mobilizes people, she does things like organizing people to go to washington to demonstrate in support of her issues and bills. I'm not in the business here of itemizing her accomplishments, people presumably know what they are, I am saying that apart from the central issue of sex, or I should say apart from and related to, here is a political leader who is actually doing something about the things that so many people are talking about, although what I still want to say chiefly is that sex is the overwhelming issue of bella's candidacy as she said herself she's the only woman who ever successfully ran for national office on an essentially women's rights social change program and as a reporter noted after the primary her defeat demonstrated that america's women voters are still not ready to put the issue of women's rights above all else and as all the venom against bella indicates the country is terrified of an outspoken woman, let alone one with real power, for bella may be making waves and introducing important legislation and even pushing a little of it through, but she has no real power and if she did as she says you can be sure that they wouldn't let her talk, as long as she's not a threat to them they're prepared to see her as interesting and dynamic, and, most of all, not boring, yet for the first time in amerikan political history we have a woman in the congress who is absolutely clear on the priorities of women's issues which include not only the pivotal question of abortion but all those concerns which involve the hopes and fears of simple people, matters of wages and child care and welfare, that consistently rate low on the scale of values to the ruling white male elite whose expensive fantasies in elaborate deadly toys and adventure vehicles continue to take all precedence over the basic needs of the people which I think we can rightly call a woman's priorities since it is the women in modern civilization who have been enfettered with the major burden of caring and the women in turn who've suffered the most when their boys grow up to care more about their toys and adventures than the daily rounds of survival business out of which they originated. The women are the warriors of peace and socialism and bella grasps the significance of her role as a leader in the movement to bring the mothers out of the political closet. A key revelation of feminism is that if women don't speak for themselves they're not going to get what they want. That seems so fundamental as to be unmentionable. Yet hordes of women still respect the assumption of their fathers and brothers and even sons to speak for them, in that spirit certainly the women are out there in battalions cheering for mcgovern because he's the nicer daddy and for the duration things would be nicer, like ryan was good enough on women's issues and he wasn't attacked for his position on women but the whole point is that women don't need the surrogate daddies any more. I asked bella about mcgovern. She says he isn't "right" on abortion, but he's the best candidate that the living generations of amerikans have ever seen and she excuses shirley maclaine from her sellout on abortion for her dedication to a good man. I don't see it that way but I wasn't into arguing as I said I didn't want to arouse her wrath or alarm her constituents and basically I just wanted to spend some time with her. I even drove down to washington and back and went to a session of congress all as it turned out to spend a grand total of two minutes with the woman. Anyway I thought I should begin my political education in earnest by visiting the capitol. Essentially I sent jill to washington to watch jill watching bella. The press section wouldn't let me in (the village voice is a weekly they said) and the visitor's gallery wouldn't let me write anything and although I went as a marine I wasn't offered any particular military dispensation either. In fact as I approached section seven or eight with my tag and gained admittance I was assailed by three guards one of whom lunged at my pendant period piece, grabbing all the metal and icons at once in his white chubby paw and demanding some explanation. I told him I was a jewelry designer for alexander's in the bronx. Then I sat down to watch our great government in operation. I heard the roll call. I watched the little man with a gavel in a high chair. I looked for bella. I listened to these speeches congratulating somebody who was retiring, one fellow saying how nice he'd been all these years and another fellow "wholeheartedly and unequivocally and enthusiastically endorsing the compliments of so & so about so & so who was retiring." I listened to an elderly upstanding type denounce dr. spock as a man who is not a "gentleman," apparently because he doesn't "deserve" the secret service protection he's receiving as a presidential candidate. I listened to lots of figures, the ones I remember being $65,000 for indian affairs and $2 million for the j.f. kennedy performing arts center. I heard the roll call again for a vote. I heard a debate in which one man said we were going down the primrose path and another said we were paying people to be patriotic and another said they were being hired to serve and not paid to kill and another called it an enlistment incentive, it was all about bonuses for reserves and bonuses for reenlistment. I wasn't looking for bella when I saw her and I leaned over the railing and a guard swooped down to tell me to sit back. I'd never seen her without a hat. I remembered that line in her book "I must admit I was so angry that I made a very shocking speech before the vote" and hoped she would do it but she was leaning on a chair in the aisle talking to the congresswoman from massachusetts and she looked ready to split as soon as she voted no for something. I ran downstairs to catch her at the door to be informed there were seven doors and I'd better leave my name for the man to announce me on the Floor so I left my name. Miss or Mrs.

Ms. I said. Miss, he repeated, and turned to enter the Floor to announce me. "I'll tell you one thing I'm beginning to realize which might shock you: It's not the reactionaries in congress who feel threatened by me. It's the liberals. Isn't that regrettable? See, I'm more freewheeling and I'm less bound to tradition than most of these liberals are.—I says what's on my mind."—"Well jill," she said, or asked. She was wearing her hat. I was wearing my aviator shades. I wished I was jewish suddenly. I wished I shopped at alexander's. I wished I'd gone to hunter college. I wished I knew something about politics. What could I say? That I'd schlepped myself down to washington to ask her if she'd ever considered having a lesbian experience? I shifted my weight and said weakly "well, I thought we might try again," thinking of our first and last disaster and of how eager bella's people were for bella to see me and how our meeting would advance the cause of the revolution. I know I was identified in her mind with the village voice the way red and matador are to a bull but either she liked me as a marine or she appreciated my schlepping all the way to washington for nothing so she controlled herself during our entire two minute walk to an exit and let me interview her by telling her about myself. I said I couldn't get into the press section and that congress was a boys club and I didn't like it and I wondered if a tall woman could be the speaker since they had such a short man doing it and I was driving back to new york and when could we get together. She said she was on her way to a new york delegation luncheon and she couldn't invite me and she didn't think it was particularly worth my while to return to the congress session either. We squared off at the top of some marble stairs. She tilted her head and hat and smiled winningly. I had to smile back. I felt suddenly quite chummy in fact and slapped the top of her arm lightly with my record book. So much for washington. I went and looked at some statues and listened to some more congressional bullshit and made it back in three hours 15 minutes. I was impressed by bella's schedule. She said she got up at 5 a m and flew to new york at 7 for a press conference and flew back on a 12 noon plane for the session. She was huffing and complaining just the way she does in her book. She complains all the time I guess. There's a yiddish word for that I can't remember what it is. I did learn a nice one from mim kelber however and that was tumler, a tumler is a person who creates a lot of excitement. Some people call that a big mouth. It's very clear to me now. We have one woman down there saying all smart things and that one woman is making up in sheer volume and determination for all the women who don't yet have a voice. As she says of the others some of the women in congress are no better than men, because they're all products of the male power structure. They come in, replace the men, act the same way as men, and do their bidding. They don't come out of a movement for social change. —A big problem facing the national women's political caucus emerges in the debate over numbers and feminism. On the one hand it could be said that the more women we get into office the more likely we'll be able to get our ideas across as brenda hyphenated explained, on the other as bella has asked do we want the kind of women who are going to vote for missiles and vietnam wars or do we want the kind of women who are going to put our tax money into housing and health and child care centers and abortion clinics and things like that. I agree with both since I think in the end the psychology of women is not fundamentally destructive, and I don't agree with any of it from the point of view of imagining that any great progress can be made within the male system proper but as I said I was suspending my stringent solutions for the cause of the rear guard. We want them out there covering for us. I want them for president. I want these dynamite women who say they've always felt that a nation can be judged by the quality of care it provides for its children and not by its airplanes and its missiles. I want these women whose voice is so big they can make one feminist quip into a national joke which sums up the whole schmiel: manny celler: "Why, women weren't even at the Last Supper." Bella: Listen, manny, I want you to understand one thing: we may not have been at the last one, but we sure as hell will be at the next one." I mentioned the joke at fine & schapiro's over my side order of gefilte fish. She said it was too obvious to say the women were out in the back cooking it. I agreed and I complimented her and I complimented her on her pink hat and I think I kept complimenting her. I rarely do that. I must've been very happy to be sitting down to supper with her and her aides in a jewish restaurant. I was glad our initial interview was over too. I got into that car I mentioned a while back and was really uncomfortable and didn't have anything to say. She was sitting in the front with the driver and I didn't know where we were going. I knew I was supposed to be firing questions. I *know* questions are foolish. So I was riding along in a strange car with strange people. Then she said without turning around from out of a huge fur coat collar: "Well, jill." Then she said "So whatdya write for that paper for" and I said "So whatdya work for that male government for." No I didn't, I made some lame excuse and said when I was president I'd put a stop to the freedom of the press and she replied that that was interesting but later on in the lobby of a teleprompter place she said freedom of the press was a precious thing. I added by the way that the voice prides itself on its multitude of voices and I don't remember what she replied if anything. I asked her about shirley and miami and betty & such and she kind of sighed and said she heard betty was up at this place (maybe the catskills) trashing her and gloria again. I said what's wrong with her. She said I dunno why don't you ask her. I said she doesn't speak to me. She said oh that's right she doesn't like you. I thought wow she must be an encyclopedia of that kind of information. I forgot to compliment her. I almost didn't make it to supper. I was standing on the corner of 86th and broadway in the rush hour while she did her "subway stop" really grokking on the whole thing and she began to pointedly ignore me again. A new york legislator was holding her elbow and piloting her into the subway people coming out of the ground saying "Meet Mrs. Abzug" or "Come and Shake Hands with Congresswoman Abzug" I was absolutely amazed at this sort of street theatre. A barker at a side show. Bigger than life on a street corner. Smiling and chatting and handing out buttons and not appearing to mind the sore heads or the obvious ones. I guessed the "subway stop" is a whole amerikan institution. Her aide told me people like to see that their politicians are real. Yeah, I could appreciate that. I was completing my political education. I was cold and her aides were pressing me to ask some questions, right on the street corner, I couldn't interrupt those little chats with her middleaged jewish women admirers, but I knew they planned to cut me out of supper so I sort of tried but she was miffed at me again, that was clear, and besides she was enjoying her subway stop, so I tried to think what I could do by analyzing what maybe was wrong. What was wrong was that four of her constituents came out of the ground and recognized *me*. Oy vay. And I thought she would appreciate the joke, after all, so I was talking to one and hailed bella on the side "hey bella" something or other and I guess I couldn't've done worse than if I'd asked her if her mother was on welfare so I waited and waited while she pointedly ignored me and then I made my move I blurted out oh I want one of your buttons too as though it was a crime nobody gave me one in the first place and she smiled and handed it over and things were mildly okay again, it's really touch and go with a great politician. I struggled to get the button into a suede jacket and then we went to supper where I was supposed to get down to the serious business of asking questions, finally. I ordered my gefilte and told her what I thought of the gay male homosexual movement and the revolutionary effeminists and how lesbians are not homosexuals but feminists I suppose she knew already. I suppose she knows everything. So I added as a sort of rhetoracle question so whatta we want a medal for being in the vanguard? and she got it. She gets everything, she isn't any particular age, she could be my daughter or my grand- mother, (if only I'd come from the bronx). She isn't even a person, she's a phenomenon. That isn't true, she's a real per- son, a real person person, a real woman person who thinks and feels lots of things in succession and all at once, a typhoon of a woman actually who blows hot and cold and forms into fun- nels that suck things up and carry them for miles and drop them in unlikely places and move on silently over the gloaming gory political landscape. One minute in her office behind closed doors yelling stamping pounding the tables "I'm very unhappy about . . . It's outrageous that . . . " and the next in a solemn quiescence in the car preparing to meet the broadcasters for a completely lucid and low key speech about her credentials as a congressional candidate. I want these women in office who're in touch with their feelings and who know perfectly well when they're bullshitting and who don't have to displace their con- cealed feelings by dropping bombs on people who live thou- sands of miles away because they (the bellas) *know* when they're concealing their feelings because they're right up front with them *most* of the time. Forsleuth I wasn't disappointed in the real woman. I wished I could spend more time with her. I know she wished she was with martin, she kept saying so. She was very upset she couldn't reach martin in the pay phone at the "subway stop" to meet her for dinner. I wished I could be solely responsible for her belated victory at the polls this week. Would she think I was crazy, for wanting to feel "like one woman risking her life going up in a helicopter to save the world when the world's obviously not going to be saved by one woman. Not even the country. Not even the state." Even so, she knows where she's going.

our time has come. we will no longer content ourselves with leavings and bits and pieces of the rights enjoyed by men. we will no longer be satisfied to remain on the outside of power

looking in. we want our equal rights. nothing more, but noth-
ing less. we want an equal share of political and economic
power. — bella abzug, june 9, 1972

november 2, 1972   221

THE HOLY SPIRIT LUCID IN NEW YORK

June 14 fell out of bed at the phone ringing and still sleeping said it must be the holy spirit which it wasn't but it was about the holy spirit. The holy spirit had been running loose in new york for at least a week I think and we were trying to keep track of the body which was getting itself in trouble. We weren't trying to keep track of it at all actually. It had been wandering around the city enjoying itself until midnight June 12 when a call came in from lyn sounding alarmed having talked to the holy spirit's mother who said the holy spirit had appeared at her house wearing two tin cans around its neck and carrying the bible. From then on whether we knew it or not we were keeping track of the body. Where was the body going and who was it with and what was it doing and how much sleep was it getting and how much food was it eating and what was it saying and what did it look like. It looked very sunburned and refracted. The gaze defocussed farsighted, literally taking in everything. Her new role creates new demands. What were we supposed to do. I thought we should do nothing because anything we did would be something too much in terms of giving anybody including ourselves the idea that there was something about which something should be done. Nevertheless the afternoon of June 13 I sped downtown from a central park appointment to see the body of the holy spirit in its apartment. Already I had done something about it without really knowing it. I had written about the end of a relationship intertwined somehow with some stories of losing things and the fears of being locked in or out of rooms or wombs or moving boxes or the enormous room itself meaning the world. And the following week about sanity madness and the family and levels altho I didn't actually know that the holy spirit was rampant again in new york city but clearly the messages were coming in. We told wendy wonderful about it

and she said everything is fucked up right now because venus
is just passed into gemini, or mercury, or something. The holy
spirit herself is aquarius with gemini rising and she informed
us that it's reigning all over the world and some people were
getting wet. A woman last night elaine by name said I happened to catch yr piece in the voice and I must congratulate
you for precipitating a totally psychotic episode and she was
marvelous. A woman last week came up and said are you and
I said yes and she akst is it just me or is it a general complaint
I can't understand yr columns and I replied I supposed it was
both and went on she could understand the most recent one
but the one the week before . . . and I said well the next one
is totally incomprehensible even to me so you don't have to
bother with it and she thanked me and walked away. Leticia
says to her they read like a roar-jacques (or jill) and that
sounds good too. We don't want to be put any more in the
position of having to try to sort out secrecy and muddlement
in the face of being muddled up over the validity of trying to
do so. All I need is a justified margin and a friendly editor.
If a fool persists in her folly she'll grow wise. So saith the
holy spirit on spring street the afternoon of June 13 after I
sped downtown from central park. This is the big year for the
holy spirit cuz she's 33 and so was christ. In 1933 gertrude
stein was bitten by a serpent and described it as a very xciting
xperience, quite biblical. The bible always gets into these stories.
The bible or black elk or lucy church amiably. From the clinical psychiatric viewpoint said ronald laing of one sarah danzig
began to develop an illness of insidious onset at the age of 17.
She began to lie in bed all day, getting up only at night and
staying up thinking or brooding or reading the bible. Gradually she lost interest in everyday affairs and became increasingly preoccupied with religious issues. The holy spirit was not
lying in bed and the bible she was into was yeats and I thought
she was fine. She had of course been into the bible. It was true
what the mother said about the holy spirit accompanied by her

body appearing at her house carrying the bible but the two tin cans around the neck were not tin cans but little tin cups and they were not around the neck but held in the hand for the purpose of drinking bourbon. Anyway the mother found the bible alarming and so did we apparently although as I said I also thought we should not do anything or we should at least pretend that there was nothing to be done in order to convince ourselves that if we began to think anything should be done it would provide its own excuse for doing so. Nevertheless we were not uninfluenced by the knowledge that the body of this holy spirit had been captured before and it showed no inclination to leave for the country, on the contrary it insisted repeatedly that its mission was in the city. It's bad enough if you be telepathic around friends that have funny stuff in their heads but if you be telepathic around thousands of people at a time that have funny stuff in their heads it means yr telepathic perceptors can be bombarded with such an input that you can't integrate it and that was what I was afraid about. When the spirit gets loose the radar set stops detecting unidentified flying objects to keep out new information and the set has trouble handling it. Overload. Very smart. She was getting really smart. She was getting so smart she was speaking in aphorisms and pronouncements. She was becoming affluent in tongues. She said get off your crosses and follow me. She said the only thing that burns in hell is the self. She said suffering burns off fat. She said shit is living clay. She said the palace of excrement is built in the place of love or the other way around. She said bring them up even if you have to bring them up screaming. She said you've gotta use words when you talk to them. Who are them I asked. I dunno, ask eliot. He dead, mistah kurtz, he dead. Sometimes when people don't answer it means they're not in. We were fooling around with words and ideas like that when lois got up and said I'll leave you two together in the playpen, I'm going out into the real world. I was still a little worried but I was having a good time and I'd secured my own radar set when i came in by consuming an english muffin and a glass of pink wine. When you come into such proximity of the transmitter of the holy spirit you can fly right off yourself in the same company of angels and albigensians and atlantians and alchemists heading for the aldebaran which is the brightest star in the Hyades right in the eye of taurus. They used to call this a contact high. So I was high and riding along on the flight of the holy spirit and sufficiently grounded by an english muffin. I thought everything was going to be all right. I didn't think we had to keep track of the body even. Probably the thing we had to keep track of was what anybody was saying about what was going on or not going on and stay ahead of the stories which are now legion. The afternoon of June 13 it wasn't much more than the bible and the tin cans. In that spirit we went out on the street and walked the humid length of the italian fiesta on sullivan which was stinking of green peppers and onion and sausage and pastry frying in grease to the corner of houston where a crowd of italian mammas was handing up its dollars to a guy in monk drag paperclipping the income to three white streamers coming off the outstretched hands of a forward tilting plastic st. anthony on a catholic float outside the church of the same saint. The holy spirit introduced me to the greek, a nice guy she said, and we ambled on through the smelly concessions. I remembered that snoopy was saved by a pizza. I remembered that in all matters of discovery and invention we are continually reminded of the story of columbus and the egg. I remembered that the hindus give the world an elephant to support it but they make the elephant stand upon a tortoise. I didn't need to remember that the proper posture is to listen and learn from lunatics as in former times. Our task is to rejoice in these condemned qualities. Aphorism is the form of the mad truth. Aphorism is recklessness. Aphorism is suicide. She said she was mission impossible. On sullivan street she yelled to the man behind the sausages stop eating that shit and I was afraid. All things had lost their definite boundaries. The world of egos is boundaries. A room full of proper people who'd gone to sleep standing up talking to themselves. All of us is implicated in some terrible aboriginal calamity. I said look maricla I know you're the holy spirit but these people are crazy and you can't run off with a can of beer like that or they'll get you that's all and I wished she'd stash her bod in a safe place someplace. I was placating five fat italians waving their arms and hurling imprecations after the thief who was 30 yards at least up the street calmly drinking the beer and regarding me approaching after I paid the 50 cents looking sheepish and satisfied out of the refracted eyes set in high relief by the sunburn and like a kid who expects to be reprimanded and still get away with it and she did and I imagined I was effective by just saying you can't do that and we went on. We went into st. anthony's and I was for going right back out but she said come on and slipped very fast down the aisle into a pew behind a couple. I followed and then became involved in a fast reverse like a basketball pivot as the spirit shot past me back toward the door a fractured second after she potched the man of the couple on his fat bald head with her hand or fist I was going actually in both directions at once pacifying the man who was looking round like an angry astonished bullfrog while going after the spirit toward the door I caught up with her and said why the hell did you do that to which she just said he was bad so what could I say. I said he may be bad, but you shouldn't do that. And we walked on back to spring street through the fiesta stopping again to talk to the greek. I wished the body wasn't wearing a dress. I guess holy spirits wear dresses. Actually she was androgynous, she said she was wearing male underpants under the dress. I don't know if the greek would've liked her any better or worse if he knew but anyway he liked her. I knew the holy spirit wouldn't be afraid of death but I was afraid of bellevue where they don't have any respect for the surviving body. Already the self was being interred. The spirit was loose and the self was dead and the bod was besieged. I'm not sure I understand too well the apparent paradox of a dead self who rises almost immediately out of its husk into the amplified self of omniscience and omnipotence and declared invulnerability to the constraints under which we seem compelled to operate in the limited plane of physics. I think it happens from becoming so smart and turning on a lot of people and not having the bread to pay for your beer and losing so much sleep you start remming while you're awake and your dreams becoming more fantastic and agreeable than your writings or your paintings which you don't do anyway and from falling in love and from people contradicting you when you've become so smart that nobody knows better than you. I knew I didn't know any better that afternoon of the italian fiesta but I could still disagree and not appear to be contradicting the oracle. I didn't mind not being the holy spirit myself, especially since the holy spirit called me a genius, and I was still permitted my own reality. The spirit may've been slipping away but the set was still plugged into the physical plane. We could still respect each other and I could admire the manifestations of her holiness without feeling obliged to fall down and worship. The subjective expedient is useful if employed at strategic times, but dangerous if mistaken for the only truth. Fantasy must be voluntarily entered. Be very careful, be careful as you can be. Don't be very careful, decide to climb a mountain with a meadow at the top and sit there in a chair where you can see everywhere, an aura of unspeakable threats will surround you. Mental things alone are real. The external world can be altered by mere thinking. There is no distinction between the wish and the deed. What did the holy spirit see close, that is what she never can tell, and perhaps it is just as well. Mystification entails a constant shifting of meaning and of position. The shrink at an emergency depot said that's a symptom of the illness when I told her the spirit said yes and then no or vice versa concerning anything and I said back that it may be a symptom but it wasn't an illness it was a state of mind and it was beautiful but impractical and when we all lived again in a world in which yes and no were the same we could all suffer the same illness and find it strange when some other monkey came along saying emphatically yes or as emphatically no like the great amerikan debating team. In the meantime what were we supposed to do about the world which was reacting both agreeably and controvertibly to the appearance of the holy spirit in its midst. People with microphones and tape recorders and chimera crews were beginning to follow her everywhere. The animals in the zoo were performing for her and the monkeys were wonderful. All the people too were beginning to know, the newspapers were full of it, even mao-tze tung knew, he was one of the first to know, coverage of the event did not begin with the report in this column. For this report I didn't have to deliberate over the disclosure of names. Morning has broken, blackbird has spoken, the revolution is over she said come out on the street with me and see. Rolling rocks, stinging twigs, the glowing eyes of animals all menace her, but carrying a blue garden chair, she keeps climbing. She said they were preparing a throne of rhinestones for her that she didn't want to sit in. Even so the ordinary furniture of her life was throne out the window. Split the stick and there is jesus. June 15 another phone call lois from spring street the cops were there and they were waiting for an ambulance and what could we do. We could meet them at the depot and get her out and I jumped into my emergency vehicle to perform my part in the play. June 15 was the day in england in 1215 of the signing of the magna carta meaning the granting of rights and privileges. It was June 15 and already we were doing something. Already for that matter the day before I had been doing something by exhorting somebody not to do anything. I said don't call up that male doctor and don't talk to the mother or the sister and if anybody else asks about the holy spirit don't even tell them the body is in trouble. The body was certainly in trouble and we were by the time of the furniture event actively keeping track of it. It was my idea that although the professed mission of the holy spirit was in the city the country was the only place to be when you can't stop telling the truth and the general population isn't ready for it. I didn't say that to the spirit who was at this time unable to tolerate any criticism of her pronouncements and policies, but I did say it would be nice if you could go to the country and she didn't disagree. Actually it must've been the only person left in the world she trusted who said they were going to the country and I merely executed the arrangements by talking on the phone. And that may have been all very well but the spirit did not appreciate the comments I made accompanying my arrangements so one more plan to save the body of the spirit went out the window along with the furniture. I was impatient. I said to myself don't be impatient and get some sleep, the spirit may not need any sleep but you do. The spirit of course desperately needed sleep and this was a certain fact that was an important source of the developing dilemma. We had neither the authority nor the means to enforce any kind of medical control on our friend and we seriously doubted our own certainty as to the necessity of it since it entailed the obstruction of justice or the thing we most value about our existence and that is our autonomy. Until the state comes to its religious senses the bodies of all holy spirits are in trouble over the absence of care and compassion in assisting at the delivery of the body from its vulnerable environment while the spirit is doing its work of running rampant and telling the truth. In same words until the state respects and exalts its spirits. The spirit herself must be educated into the control of her body to insure the effectiveness of the message. The new amplified self of omniscience and omnipotence must be as I see it some extraordinary reaction to the problems of moving through the world with a dead self or ego or self devoid of its sense of boundary and division or of its separation from objects. I am pure energy, she said. She was pure

energy and her physical and mental activity had become undif-
ferentiated. If this is the pure state and I think it is then what
was the matter with the world and why was she getting so
angry which amounts to the same thing I guess, the matter with
the world still residing as it were in the body of the spirit
which is not yet completely detached. We made new efforts to
get around a defeated situation. The most difficult thing is
maintaining an attitude of suspended realities in responding or
I should say in trying not to respond to the primal outbursts
and unpredictability of a body gone astray, especially when
the body expresses its displeasure over your own and taxes
your natural or conditioned tolerance for a certain amount of
daily assault by lunging at you and looking dangerous. That
shrink at the emergency depot for instance the second time we
arrived the night of June 16 over the destruction of a plate
glass door really blew her cool when she reacted in our one
dimensional reality plane to a pronouncement of the holy spirit
regarding her wishes to be sent over to bellevue by changing
her mind about admitting the body to the superior prison we
were already in (in its emergency area) and taking the spirit's
word for it about bellevue by signing her over with papers and
phone calls you know like a mommie playing that game of if
you don't like the favor we're doing you see if we care we
don't have to do you any favors in fact we're going to punish
you for not liking our favors although she didn't say that and
she wouldn't have said she thought it if you told her. What
these people say they say is always bewilderingly incongruent
with what they say. Their attitude in any case is that the holy
spirit is a criminal and it's *these* damn people who have the
equipment for doing something effective however brutally in
saving an overexposed body. They save the bodies and destroy
the minds. For in saving the bodies they reinforce the original
problem rooted in the material state of doubting the necessity
of becoming the holy spirit in the first place. In this dilemma it
isn't surprising that the spirit in its journey encounters such

obstacles to its fulfillment that it begins to feel with some real justification that she is the only holy spirit in the world and the rest of us are traitors to its purpose. All of us is implicated in some terrible aboriginal calamity. Anyway our friend mirac-ulously escaped bellevue at three or four in the morning by telling the shrink over there that she happened to be standing outside a combination whorehouse and buddhist temple next to a plate glass door that somehow broke or something like that, she was able of course to comment quite lucidly on all her mystifications. Whatever she could do it still seemed equally urgent both to do something and to do nothing. In the name of authority something was required. In the name of autonomy nothing.

june 22, 1972

R. D. LAING: THE MISTEEK
OF SIGHCOSIS

All that is certain about 'mental illness' is that some people
assert that other people have it (Morton Schatzman).

Not since approaching Richard Alpert in '69 have I felt it
furthered me to see "the great man." Approaching R. D. Laing
last week was for me something of an exercise temporarily dis-
carding a new frame of consciousness for an earlier one still
very much with me but not so visible or accessible. Thus I
approached with a certain ambivalence. I should've seen the
man in '69 when I was in london and made inquiries and went
out to kingsley hall and let it go at that. He seemed as unavailable as the queen. It was just as well. Had I located him I think
I would've been prostrating myself as a sort of a "patient" and
my mission essentially was a lonely one, I spent a week in a
fancy hotel reading oedipus rex and dissolving in the bathtub
and then bought an old black ford prefec and went traveling
into myself into the heart of france accompanied part of the
time by a very young british boy who made the big trek to
india and acted as my "great man." We were certainly always
into some great man or other. The addition of Laing to my
roster was a fairly recent one. It must've been '67 that a fellow
in new york put The Divided Self into my hands, and that was
the year that The Politics of Experience had become available
in this country. I didn't read The Divided Self at that time
and I resisted reading The Politics of Experience because it
was written by a psychiatrist. I didn't have to wonder what a
psychiatrist could possibly offer me at that time. So far as I was
concerned the entire profession was a shuck and the sooner
western civilization had done with it the better. And I didn't
think so because I was a woman, I had not then linked the profession with the patriarchal status quo, I thought so because I

had been personally brutalized by it, and although I respected other people's judgments of themselves being helped by going to somebody's office, I didn't think *any* of these doctors in offices could be trusted when the chips were down, I mean I knew they were all in collusion with the hospital-prison system. I had witnessed the entire system in its operations at every level and I knew. The primary function of the profession was (is) to help people 'adjust' to their roles in the self denying hierarchical structures of this scarcity oriented work-pressed society and to lock them up if they couldn't. Helping was to help people function better. A person was thought to be "breaking down" when it was observed that they weren't functioning. Other expressions, of violence and withdrawal and apparent unintelligibility, were naturally viewed as acts of defiance accompanying the inability to function and threatening the social order (represented in the authority of the psychiatrist) and requiring punitive corrective measures to maintain the general level of fear and terror at the possibility of one's own individual deviation. The attainment of true individuality through therapy was either a thing of the past or the privilege of the rich or a rare misunderstanding of certain deeply concerned people like carl jung who in any case had an unusual historical grasp of prototypical figures of deliverence in the dramas of rebirth; but this is a mystical tradition to which the psychiatric profession never laid claim, outside of such exceptions as jung the profession emerged as the guardian and the beneficiary of the state. An army of medical bureaucrats. Here and there a stray individual who had suffered who happened to have the same credentials. Such a one was wilhelm reich too, one driven mad if not by his own perceptions by the opposition to them within and without the profession. In scotland in the '50s another such a one was emerging and this was Ronald Laing from a poor middle class family in glasgow. By the mid-'60s Laing was in london at the center of a revolutionary group of ex-"psychiatrists" developing the communal idea of their vision at this place called kingsley hall in a working class section of london a place where people could go and freak out or 'go down' as Mary Barnes put it anyway to *have* this experience that the psychiatric profession cum society has been so determined to prevent people from having. This was 1965. As Joseph Berke the amerikan trained doctor who 'assisted' Mary Barnes put it "Ronnie and his friends and colleagues very much wanted to get a house in which they could live and personally provide an efficient life support system for one or two people who would be undergoing a psychosis 'trip'" and as he said of himself ". . . to *stop* acting towards others as taskmaster for some agency of institutionalized brutality." 1965. A pivotal year for the mind of the western world. It isn't insignificant that while Laing and his associates were launching their freakout center in london the psychedelic movement in amerika was going into full bloom. People like me just happened to be in the wrong place. It was one thing to go off the end on an acid trip but it was still quite another to go on one of those unpremeditated journeys identified as madness. What was happening in the west in the '60s was an unprecedented convergence of two traditions: drugs and madness. The one was elucidating the other and together constituting the first widespread challenge to the civilized insanity of western rationalism. A number of individuals had made the proper connection between the psychedelics and states of madness or so-called schizophrenia, but this was not popular information, and if you made it yourself it seemed the wildest supposition, thus Laing's The Politics of Experience was the first official news linking the two experiences although he never actually says so in the book it's clear that the model for his revolutionary view of madness is the psychedelic one, transposing as he did the psychedelic terminology (guides, trips etc) onto the madness experience and coming up with an apocalyptic vision comparable to the great pronouncements of high priest timothy leary regarding the purgative effects of the psychedelics. Popularly a good fullranging acid junket was considered an induced 'psychosis.' A year ago I wrote that having read The Politics of Experience again recently I was disappointed that Laing wasn't explicit about the source of his

revelation and transposition. It was either in high priest or the politics of ecstasy that leary described his meeting and tripping with laing in millbrook and later in london and in 1969 richard alpert told me about flying to london and tripping with laing so I concluded that laing must've been protecting himself professionally by coming on as the high priest of madness without any direct personal information as to how he got there and I determined to ask him why. Any Laingophile can find a logical continuity between his earlier books The Divided Self and Self and Others written in the late '50s and The Politics of Experience written roughly from '61 to '64 although not available here until '67. Yet the break between the books is such a before and after affair that you know the transition must've been another modernday crucifixion and conversion number. The question was was the man revolutionizing the profession or was he just going round the bend or what. The profession itself reacted with predictable hysteria and dismissal. As Laing said on the cavett show november 9 95 per cent of professors of psychology in this country declared that he was a dangerous lunatic at large. The threat to the profession was perfectly expressed in a book published last year called R. D. Laing & Anti-Psychiatry which sums up the range of agreement with and antagonism toward Laing's positions and pronouncements. A respectable member of the profession one Theodore Lidz for openers said he had relatively little quarrel with The Divided Self. While he considered the book a different type of approach than he would use, he thought it a "brilliant work" that "held out the promise of a really great mind in our profession." He went on, "Politics of Experience, on the other hand, is a wild and whirling commentary that demonstrates little grasp of the reality of human development." Within a few years it appeared Laing had turned traitor to the profession. How had this happened? How had a brilliant young scotsman obviously on his way as an important figure *within* the profession been so foolish as to turn his back on an already considerable reputation by writing a crazy book like The Politics of Experience? Why is the profession still so threatened? This same fellow Lidz I think provides the answer, saying things like "the idea of breaking down distinctions between doctor and patient doesn't appeal to me at all." Or "I was upset at first when I found that Laing was writing for a general public rather than for a professional audience." Or "I think The Politics of Experience is doing a real disservice to a number of people who take it very seriously. I am speaking of the notion that it is good to be schizophrenic, or that one should force himself into a psychotic experience." There you have the three central expressions of the problem: A man anxious to maintain his role as doctor will be just as anxious to withhold the 'secrets' of the profession from the public and that includes the necessity at all costs of upholding the notion that there is actually something called schizophrenia. A doctor needs a patient to complete his identity, I'm reminded of genet's judge pleading with the thief to go on being a thief, and a doctor needs his profession to institutionalize and legitimize that identity, and the profession needs a terminology to label those objects, the patients, through whom they've established their identity in the superior authoritative half of the bargain. I've observed before and so does one of Laing's colleagues in this collection of essays I mentioned the name-calling nature of the psychiatric textbooks. And I've experienced this situation that Joseph Berke refers to: If his 'patients' claim they are not ill they challenge his pretensions . . . mental patients can find themselves in a special bind. To get out of the hospital, or to ease their life within it, they must show acceptance of the place accorded them, and the place accorded them is to support the occupational role of those who appear to force this bargain. Endquote.

Most 'patients' have been successfully brainwashed into a career as patients. Those who haven't and who become temporarily trapped by the profession may view themselves like the blacks as political prisoners and indeed they are. In 1965 for no reason other than that I had gone out of my mind (or into it) I was locked into a gray walled dungeon with no way out and shot full of paraldyhyde and 1000 mcs of thorazine and locked into a cell within the dungeon a room containing a peestained mattress and the dents of bludgeoning heads and trussed up to a bed and laced up into a straightjacket and left to die for the night I did and I've never been the same since I'm just beginning to get in touch with the phobias I acquired in one night's time an elevator problem is the least of it and I stand as witness for thousands like me for whom The Politics of Experience came like a belated vindication against our censure and invalidation by the Modern Inquisition. I've written in this paper before that people like me were leaning out of our disaster areas waiting for *any* parchment of evidence to verify our trips, just to indicate that we had actually been someplace, never mind that we saw something interesting where we went and that there might be some value in it. The total invalidation of the "inner journey" by the psychiatric profession was a damnation from which few were lucky enough to recover. And you couldn't expect any help from your friends, who believed in the profession. They'd be "kind" to you as a "sick person" but they weren't about to find anything interesting about your trip, much less think you'd actually been anyplace, except to the bin, which was a legitimate enough place to go since they helped to send you there. It is then in the continued spirit of the refusal to respect *other* people's experiences and these same *other* people's *assessment* of their experiences that the critics of Laing have the exquisite gall to go right on trying to tell us all what's good for us, i. e., in this R. D. Laing & Anti-Psychiatry book: "Bright young schizophrenics, like bright young people generally, are interested in reading about their condition. From the vast and varied selection of literature available to them, they appear to show a marked preference for a book called The Politics of Experience. The authors, like other members of the 'square' older generation, are of the opinion that they know what is best, and that this book is not good for these patients." (!) The authors are miriam siegler, humphrey osmond, and harriet mann. The authors would still be telling us what's best for us. "Laing's psychedelic model is its implication that schizophrenics will benefit from being seen as persons embarked on a voyage of self-discovery. It would be closer to the truth to see most of them as voyagers who have been shanghaied, for unknown reasons, on to a ship which never reaches port." Exactly. But not for the reasons provided by the authors, who note the voluntary aspect of psychedelic voyages as compared to the spontaneous nature of the psychotic episode, concluding that any involuntary trip (uncontrolled, unplanned) is necessarily bad, like being "shanghaied . . . on a ship which never reaches port." For one thing it's quite rare, in fact as I see it apochryphal, that anybody on a voyage, whether shanghaied or not, doesn't come back, it's impossible really to go anyplace you can't get back from, I'm not completely certain about this, I just don't know anybody who didn't."come back." (I just read this bit of corroboration in David Cooper's Death of the Family: "I have never known one person who did not go fully into his particular madness and come out of it within about ten days, given a certain lack of interference in the guise of treatment.") At one time a few centuries ago in europe mad people were herded onto ships of fools and these ships of course never did reach port, and this is not a bad description of contemporary psychiatric practices by which innocent people abroad in their minds are deterred (or "shanghaied" if you will) from reaching port by coercive detours to familiar dumping grounds of social neurotic adaption. My own cliche for this experience has been that my trips were aborted until I did it myself and

239

went the whole way round and back to port in my own good time and without significant interference from those who like to tell people where to go and how to do it, and the port I reached then naturally was precisely the place these people are determined to prevent you from arriving at. I mean the port of some semblance of detachment from the great civilized neurosis of normalcy. Cooper says what we all have to do in our first-world context is to liberate ourselves personally by a Madness Revolution and I agree. He says we can perhaps talk about "madness," which is the genocidal and suicidal irrationality of the capitalist mode of governing people, and "Madness," which is the individual tentative on the part of actual, identifiable people to make themselves ungoverned and ungovernable—not by undisciplined spontaneity, but by a systematic reformation of our lives that refuses aprioristic systematization but moves through phases of destructuring, unconditioning, de-educating, and de-familializing ourselves, so that we at last get on familiar but unfamilial terms with ourselves and are then ready to restructure ourselves in a manner that refuses all personal taboos and consequently revolutionizes the whole society. Speaking of Cooper and his book The Death of the Family I recommend the current flick Wednesday's Child in which we can see all of our parents in caricature in their collusive authoritative madness which society calls sanity. These parents "know what's best" for their child, and this child is torn apart by her need to become herself and to satisfy her parents' expectations at the same time. It's an understatement to say that the tradition of Laing and his colleagues stresses that civilization impedes the development of human potential. As Berke puts it we're up against a whole society which is systematically driving its members mad. I would go further and say that most all of us are mad practically from the start, and by mad I mean what Cooper means, that madness cultivated in every family to ensure the proper functioning of its offspring, and that madness which is the effective uncoupling of our inner and outer realities with a persistent valuation placed on the outer such that our inner worlds recede and shrivel up and petrify in forgotten ruins beneath a one-dimensional reality of consciousness devoted to a grasp of concrete things and objective facts and goals and principles. We are, as Laing wrote in The Politics of Experience, socially conditioned to regard total immersion in outer space and time as normal and healthy. Thus the madness with a capital M that Cooper refers to is this fantastic eruption at some later stage of living of that forgotten inner world, I suppose a kind of convulsive involuntary natural effort of the organism to reunite the inner and the outer by grandly retreating from the familiar outer and embarking dangerously on a voyage through the regions of the lost interior, regions traditionally accessible to people identified as crazy visionary artists, say. A well-known passage in Laing's own visionary work reads "We respect the voyager, the explorer, the climber, the space man. It makes far more sense to me as a valid project—indeed, as a desperately and urgently required project for our time—to explore the inner space and time of consciousness." *Humanity is estranged from its authentic possibilities.*— The reason the psychiatric profession proper finds Laing's The Politics of Experience so detestable is that in this work Laing was closing the gap between Self and Other (Patient and Psychiatrist) and identifying his original schizoid model of his early clinical work as the norm of human existence. Split between inner and outer, split between body and mind, split between spirit and matter, split between form and content, split between experience and behavior, and so on. As he remarked wryly on the cavett show after cavett asked if anyone here could define schizophrenia and nathan kline the Inquisitor (director of rockland state) said it was a split between feeling and thinking and behaving this description applies to most people he meets, most psychiatrists for instance. The word schizophrenia is applied indiscriminately to most anything. Laing and his associates deny that there is any such thing as schizophrenia, except as a term of personal and social invalidation. "I emphasize that schizophrenia is a term rather than a condition, and this is an important part of our work, showing how people are invalidated in their own life styles, their life experience, by having this term applied to them" (Berke). The label is a social fact and the social fact a *political event*. The person labeled is one of Them. There's Us and there's Them. The Self and the Other. The Other is the Enemy. In any interpersonal theory of psychiatry the person who gets to be deemed mad is the loser in the hide and seek games that people play as the Self and the Other. Laing is the first hero of the psychiatric profession, he gets the molten medal of honor for finding himself in the Other, and by so doing exposing the profoundly schizoid nature of the profession itself. By now I've read the early 'brilliant' book The Divided Self and you can see how refractory the young scotsman was even then, applying as he did a Sartrean existential-phenomenological method to demonstrate the *intelligibility* of madness states, and further of perceiving the individuals held prisoner in the hospitals he attended in relation to the world around them, both at home and in the hospital setting, and not in that clinical abstract isolation by which people are instantly typed as the Other and imagined to be suffering from purely *individual* disorders. Even so, it makes me very nervous to read such a book. That Divided Self is still the Doctor and the Patient. Only a Divided Self could be so authoritative on the subject. But he was still talking about Us. That one or the other of those two selves was you or me they were talking about, they were talking about us behind our backs again, writing us up as clinical studies for "professional audiences." Anyway the author of a work I first saw in '67 in the form of a Divided Self which I couldn't read who followed that up one year later with a work that entered the mainstream of the subversive psychedelic literature of the '60s seemed a strange man and I wanted to meet him. It didn't matter by the way that The Divided Self was written and printed in the late '50s. We don't all keep up with everybody's chronologies. Then when I knew the chronology better I still wanted to know how he got to The Politics of Experience, and why he was still hiding, in a sense. I heard he was coming to amerika for a talk tour so I arranged with difficulty to go see the man the nice woman working on his tour was afraid I'd challenge his manhood or something by bringing up a subject as irrelevant as women's liberation. She kept saying he was in very good shape. I thought he could take care of himself in any case. Better than I could take of myself. I mean it costs you something to go and see any "great man" these days. Especially any great man who claims to be one of us. I went at the ungodly sunday morning hour of 10 to room 608 at the algonquin and expressed my ambivalence as soon as I walked in the door. I'd seen him the night before at hunter college and I said so and I said it was difficult to imagine a woman sitting before such a big audience with that kind of confidence and authority and commanding that sort of ultimate attention. Any woman, that is, who isn't a "performer" in an entertainment medium. His wife, Uta, agreed readily and he didn't say anything but he wasn't hostile either. I liked them both and made myself comfortable right away by talking about myself. I wondered suddenly what my *real* motivation was for going, and was I just presenting my credentials as a true crazy to establish a peer identity if that was possible or was I after all this time since '65 attempting to prostrate myself as a 'patient' and if so was the algonquin early on a sunday morning the proper place and time for a cure. I don't know. But we got into ourselves and I had a good time and I did find out what I wanted to know basically about the morphology of The Politics of Experience. He said he first tripped in '60, which makes sense, and he wrote P of E between '61 and '64, and he tripped with both leary and alpert in london on different occasions in '65, and in answer to my suspicions concerning professional

protection he said he was and is one of about 18 medical people in the british isles who are authorized officially by the
home office to do as they will with the psychedelics and that
this authority has given him a certain significant pivotal function as a buffer between the kids and the government. At some
point when we were fairly deep into it, into ourselves, he
said he always was peculiar. I said well the scotch are peculiar
and later I told jane who said that was scotch chauvinism and
that's okay I know my name is scotch and laing said yes it was.
Anyway he qualified what he meant by peculiar by telling
me he always was able to get into himself. I'm not sure that's
how he put it. I knew what he meant. Like he could induce
himself into that other world and bring himself back. If you
can dig that. And he reminded me in case I didn't know which
I didn't really that in Self and Others (also a late '50s book)
he put forward the case of a 34-year-old woman in a kind of
death trip lasting five months after the birth of her third child
as an example of an experience of psychic disintegration and
rebirth that later became the very heart of The Politics of
Experience. "She went out of this world into another world
where she was enveloped in a tapestry of symbols."—"She
came back from that world of the dead and unreality, to this
world of the living, in flashes of realization. She came back
in the spring, after the strangest winter of her life."—These
were not the remarks of any conventional doctor judge. And
in fact in his commentary on the case he includes this prophetic
thought: I have alluded elsewhere to the possibility that what
we call psychosis may be sometimes a natural process of healing. (A view for which I claim no priority.) Possibly this
was a key case, or experience, for the later visionary. I suppose the turning point was '60 and that first chemical trip.
All things combined there's not such an illogical transition.
What he tentatively suggested in Self and Others is merely
realized or unfolded and evolved in The Politics of Experience in which he moves simultaneously into social criticism

244

and a mystique of psychosis asserting in effect that the very states of mind that society in its delegates of psychiatrists had condemned and consigned to its jungles of justice were in reality states of grace visited on any one of us normally fucked up schizoid individuals passing by chance into forbidden territory. "No age in the history of humanity has perhaps so lost touch with this natural *healing* process that implicates *some* of the people whom we label schizophrenic. No age has so devalued it, no age has imposed such prohibitions and deterrences against it, as our own. Instead of the mental hospital, a sort of reservicing factory for human breakdowns, we need a place where people who have traveled further and, consequently, may be more lost than psychiatrists and other sane people, can find their way *further* into inner space and time, and back again." Such became the place called kingsley hall, opened in '65. At the algonquin I told Laing and his wife I went out to kingsley hall in june '69 and was quite depressed by the place and wondered what if anything went on there. They told me people very often walked in there under the impression that nothing was going on and in fact something very much was but it wasn't immediately visible. Even so, the physical structure was extremely dismal, a huge brick mausoleum of a place with a barren cavernous interior and broken windows stuffed with rags. I remember a glimpse of some big suffering christian paintings in a huge room. I was offered some undrinkable brew by a fellow who talked simultaneously about mathematics a girl friend and witchcraft and bore a heavy crucifix on a hairy chest. I saw two other people waft in and out and I left within a half hour. The paintings were Mary Barnes's paintings and the fellow was John Woods, who appears in Mary's book (Two Accounts of a Journey Through Madness, with Joseph Berke). I think Mary was still there when I stopped by. The place closed a year later in '70. This book by Mary Barnes and Joseph Berke is a fantastic document. The way Mary put it she had come to the place where she could 'go down' to before she was born and grow up again—to come up again straight. She said it was all about coming to know what she wanted. The 'right' thing had always been what someone else wanted of her. For his part Berke said Mary was the right person at the right place at the right time. As soon as he got to kingsley hall he realized that the best way to learn about psychosis would be to help mary 'do her things.' Berke played the part of 'good mommie' to the regressing 45-year-old woman who successfully embodied the thesis of Laing and his friends that psychosis is a potentially enriching experience if allowed to proceed full cycle, through disintegration and reintegration, or death and rebirth. Berke comments that Barnes had elected herself to the position of head guinea pig, but the nature of the experiment had been determined by *her,* that she had her 'trip' all worked out for years before she ever heard of laing or berke or the rest of them. One of Laing's projects in new york this month was a showing of a movie called Asylum made at the quarters they acquired after kingsley hall shut down. A young woman by name Julia appears to be on a trip similar to Mary's. On channel 13 after the showing the interviewer asked Laing what happened to Julia and Laing said the last he saw her she was on the continent and seemed fine and was married. I forgot to ask in turn whether he thought she was fine because she was married or what. But we did talk about feminism. I said he shouldn't say "women's lib" in amerika, supposing he said "black lib" or "black libbers" and he took note of the correction. I know he has a heavy early marxist lenin engels trotsky socialist orientation to the world and he grasped immediately the concept of "men as a class" whether this was his first introduction to the idea I don't know but he said after a few moments' pause he thought he would have to agree that sex discrimination historically preceded class distinctions in structured hierarchies. That was all, except when we were getting ready to leave I said the tour woman was afraid of my seeing him, maybe she thought I'd appear like solanas at the door with a rod at which he pantomimed the result of this kind of entrance screaming and falling backward onto the couch and clutching his balls. Suzi Gablik was there by then and she asked him to repeat the performance and he did. That wasn't all actually. I recommended Philip Slater's The Glory of Hera he wrote it down promptly in his record book similar to mine only bigger and he recommended a fat paperback he flashed at me Malleus Maleficarum concerning women and the Inquisition he said a *woman* should write this and I wrote it down in my record book similar to his only smaller. I wondered if I felt an affinity because we're both scotch and peculiar or because we've read a lot of the same types of things or because he's just a nice bloke and I like myself okay too or what. But I didn't forget my ambivalence and resentment at knocking on his door in the first place. I said in fact that I resented his credentials. He said but you have your certificate of insanity. Yeah but I want *both*. And what could he say. I mean I'm still quoting these authorities. I want to know when I get to be my own authority. For a year I worked on my crazy book surrounded by dozens of three by fours of typewritten quotes by the authorities not the least of whom was Laing and I abandoned the project to write my political book and when I start in with the crazy book again I'm promising myself not to look at a threebyfour. It isn't just the world out there that's reluctant to grant any person their own authority, it's the world inside yourself and a part of that world for me is the internalized Inquisitor of the hospital system who indicated by the most elaborate punitive modern machinery that if I thought I wasn't much of anybody *before* my "experience" I could be certain that what I had become was a total non person in a non environment of my own non making. The internalized Other. I don't romanticize the crazy trip any more than Laing and his people do and this is a big misunderstanding. The thing is although it isn't the perfect solution to anything, it *is* a *way* and it's a way we need to know a lot more about and I'd even hazard the thought that when we have a body of literature descriptive of the "inner journey" comparable to what we have in space and mountain and jungle and underwater exploration that we'll be a civilization on its way to recovering a lost unity of inner and outer. I mean that that would be an indication. There is something called schizophrenia and it means brokenhearted. Much of the misunderstanding concerning the word and a state or states to which it's supposed to refer has arisen over its unfortunate association with the similarly derived word: schizoid. If the latter indicates the *split* nature of all our normal functioning lives of civilized sanity, schizophrenia means to me the cataclysmic brokenhearted experience of fragmentation and disintegration of those normal processes in some weird counterdynamic of a *fusion* of all those dualities. Laing has been criticized for encouraging people to plunge into their madness and of course he does but he doesn't romanticize the state at the same time. He says madness is an understandable reaction, not a proper adjustment to the world. He's surprised actually that more people aren't screaming and having the creeps in the world we live in. He says madness is *potential* liberation and renewal. The point is that we don't even know how liberating it is yet because a schizoid culture naturally validates only its schizoid members and punishes both voluntary *and* involuntary efforts of certain of its members to (re)integrate themselves. "This process could have a central function in a truly sane society." Those who had been there would help others to get there and to be there and to go through there and to come back and to assist others and so on. For, as many who've been there have said and written (including people like Zelda Fitzgerald by the way), the sudden unexpected and unprepared-for plunge into the forgotten ruins of the inner world can cause great terror and confusion between inner and outer realities and cause others to panic and take police action of some sort in response to the "peculiar" behavior of their friends or relatives. I suppose at some moment of exit or re-entry the moon travelers experience this (con)fusion between this world and the other. They might at that point wonder where they are. They've been trained for the other world, they know what to expect, and they have plenty of guides pressing buttons down in this world, and they have all these back-up systems, but re-entry is a terrific burn for the ship and I can imagine it's a wild moment for the mind too. Burning and fusion are the same thing. The first indication I had in '65 that I was going someplace was a slight burn in my foot. You may think the analogy is far-fetched, but I had a friend gene swenson who went on an intergalactic journey in his own space ship, I've forgotten the details, but I know he went, possibly the reason nobody believed him was that it wasn't written up in the papers. The splashdown occurred on the roof of his tenement on 4th street and the recovery operation team was the local precinct police and the check-up took place at the hospital. I suppose the astronauts get the psychological test treatment too. And you remember originally they were locked up in a trailer or something on the carrier after the frogmen pulled them out of the water. The analogy breaks down at the point where you might say gene was on a more dangerous trip since he had to improvise his own guide and preparation system. I remember him for example bending intently over my radio one afternoon listening for "number signals." As for preparation there was none. The trips were a little on the sayonara side. He did come back however. He came back three times, and after the third time the Medical Inquisition Recovery Team and all the rest of their frogmen had at last convinced the guy that he was a "case." He was ready then to take their tranquilizers forever and get a nice nine to five job filing something and wear a suit and a tie and go to a shrink very often regularly to keep himself straight. The last thing that happened was he biologically died in a carcrash in kansas with his mother. At 35 he was still going back to kansas to see his crazy parents who were never his most avid supporters. I'm sure I wasn't the only one who kept saying don't go back home gene, there's even that famous book title you can't go home again, but who were we but an extended family still telling him what not to do. I don't have any idea what the complex dynamic fuel system was that launched gene on his trips, who could ever know what that is, much less the chief passenger, but I do know that his life situation was basically untenable to himself and that a journey to "other regions" was in order and that as a one way ticket to bellevue he became a two-time loser every trip he took. No credibility anywhere. One day he came over to my loft with ann wilson who brought a taperecorder and a cardboard mobile of the galaxy she strung up from the ceiling the idea being gene was going to recount his journey but we got into kansas and the family instead somehow and somebody said what's that got to do with the big trip and I said oh it's all the same thing but I didn't know what I was talking about and even if I did we didn't know what to do really. We didn't know what to do about ourselves. The journey solution was no big deal if you couldn't come back and seriously change the conditions of the place you found it necessary to leave. No roles for the mad. The point of black elk of the oglala sioux is that the 'illness' of black elk as a young boy, his passage into the ancestral realm of the dead, actually *qualified* him for his future assumption of the role of healer of the tribe. Who else in fact could 'make whole' if not the one who had 'been there' if by whole we mean the (re)unification of all our past presents and futures. By contrast the artauds in wasichu land are a weird breed of outcast, tormented by the keepers of real time and real place. And if the old indians could read and witness some of our stumbling efforts to recover ourselves I wonder what they'd make of it, i. e., a passage like this out of david

cooper's Psychiatry and Anti-Psychiatry ('67): I shall con-
centrate on afterdeath experiences within the biological life
span. These occur in so-called psychosis, in experience called
mystical, in dreams, and in certain drug states. Also they can
occur, rarely, in certain waking states where the person is not
engaged in any of the four types of experiences that I have
expressed above in a hateful language of categorization.—
Maybe this is what we have to go through in order to get
back there. I don't mind cooper myself since he's been there
personally. When in fact all these doctors go there and the
personal testimonies begin to replace the clinical studies, the
patients liberating their doctors as it were, the self recognizing
self in other, we'll have the makings of some authentic initiation ceremonials into our cosmic heritage as members of the
primeval slime. Whatever you say about leary he's a true mad-
man, he's one who did it, he forfeited his earned rights to the
rewards of a mad culture, he can't come back any more than
gene could, but he created something of a role for himself
out of the credentials he had, out of *that credibility,* his experience as a professional in matters of the psyche in fact
was not only a credit but a certain sort of preparation as a
successful navigator of his own trips. Problems of control.
Problems of navigation over an eight hour period however
not being the same as for three weeks or five months. The
thing is in a sense that we're not able to realize yet that the
profession through these fellows did remain intact. A bunch
of doctors of psychology went 'round the bend not too long
(about 10 years) after the momentous invention of acid in that
laboratory in switzerland, an event that put them in touch
with the ancient religious traditions of the profession, that
is, with its potential shamanistic functions of exorcism and deliverance, long predating its modern police function as guardian
of the state. Laing's analogies between the Inquisition and the
Modern Psychiatric Profession should be well taken. It was
a bit spooky to see a medieval Inquisitor facing a modern

shaman as it were, on the cavett show no less. It wasn't hard to catch who was who. The one a kind of transmigrated viennese patriarch (nathan kline), the other a scotch mystic, the two in the middle (cavett and rollo may) ordinary confused men of our times, may's big line is that society is crumbling (oh dear oh dear, and his jowls quiver a little, like a disbelieving old maid aunt), cavett hopping around for answers in front of his not too well concealed layers of masks, as I saw it quite threatened by the scotch mystic whom he sensed rightly to be capable of penetrating those layers, and who was as Laing told me a few days later probably relieved and appreciative that Laing didn't take advantage of the vulnerability. Anyway the classic antagonists being Laing and kline. Laing: " . . . who sets the computer . . . who controls the system that determines who needs treatment . . . sometimes the patient thinks the psychiatrist needs treatment and then the psychiatrist takes account of this as proof of how much treatment the patient needs . . . who is to administer treatment . . . who is the transgressor? . . . who is out of line . . . and out of place . . . who should get back to their corner and stay there . . . should we give treatment to the president (those who are really at it [applause] or to those who drop out and say I'm checking out, and I'm not coming back) . . . who would be giving "Tranquilizers" to whom in the days of the witches . . . 100,000 women a year killed . . ." And up kline with his medieval reflexes: "Many of these women were self confessed witches. Today we would view these people as mentally ill." It went on like that and it was all very clear. We exchanged some remarks about the man at the algonquin, I said he's a scary character, Uta (Laing's wife) said he was extremely threatening, Laing said you have to back off from these guys, I said yeah but I think anyway he's more threatening to women and we dropped it. Laing was never an inmate at rockland state, but he makes the proper historical connections. And he didn't let the impotency question raised by cavett into the hands of the inquisitor. He took charge of it right off. Q: Can the startling rise of the women's movement be responsible for male impotence? A: It was said in the old days that men's penises had disappeared and sometimes other people couldn't see them either and this was called *bewitch-ment* and the *Hunt* is still going on . . . to blame women for our own ineffectualness. Agreement by rollo may (society is crumbling anyway) and change the subject. End topic. I wasn't ready to get into the women aspect of the whole crazy question and the profession etc. I was trying to restrict myself to sorting out the males, in so doing the level of my ramblings is post-revolutionary, as though we're all people again and nobody takes count that these people we're talking about are in fact males. There are two healing traditions in the west and one of them is female and that was wiped out and that was actually the tradition of the witch. Certainly the witches were the midwives and had charge of all matters concerning women and childbirth. The professions are presently mightily confused. What is thought by many to be a psychiatric profession is in reality a law enforcement agency. Hospital treatment is exclusively moral. To frame the activities within a medical model a trial is called an 'examination' and a judgment a 'diagnosis' and a sentence a 'disposition' and a correction 'treatment.' The lost true profession is the ceremonial deliverance of childbirth and all true doctors are midwives. The grave of the self opens and a child is born again. Birth and death are the same event. The "inner journey" is in reality a return to the labyrinth of the womb or tomb. "The process of entering into *the other* world from this world, and returning to *this* world from the other world, is as natural as death and giving birth or being born" (Laing). We might thus understand better the great (con)fusion that may occur at moments of exit and entry. The burning up of the ship. The demolition of the boundaries between self and other. The re-entry into mother. The movie played backward. The splashdown on the roof of a tenement. The launching pad at carnavarel. The carnival of comings and goings. All this and purgatory too. The death-in-life situation of the normal dead(ly) civilized condition is a desperate clinging to life in fear of the death that has already happened countless times. *The Dreadful Has Already Happened.* It's a memory problem. We've been sleeping for centuries. How do we get lost and become ourselves at the same time. To be both separate and the same. To be at once the mother and not the mother. To become one's own mother. Pure Mind. "In certain forms of 'psychotic' experience there is, at the height of the experience, a pure anoia in which the 'outside' becomes continuous with itself through the 'inside' so that all sense of self is lost" (Cooper). The terror of the loss of self. The madness of it. The birth of our selves from our false selves, our social selves. As Mary Barnes says, we go from false self, to madness, to sanity. The dire extremity of madness as a last ditch solution. The burning up of the masks. A little egg of a self inside a box inside a box inside. The chinese boxes. The dissolution of their walls. Going further back down to the Void. The Matrix. The Chaos. "Human societies in diverse times and places have relied upon a method of 'psychotherapy' which western man has forgotten and suppressed: the return to Chaos" (Schatzman). There is now a new (old) male tradition of therapeutic ritual rebirth, the gravedigger and the midwife, in one, the assistant at the delivery, the old men at their own tribal initiation ceremonial pushing their members through some surrogate male legs. To become their own mothers. To come. To deny the mother. The question now I think is what about the mothers. What about feminism. The delivery of Mary Barnes by a male midwife is really something. And I think laing and his associates have been all along particularly sympathetic to women, but that doesn't mean they would encourage or even permit the (re)emergence of the female healing tradition proper. In all their writings to date their feminist consciousness is totally marginal. They know about the sorry state of women but their political understanding of the world stops with socialism. It isn't fair, at the same time, to criticize their early writings on feminist grounds, if most of us here were not exposed to feminism before '68 or '69 why should they have been and what can the males do with it anyhow. What in any case can this handful of crazy doctors do. I blurted across the hotel room to laing's wife Why didn't YOU go to Ceylon? Last year laing spent two months in a monastery in ceylon in intensive mind training. The doctors have been going east too. *Orientation is knowing where the orient is.* The control mastery of the yogin. The craft of dying in the tibetan book of the dead. The males wandering into their sanctity. Over the dead bodies of women. The womb traffic is heavy. I didn't have to argue with Laing and his wife, who did in fact go to ceylon to visit, and Laing demonstrated her reception there, the monks would shake her hand, with body and glance averted. I said the same thing goes on here and he replied well at least they're up front about it there. Behind every great woman is a man, uh rather a woman. Most of those accused of being witches were women . . . the whole campaign against witches was permeated with the spirit of aversion toward women. Civitas dei. Civitas diaboli. The law enforcement agency of the Inquisition in its older form of the Church and its new form of the Modern Psychiatric Profession is primarily an agency to keep women in their place and exterminate them if they can't. The office procedures represent the initial stages. The hospitals the final solution. I didn't mention that gene swenson was homosexual. He had an Inquisition installed in his Head. By the sights of family and state he was a Bad One. He had a normal false self system that occasionally just crumbled. Being pedestrian about it they say he'd be labeled insane because he would be seen as trying to escape from 'crazy' or disturbing relationships (read 'society') and that was true and he went to the orient too, he was very involved in chinese characters and confusions. "One is even tempted to ponder on the daring hypothesis that in the 'psychotic' families the identified schizophrenic patient member by his psychotic episode is trying to break free of an alienated system and is, therefore, in some sense less 'ill' or at least less alienated than the 'normal' offspring of the 'normal' families. In so far as he enters a mental hospital, however, his desperate attempt to liberate himself would seem to fail in terms of his deficiency in the necessary social tactics and strategy" (Cooper). Problems of control. Moving from false self to madness to sanity. A midwife at this point in civilization seems imperative. It's a mother problem all the way around. The bad mother is rampant in the Laing and Esterson book Sanity Madness and the Family. There's no analysis of how she got that way. That's why I recommended Philip Slater's The Glory of Hera because I think he's one contemporary writer (male that is) dealing with the hopeless position of the mother in the family, and state. I also think laing is finding out something about feminism and that eventually the orient and the new therapy and the new sexual politics are going to merge into a comprehensive political-psychological theory and counter consciousness that will be a more effective subversive deviation from the patriarchal authoritative hierarchical law enforcement reality oriented materialistic sexually repressive fucked up culture in which we live. I can see the Laing people for instance getting together with the radical therapists in amerika, a sexually mixed group which puts out a rag called rough times (originally called the Radical Therapist) there's quite a bit of heavy sexual political consciousness. In a paperback collection of theirs called The Radical Therapist there's quite a few essays by feminists, including Mary Barnes (feminist?) In an Editorial Judith Brown says Male supremacist behavior in psychiatry and psychology is perceived by radical feminists as one of the single largest enemies of women's interests. Maybe the two groups are blending already. Berke and Schatzman are in the book too. I don't know. A Madness Revolution. Berke: The reason why most psychiatrists are unable to communicate with people who have entered the deeper levels of regression is that they do not utilize their own enormous reservoirs of primitive emotion to make contact with such individuals. They try to force the other to speak in rational modalities long after he or she has decided to declaim in an 'irrational' tongue. And I do not mean by irrational unintelligible. I am referring to the language of the infant, the melodies of primary feeling, which are, in themselves, quite comprehensible." A stray case of normality!

november 30, 1972

TIME WOUNDS ALL HEALS

i'm bored with the michigan wisconsin story and i'm already
in england where i've promised myself to be by the time anybody reads this. the winter odyssey is over. it's all about books
and bells from here on in. the story has been told many times.
some parts of it may be true. the sequence is unconscious and
the unconscious is the most orderly place of all. nice play,
shakespeare. amnesia is a social event. i'm reactivating the
father investigation and other cocoons. there's a girl called
rosemary i haven't met yet. and a boy called arthur. and some
other nights of the squaretable i presume. the romance family
is not necessarily an invention. in any case the feminist project
is to recover possession of the paternal titles. see sleuth with
olivier and michael caine and substitute for caine a girl. sleuth
is a fabulous flick. the sleuth is the grail quester or so i read
it. the british are the masters of this modern detective story.
the problem is how to take the bull by the udders. the bull
or minos or olivier is first found by the quester at the center
of a maze constructed of tall hedges just outside the palace
or manor house where he is recording a new episode in his
next detective story on his tape recorder. he's a famous author of such novels. he's at the center of his prize possession,
his woman, whom we never see. minos's palace at cnossus
was a complex of rooms, ante-rooms, halls, and corridors in
which a country visitor might easily lose his way. according
to some historians the labyrinth was so called from the labyris,
or double-headed axe, a familiar emblem of cretan sovereignty,
shaped like a waxing and waning moon joined together back
to back and symbolizing the creative as well as the destructive
power of the goddess. according to every feminist's favorite
author, elizabeth gould davis, the labyris was symbol of the
goddess and of matriarchal rule, not only in crete but among
the lycians, lydians, amazons, etruscans, and romans and it's

been found in the graves of paleolithic women of europe buried 50,000 years ago. there's a feminist bookstore called labyris just a few months old in new york owned and operated by two women on 33 barrow street. there's a feminist restaurant on 11th street near the docks called mother courage after the revolutionary woman of the brecht play. the women possess their own means of production and nurturance. the women are inside themselves, their own food establishment, and they sit down and talk to you as if they owned the place, which they do. the intestines of the labyrinth of the woman. if you're a woman it's an easy place to go to. an insiders hangout. i don't go to england as an insider exactly. hardly. i don't know what i go as and i don't know what for particularly either. the queen is in good shape, so it can't be the grail. and i don't need any souvenir bells. and i don't need to meet arthur and rosemary, who might not be dying to see their name contaminated by a dishonorable relative. the project actually might boil down to a hunt for the proper sort of derby hat. the hat i might then set up as a still life with a toy tommy gun in metallic blue i bought at a grant superstore place. the bowler hatted man is more like a figure in a book than a human being. that's where the books get thrown in with the bells. my earliest idea of my father was out of a book. the book was called carillon music and singing towers. a later idea occurred in a book called the banquet years containing a photo of apollinaire in a derby and a moustache. one of his transmogrifications. the one who died young of the spanish influenza. the one who said please doctor i don't want to die, i still have so much to do. the other image was of this one was a head swathed in bandages. at four o'clock in the afternoon of march 17 in the year of 1915 second lieutenant apollinaire was sitting in the trenches reading the latest mercure de france to which he was still sending his regular chronique, la vie anecdotique, when some blood started dripping onto a page from a shrapnel that pierced his helmet over the right temple. i should add the bandage to the tommy gun and the hat. that would be very obvious. the choice of effects is not difficult. it's their juxtaposition that matters. the arrangement of new mysterious associations. the coordination as equally present of a variety of times and places and states of consciousness. the labyrinth could be the bowels of the old man too i guess. to reach the king a visitor is passed from one guide to another to be led thru the maze. the first objective of the young aspirant in sleuth is to reach the lord of the manor in the center of his perfectly symmetrical maze of hedges. the game of troy, the siege of troy, was the penetration of the maze to win or capture a maiden, and that is the apparent quest of caine as an unwitting sleuth. the maiden as it turns out is the middleaged wife of the lord of the manor, the famous author of detective stories. the author of course has invited (lured) the lover of his wife to his house. he is the king in the sense that he appears to be the correctly descended englishman. the challenge to his throne is distinctly from an outsider, an upstart, a hairdresser of some italian origin putting on fine airs and manners. he is the traditional hero. the hero sets out on his journey with no clear idea of the task before him. he comes in red sports car and parks in the circular gravel driveway. whither he rides, and why, he does not know, only that the business is important and pressing. he hears the voice of the man who called him, a garble of overtones emanating from the hedged enclosure dictating to himself the new episode in his novel. traditionally in no case was the fisher king a youthful character. that distinction was reserved for his healer, and successor. the main object in the quest of the grail was the restoration to health and vigor of a king suffering from infirmity caused by wounds sickness or old age. the grail stories were medieval romantic evolutions of the ancient fertility rites centering round the death and resurrection of the divine king. one of the fatal symptoms of decay was taken to be an incapacity to satisfy the sexual passions of his wives. the custom of putting divine kings to death at the first symptoms of infirmity prevailed until recently. when he had ceased to be able to reproduce his kind it was time for him to die and to make room for a more vigorous successor. in certain tribes a king even while yet in the prime of health and strength might be attacked at any time by a rival and have to defend his crown in a combat to the death. sleuth is a combat to the death. one might assume that the author (olivier) is still hearty, though hardly young, he's certainly intense and energetic, effusive and extravagant in his outpourings, yet the subject of his impotence arises, the pedestrian justification for a domestic tragedy. his wife had been looking elsewhere, and his mistress confided to the hero that he hadn't been able to get it up in a year. the health of the king was always absolutely intrinsic to the state of the land. the king is ailing and so is england. the restoration of the land and the survival of its inhabitants was at stake. this is why the status of the author is made very clear. altogether this is a time of mounting and unendurable distress. the life of his wife has been a perpetual surrender of ease and comfort to the service of others. it's no wonder the two male antagonists are so desperate to have her. even though she remains invisible. one wonders what they do actually want. the grail is still a mystery. the symbols of the great search were the cup and the lance. there was also the sword and the dish. hearts diamonds spades and clubs. the four suits of the tarot. the labyrinth is the form of the detective story. the story is the seasonal wanderings through the landscape of the woman. the ups and downs of the man. the men're hung up on legitimacy, because theirs is so tenuous biologically. i never did go through the proper channels, i attempted to make contact by jumping in a pool. i appreciate however the artifice of the search. famosus ille fabulator. the details of the symbols. the reactivation of the father investigation. the romance family is not necessarily an invention. i lay the derby upside down to achieve the chalice. i lean the toy tommy gun against the chair to signify the sword. i make a reservation for london on boac on washington's birthday. i note that christ was crucified march 25th and resurrected the 27th and the pub date of my book is the 30th. i note that my son's birthday is the 31st. i arrange to travel with susan b. whose best friend in england is named rosemary who will meet us at the airport. i remember that rosemary who went to cambridge to study history is also a british bastard. i am notified by my unconscious that at my age my father was traveling the atlantic by boat to install his goddam bells in all these episcopalian towers. i remind my readers that the belle in the tower is the captive virgin, the maiden (head) at the center of the maze, the garden of even. you remember poseidon built rings within rings of a fortress to protect himself inside at the center with his wife and mistress clito. during the day the king surrounded himself with his friends and bodyguards such that an aspirant to the throne could hardly hope to cut his way through them and strike home. a belle in a tower in the form of a huge hunk of metal is a very permanent fixture. in the movie sleuth the expensive effects of the lady in question, her invaluable jewels, are hidden someplace in the wall in a safe, naturally, and the first task of the hero is to locate said safe (it's behind a dartboard, naturally) and then to help the ailing author dynamite the thing, which they do, causing the dartboard to erupt at its center into a gaping smoking perfectly circular hole. from some ancient point of view kindness could be anticipated from a woman only so long as she remained a virgin. the hero (caine) the hairdresser descendant of an italian is an offender of the prime water. he presumes to violate the woman of the palace. the woman herself is a mere plaything, a *femme a homme,* the object of her crazy husband's fantasies, she's all over the house as a windup doll performing acrobatic tricks or pouring tea or smiling approvingly or playing the harpsichord. he touches a button in his pocket and his toys do their tricks. his real woman hasn't been responding correctly, she's been playing around on

her own. he wants her back and he wants to murder her, he
hates her, his pride is wounded, he's a furious fellow, he's
falling apart. the malady of the king is always antecedent to
the visit of the hero. in the least contaminated version of the
grail story the central figure would be dead and the task of the
quester that of restoring him to life (my prime source is jessie
l. weston). this of course is precisely what olivier has in mind,
and by inducing his victim (savior) to jump through a series
of hoops, i mean an elaborate obstacle course or labyrinth of
clues and objectives, as a sort of test of his worthiness as it
were, even persuading his victim that he actually wishes to be
rid of his wife and that he is helping him to have and to keep
her by setting up a phony theft of her jewels so that the interloper can maintain her in style through the collection of bur-
glary insurance, he leads him expertly into a scene of mortify-
ing humiliation and a mock murder in which the hero victim
savior hairdresser etc. is literally almost scared to death, and
following which we witness the amazing revitalization of our
author and his household of rejoicing toys all gyrating and
laughing and bobbing and sireening at once, the most clamor-
ous being his mockup sailor (sinbad?) his alterego i presume,
a mortimer snerdish puppet who laughs and applauds alarmingly. anyway thus endeth the first chapter of the flick, the
victory of the incumbent. at some point the two figures begin
to merge. i won't give away the rest of the story. the horror of
the occasion is by every means magnified and funereally en-
riched. what we are witnessing is the crucial matter of the
possession of the proper woman. such preferences and priorities are not easily and effectively transmitted. the class struggle
of the movie may obscure a more fundamental contest between
the forces of life and death, of spring and winter, the safe-
guarding of the cup of plenty, the problems of the broken
lance. the class struggle is merely a civilized decadent form of
its embodiment. the morality play that is sleuth leaves the
paternal inheritance in question. the men have outwitted them-

selves, for both are the losers. the bandage on my head of apollinaire is an essential prop for the play. apollinaire was in love with madeleine, a young girl he met on a train. "The shells were bellowing a love-till-death/ the loves which leave us are sweeter than the rest/ rain, rain, go away and blood will staunch its flow/ the shells were bellowing listen to ours sing/ purple love saluted by those about to die!" in certain versions of the grail the king is wounded, as a punishment for sin, for having conceived a passion for a pagan princess. what one should note here is the invention of a discipline of disintegration. the men of sleuth are properly living and dying in the ginnunga gab, the time of transition as the virgins travel round the world of their mothers reclaiming their paternal titles. la belle dame sans merci hath thee in thrall. the labyrinth of error will be the initiation of the daughters into the wombs of their selves. patient, reliable, uncomplaining, bowing to the inevitable yoke of her sex, she accepts her tasks. she has no idea where to begin. she makes reservations, she reconstructs her virginity, she exposes herself to the media (: scenes from the execution), she collects and disseminates bad news, she advertises feminist restaurants and bookstores, she makes the kind of collage you put up on the wall, she practices being simultaneously overt and mysterious, she exploits her expansive personality and celebrates it in her writing, she assembles the symbols of her death and her future, her farther unknown. usage externe. the bowler hatted man may be the perfect vehicle for anybody's projections. he takes on an. increasingly mythological aspect. he has come to represent all men. he walks around anonymously with his chalice on his head. his mother will serve him his supper. time wounds all heals.

february 22, 1973

AGNES MARTIN: SURRENDER
& SOLITUDE

going to see agnes martin in the desert came to seem to me
like a pilgrimage and i don't see why not. a pilgrimage is a
long, weary journey, as to a shrine. a shrine is a tomb of a
saint or other sacred person. none of these words may apply
to any contemporary venture, at best perhaps they have exotic
unreal connotations, but agnes martin is a spiritual woman
and she isn't easy to find. unless you happen to be in los angeles
when she's speaking at the pasedena museum, which was just
my luck last month while passing down the coast. i was mildly
disappointed since i wanted her to be as hard to find as i'd been
told she was and i guess the last place i expected to see her first
since she disappeared from civilization was in the civilization
of a museum. yet i was relieved in a way, just to see that she
was alive for one thing, and to have the opportunity to see how
she felt about me before i made so bold as to trek into her
wilderness with only a one-way advance telegram to recommend my arrival. i was disappointed in general to hear that
agnes had been emerging at all. she has in fact made six museum appearances this past year, and she told me she flew to
germany recently to negotiate the sale of some prints. it seemed
therefore that i'd be visiting somebody who was just very inaccessible and not a recluse from civilization. nonetheless she is
basically a recluse and she always has been thus it doesn't matter now any more than before how far you go to see her unless
you like to travel and see deserted places. i used to see agnes
in her loft on the battery and i don't know if she's any different
now than she was then and she left new york in 1967. i think
if anybody's different it's me and although i thought she was
very special then i doubt that i heard what she had to tell me.
i was just awed to be in her presence. i knew she was one of
the great women. it was a pleasure finding a great woman in

new york city during the terrible times of the '60s during every terrible decade it's a pleasure finding a great woman. a great woman may be a woman more interested in herself than in anything else. one way you knew agnes martin was great was because she lived decisively alone and that this was an active irrevocable choice and because she put very little stock in people at all and another way you knew she was great was because her paintings were. i know agnes would say the work is completely apart from the person and i have no quarrel with that myself but i see the work and the person as inseparable too. my earliest memory of agnes is of her work alone but then a little later on i saw agnes and her work together and in fact i rarely saw them apart since whenever i went to her loft almost always as i remember she showed me her paintings and sometimes her drawings too and so for me agnes was agnes the painter although i understand her detachment. her paintings are not about the world and i suppose her paintings paint themselves and in this sense she has nothing to do with it. i think it was 1964 when i stopped in at the elkon gallery and saw all these six by six foot paintings washed out whites and tans crossed by close vertical and horizontal lines muted and irregularly perfect and i called up dick bellamy and said do you know this woman agnes martin why aren't you showing her i thought at that time that if anybody good was around he was supposed to be showing them but of course he knew her work and he wasn't showing her elkon was anyway that was my introduction to the work of agnes martin. a little later on either by design or accident i was knocking on her door to review her most recent show for art news and that was how i met her. already i thought her paintings were beautiful and i wanted to meet the artist. i wasn't the least bit disappointed but socially possibly i was more awkward than she was so i wonder how we impressed each other. her hair was long then and she had lots of it and when i came in it was all loose and she was busying herself putting it back or up and sort of apologizing for being in some dissarray. i know we had tea and i looked at her paintings but i don't know what else. looking at agnes's paintings with agnes was a quiet concentrated cere- monious ritual. there was a very certain distance she traversed from the point in her loft where the paintings were stashed to the spot right next to the door where she showed them. one by one without any hurry or hesitation she would carry them from one place to another, back and forth, and when she reached the showing place next to the door there would be a certain gesture of hiking the work with her foot under the canvas up into position on the nails sticking out of the wall. then she would sit down next to you and contemplate the work with you and wait as i imagined for you to speak your thoughts. i can't imagine what i ever said if anything. i know we discussed the titles. i think very often she wanted to know if some particular title or other was appropriate but i'm not sure. i liked them all myself. desert. islands. mountain. blue flower. hill. starlight. ocean water. leaf. untitled. i liked them all. i thought i could see what they were even though every- thing was a graph. i used to say to people there was this painter painting mystical geometries as though nobody else had thought of that. nature paintings ruled by the horizontal line or was it vertical. when she was young she painted the mountains as they were or as we suppose we see them or anyway the way you see them at the washington square outdoor art show. in the desert agnes told me she could see in nature there weren't any *real* verticals or real horizontals and right then she gave up nature. in the desert there weren't any paintings at all. there was a rectangular pit maybe six feet deep and 15 feet from corner to corner next to her little adobe that she said was the foundation for a studio. she abandoned new york and painting both when she left in '67 and now she is beginning to begin again. it isn't altogether clear why she left new york and why she stopped painting but if you heard the story it's the sort of story you accept and understand without any explanations.

leaving new york has become as much a ritual exodus as going to new york is a ritual initiation. people said oh agnes martin left in a dodge pickup, and nobody knows where she went, or you'd hear vague reports that she ended up in the new mexican desert. i asked agnes how she ended up there, why she chose cuba, and she said she saw these mountains on this road leading northward into cuba in her minds eye in new york and that was how come. i was amazed to find the place. i sent a telegram as i said but i never made the 6 a. m. bus out of albuquerque that i declared i would, the reason being that jane was flying in from new york and arriving 11 a. m. and i didn't know that till after i sent the telegram and i didn't send another because i didn't want to make any more declarations. anyway about 3 p. m. three women of albuquerque drove us north toward cuba where i enquired in the postoffice if they knew where agnes lived. they said no but a man down the road did. down the road the man's daughter explained carefully and i thought it sounded pretty clear. basically she said there was a gate a dry river bed and a little forest. i don't see gates dry river beds or little forests very often so i heard it all in the singular. i'm still certain she said it that way too. well there were lots of gates and dry river beds and little forests. first you had to drive some few miles out of cuba way off the main drag if you could call the road through cuba that. the gate the man's daughter mentioned was obvious enough, an impressive barbed wire gate the sort you have to get out and unhinge and swing away for the car to pass and then rehinge again. then we were on a soft red clay road. then we crossed the dry river bed. then there was a little forest, midget gnarled trees of some sort. then i expected to see agnes's adobe. but what there was was another gate. i didn't think we should go through it but we did because there wasn't any other place to go in order to reach a dwelling unless you went careening off into the sage and the arroyas, those dry river beds in the form of drastic looking jagged ditches that snake around all over the place through those parts. so we went on and everything began to look like a dry river bed and a forest. i asked one of the albu-querque women what we were driving through actually. she said it was a short grass prairie with incursion of sonoran desert species running into pinon-juniper forest. that sounded good. i liked being there and all too, but the apprehension was mounting, especially when there was not only a third gate but a fork or a choice of going off or on the same road unimpeded by a gate. moreover we had passed the half eaten carcass of a cow right long the side of the road and that seemed to create an adage in my mind that when you see a dead cow you should turn back. besides i had the feeling we were within a clods throw of agnes's adobe but some part of my head said we were going to die in the desert. anyway we were all neurotically consuming a bag of nectarines and i was about to die laughing. i thought i'd never be able to travel in the desert with lucia since we were both particularly dying laughing. i said we should turn back. it was quite a few miles inching back over the soft clay bumpy road and reopening the gates and closing them behind us and wondering where the hell agnes was. back on the macadam we went a half a mile up to a little ranch farm to ask this man and his wife if we'd been on the right series of gates river beds and forests for agnes martin and the man said yes and his wife drew diagrams in the dirt and the man gestured out across the plain and said that's her mesa, right there, as though i should be able to see it and there was a curl of smoke out of a chimney that i was missing. it was clear anyway that we had to go through that third gate where the fork was where we'd turned back so we did it again and we came to a real little sage and juniper forest and there it was a small complex of vehicles and structures that had to be agnes. agnes the classicist. classicism she says is not about people and this work is not about the world. classicists are people that look out with their back to the world. it represents something that isn't possible in the world. it's as unsubjective as possible. the classic is cool. it is cool because it is impersonal and detached. if a person goes walking in the mountains that is not detached and impersonal she's just looking back. to a detached person the complication of the involved life is like chaos. if you don't like the chaos you're a classicist. if you like it you're a romanticist. painting is not about ideas or personal emotion. painting the desert in her head. the horizontal line. there's very few verticals in nature. and there she was as vertical as i remembered her which was only a week ago at the pasadena museum sitting on a chair in the middle of the stage surrounded by an overflow audience her hair short to the ears and still brown and wearing a sort of tangerine velveteen skirt to the floor with a white starched blouse slightly femme flared at the elbows and twisting a white handkerchief in her lap as though it was worry beads and my friend with me said she looked a dead ringer for gertrude stein. picasso said he was impressed by gertrude stein's physical personality and anyone might say the same of agnes martin. she's extremely handsome and she has the most brilliant twinkling blue eyes and her body is full and she's very solidly there yet shy and a little retreating at the same time. she giggles and jokes a lot and laughs at herself and i'd never seen her so solemn and formal. and i'd never seen her in a skirt or any sort of a "blouse." i could see she was on her best behavior, even as though it was sunday school or something. the audience too was reverent and expectant. it was a new aspect of agnes to me, although not one i wouldn't have envisioned. as i said she was for me a spiritual woman and i was awed to be in her presence and i believed whatever she said i knew she was a right person a natural woman a presence of the universe. she made pronouncements and spoke in aphorisms and she was known to go into trances and she proclaimed the future and she had no pretensions about herself except perhaps as a painter which may possibly be the subject of her intimate and abstracted speech that she's given lately in several of these museums. it's called the underlying perfection of life and almost the first thing she says is we are blinded by pride and that living the prideful life we are frustrated and lost that we cannot overcome pride because we ourselves are pride but we can witness the defeat of pride because pride is not real and cannot last, when pride is overcome we feel a sudden joy in living, the best place to witness the defeat of pride is in our work . . . all the time we are working and in itself . . . all the time in your working your self is expressed in your work in everyone's work in the work of the world we eliminate expressions of pride. her speech is 4000 words long she told me, and she memorized the whole thing. she speaks of pride, and pride, and perfection and solitude and fear and helplessness and defeat and disappointment and surrender and discipline and the necessity of all these and the necessity of the defeat of pride. besides knowing why she left new york i wanted to know why she left new york but i had no way of asking. she was glad to see me by the way. she baked an apple pie for the occasion and then when i wasn't on the 6 a. m. bus from albuquerque she was disappointed and ate some of it. i was glad she was glad to see me and i was glad we drove past the dead cow again and found her. i left jane and the three women of albuquerque in the car a discreet distance from her adobe and walked over there and hailed her and she emerged from the door beaming in dark blue work clothes very tanned or desert weathered i thought and that makes her eyes bluer and more sparkly. she was pleased i didn't bring everybody to the door at once because she wanted to change her clothes. she put on a clean shirt and pants and i explained that the three women of albuqurque were going home in case she wondered. but first we all had the apple pie and a french fish soup bouillabaisse with salmon okra and tomatoes. i was very nervous. or very high and nervously attuned to her emanations and expectations. later jane and me agreed we were afraid of her. i couldn't remember being afraid of her before so i decided i'd changed a lot. i must've been more presumptuous about myself before. or not so aware of the extraordinary presence i was in. or we were both crazy and i thought she was my peer. i don't know. i *was* in awe, but less conscious perhaps. there was the most incredible evening in '66 i think it was when i brought five or six people over to her loft and we sat around in a vague circle in a sort of a trance as though it was a seance although nobody mentioned it and there was at one point this great overhead crash i don't know what it was it wasn't thunder and lightning it might've been a skylight on the roof or even her skylight but whatever it was she didn't bat a lash she went right on talking and asking us all what sort of a wall or body of water we imagined in our minds eyes and when we saw the wall or the body of water would we cross it or could we and if so how would we do it she went right on with this exercise testing us i imagined for correct answers anyway as though nothing had happened which is her basic approach to life. nothing happens. no verticals. everything the same. a quiet existence. not much time for other people's problems. lots of time to herself. solitude and loneliness and contentment with one self. the union of opposites without trying to do so. the friend who went with me to the pasadena talk wrote and told me the whole thing seemed much stronger now than it did at the time but what she absolutely remembers about it is that everything she said she also negated completely, and she doesn't know how she did it. she does contradict herself all the time with the most bewildering confidence. she'll say all conventional people spend 90 per cent of their time wondering is it right or wrong. what you do is right, that's it. then she'll be cato the censor and tell you how absolutely wrong you are. she'll tell me one moment that associative thinking is the basis of all our distraction and the next that i'm exceptionally lucid when i'm at the typewriter. she'll tell me i'm very prudish and priggish (and she *knows* i'm a snob), and later on she'll say i shouldn't use four letter words. she'll say she wanted to ask me something although she wasn't into winning anything and then suddenly there's an argument and it seems as though somebody has to win something if we're to proceed to the next. i think she's delighted to see people but her fear of being disappointed by people is intense. she says she talks all the time when people come in order not to know more than she wants to know, she said you mean you realized how mean we all are? she said about people who come to see her believe you me, i run em off if i don't like them, if they're inconsiderate. she said it with a little chuckle. and told about a couple who came and lived off her for two days and the woman ate a peach from their car right in front of her and didn't offer her one. she doesn't know really why people come to see her. i wasn't sure myself, being such a pilgrimage and all. i just know she's important to me. and i was very curious to see how she was living in the desert. and i still wondered why she left new york even though i knew. i didn't know how to ask but she offered a number of hints gratuitously. she said i don't blame people for not being able to see the paintings, goodness knows, i have no idea why i did them myself. she said i had 10 one-man shows and i was discovered in every one of them. finally when i left town i was discovered again—discovered to be missing. she said she didn't know if she had left the world behind or the world had left her. she said she left new york because of remorse. she said that out at the edge of the canyon after we walked out through the sage to see the sunset. i didn't say anything at all. i guess it isn't necessary to clarify everything or anything. the canyon and the sunset were what seemed to matter and that didn't matter either. a glow was on us though and agnes extended what i thought must be the rarest compliment for her. she said everybody who comes is very conventional except me. it was after that that we were walking back to her adobe and she said she wanted to ask me something although she wasn't into winning anything. it was certainly a difficult moment. i knew it would be some sort of political question which would mean she would stop liking me having just said out at the canyon that everybody who comes is very conventional except me. i have no idea what she meant by the question all i can say is it concerned domination and i think whether i hadn't experienced domination or being dominating. i thought possibly she was alluding to women as role players. i had no intention of mentioning the despairing word feminism, agnes was born in 1912 and it doesn't take much ingenuity to see that she's better off in the desert throwing mud at her adobe and polishing her green truck than i am going around meeting hundreds of strange women who might have nothing more in common than electricians and philosophers but who in the name of feminism take issue with your four syllable words so that we can all be the same that is to say feminists, thus i believe i was appropriately evasive and the only remark i remember is agnes saying her sister says she believes in men women children and dogs and we left it at that although that wasn't the end of it. the thing is in any case one remains modest and gives honor to the sage who stands outside the affairs of the world. out around her adobe she pointed out the loco weed. which drives horses crazy she said. she explained how you make adobe mud bricks by filling up four rectangular sections of these open wooden frames with the mud stuff and then leaving them out to dry or bake in the sun. she talked about animals having thoughts and how she doesn't keep domestic ones any more, she doesn't want them around any more than people. what she keeps exactly is five vehicles in perfect working order and a beebee gun and a regular .22. not counting the small adobe in which she cooks and eats and possibly reads and undoubtedly muses, an open tall shedlike garage where she was parking her new shiny blue vw sports model, an outhouse, a tiny cave log room guest dwelling and a compost affair and she still sleeps in the dodge pickup or the pickup detached from the truck in which she lived for a couple of years riding all round the u.s. and canada till she found the proper mesa. when we drove away i said it didn't seem as if we were driving off a mesa, she said that's because we drove off the back end. anyway she keeps all her machines in good shape. before we woke up she polished her green truck, a '48 chevie, she said. the jeep we didn't see because she keeps it in town in case the roads've been more washed out than usual. i didn't see how we made it in in her white dodge truck returning from taos there must've been some rain and the dodge had zilch traction so i kept ditching off to the side to a stand-still and somehow retreating backtracking and then racing forward as though to hit your mark meaning staying on the road as in archery if there's a wind you shoot or aim way off target in order to hit it or even boomerang yourself. after the first night there she gave us a vacation and we went to taos. i was relieved in a way since the telepathy is pretty heavy and i had had a nightmare and the scrutiny is relentless and while she completely disarms you she then flatly contradicts you and as i've indicated i was fearful of exposing what could only be a profound political disagreement between us. i read a hilton kramer review she had there of her retrospective in philadel-phia and couldn't help saying the reason she doesn't have the reputation hilton kramer says she should have is because she's a woman. but agnes knows exactly who or what she is or isn't she shot back i'm not a woman and i don't care about reputa-tions. i said well i wouldn't come to see you if you weren't a woman. she concluded the argument saying i'm not a woman, i'm a doorknob, leading a quiet existence. in taos jane thought of buying her an enamel doorknob we saw there but we brought back some cheese and syrup instead. also jane bought some eggs milk and apples and agnes said that was exactly what she needed so as concerned the food we were in perfect agree-ment. another safe thing was finding out more about agnes, i never asked her much before, i never seriously wondered why she was so different and a natural woman of the universe, or even why i felt close to her while knowing she had her life a lot more together. i never knew she was scottish for instance, but i didn't know how scottish i am until recently either. i think the first thing i asked her over the apple pie and french soup bouillabaisse was where did she come from. then i asked her if she likes the bagpipes and she replied oh yes. a half a mile

away. she doesn't come from scotland herself actually. she was born and grew up in saskatchewan, somehow i always thought it was vancouver. i thought vancouver was a wild uncharted territory, but i happen to be in vancouver right now and i can see how agnes couldn't possibly have come from vancouver, i never inquired what saskatchewan is but it sounds northern and wild and right for where agnes would have to come from. she's a mountaineering camping pioneering frontier type of woman whose unnatural habitats for reasons of turning out to be a painter were vertical claustrophobic cities like new york. she's climbed big mountains alone for years so i can only imagine how she felt going three hours upstate new york with me and thalia poons one summer for a little two day cook and sleep-out next to a crick river and 20 yards in from the macadam but she never mentioned what an elementary tourist trip it was. the crick was deep enough to submerge and swim a few strokes around where we camped and she seemed happy tearing off her clothes yelling at last at one with nature and doing so. it was there that she divined my future and said i would go insane again which i did. another fairly safe thing to talk about is insanity since i suppose we would both agree that nobody knows anything about it except the insane. i think it was at the very end of that summer that i did go out again and agnes and thalia were the ones who rescued me up in brewster where i abandoned my car and called them and waited for them to drive up in somebody's vw bug and didn't take the whole bottle of thorazine that agnes suggested i should but rather about 400 mcs or mgs or whatever they are. possibly agnes asked me what was wrong with me and i said i was afraid to die. yet in her wall and body of water game in which she asks people what sort of a wall you imagine or body of water and when you imagine it if you could cross it or go over it and if so how you would do it i was the one apparently who had the correct answer, at least to the wall question, and that was that the wall was transparent so naturally i could walk through it and whatever was on the other side was the same as on this, so it doesn't seem reasonable that i was afraid to die unless the game we played occurred later on and i was by that time dead or dead on the one hand and alive on the other so it didn't matter. on her mesa in the desert agnes told us the women in her family live a long time although her mother died young, at 75. she told us all about how she died, how it took two years and how happy she was when it happened, i mean how happy her mother was, and agnes's final pronouncement on death was that you go out either in terror or in ecstasy and clearly her mother was ecstatic. she said her mother was one of the little people. agnes isn't very tall herself but partly because of being full and solid of body she appears a medium height. she says at 60 your body begins to fall apart, whether she is or not it doesn't seem to cramp her style, when we emerged that first morning from the log cave guest dwelling she was standing on a ladder hurling handfuls of mud at the wall of her adobe. by little people i believe she was alluding to the fairies of old celtic scotland. the rest of what i found out about who she is or where she comes from was that an ancestor was the scottish poet who was the author of flanders fields and her father was an essayist and there weren't any painters in the family. she thinks everything happens according to destiny and i objected on grounds of social oppression which was one more instance of my political tactlessness. i was saying that my mother painted lobster pots and boats in the harbor at sunset and that her potential for being an artist or an artist's artist or an artist to herself and nothing else was undeveloped for social reasons but i was saying altogether too much. someone has to be absolutely quiet when the other holds forth agnes remarked. and she talks all the time when people come in order not to know more than she wants to know. but i was thinking some of the time how to get agnes's attention. jane had the idea that sometimes she must feel awfully heavy to herself and then i thought she hasn't had enough people respond to her humor and jane said yeah they're probably too busy at her feet. were we supposed to ask her the meaning of life questions. do people go in order to ask her the meaning of life questions. i guess they would. but she doesn't have any answers, for nobody can tell anybody something they don't already know. she says what she knows for what she knows is what she is and what that is is perfect for her and she is still on the path herself. she says one thing she has a good grip on is remorse. and that suffering is necessary for freedom from suffering. and that the wriggle of a worm is as important as the assassination of a president. and that our work is very important but that we are not important. and that what you want to do is your work and what you want to want to do is your work. and that people ask her whats going to happen in art, where is art going and she says gosh, i hope it's going to go in all directions. and that a sense of disappointment and defeat are an essential state of mind for creative work. a working through disappointment to further disappointment to defeat. what does it mean to be defeated. it means we cannot move . . . but still we go on, without hope, without desire, and without dreams, then it is not i, then it is not us, then it is not conditioned response . . . without hope there is hope, we go on because there is no way to stop, going on without hope and desire is discipline, going on without scheming or planning is discipline and without striving or caring is discipline . . . defeated you rise to your feet like dry bones, these bones will rise again . . . undefeated you will only say what has already been said . . . defeated having no place to go you will await and perhaps be overtaken . . . defeated, exhausted, and helpless you will perhaps go a little bit further.helplessness is very hard to bear, helplessness is blindness, in helplessness we feel as though some terrible mistake has been made, we feel cast into outer darkness as though some fatal error has been made . . . feelings of loss and catastrophe cover everything and we tremble with fear and dread but when fear and dread have passed as all passions do we realize that helplessness is the most important state of mind . . . lack of in- dependence and helplessness is our most serious weakness as artists. and that's the way agnes goes on in her 4000 word speech that i heard at the pasadena museum and a few of those things she said to me too and i think her critical attitude her relentless scrutiny her voices of perfection her examination of your words and deeds is all in the spirit of improving your character for otherwise why would you go such a distance to see a woman who is herself on the path of perfection which is to say to becoming most totally who she is. she said sitting in the adobe or someplace if only i could get non resistance. she understands remorse but she needs non resistance. that's clear isn't it. yet while walking seems to cover time and space in reality we are always just where we started. i went for a little walk along the rocky edge of the canyon behind her adobe and was amazed to see a tremendously long procession of small black ants in an orderly line up and down this rock facing down into the canyon some going up and some going down with a few stray dissenters or were they the lost ones. i picked up a sandstone to take back to the world. i returned to eat supper. i didn't do much else there. i did take a shot out her door with her beebee gun at a can she placed for my aim after a quick lesson in how to hold the thing i hit the can and quit while i was ahead. also i thought there was a sudden rainbow just to commemorate our visit and i said i'll bet you rarely have a rainbow here and agnes replied yes we do, all the time, it's forever raining when the sun is shining. but the last per- fect double rainbow i saw was a couple of years ago in mendo- cino so i was in and out of her adobe ooing and ahing catching it out in the open or through one window or another watching its aspects and fading disappearing act. about 6 p. m. the wind was blowing in the canyon. by nightfall we were in bed, there isn't any electricity, and i had another nightmare. there was of course just a little bedtime story, of multiple rapes in cuba, a most dangerous part of the country apparently. but agnes had a nightmare too, she was quite indignant about it, she said she knew those nightmares weren't hers, and that's why she can't be around people, because she takes on their . . . she picks up their . . . and jane told her i needed to live among people and agnes said then i must have more pain. i could of course consider exchanging the pain for the nightmares in the desert. yet i could say like her that pain is necessary for freedom from pain. anyway if we are always just where we started there isn't anyplace to go and we might's well be where we are. i was reading recently about merlin who retreated from the world into his forest hermitage. it was said that at the sight of a crowd of people his madness breaks out anew. it was said also that his laugh was especially well known, the result of his more profound knowledge of invisible connections. agnes has this laugh or this cosmic giggle, but i wish to say she isn't any magician. she disavows magic adamantly. she hates magic and fetishes and superstition and the i ching, she says superstition is a belief in power, that there've been whole ages where art was only fetishes and that superstition is the enemy of art. she is also as a classicist as a cool artist a woman who looks out with her back to the world a painter who paints not about ideas or personal emotion but who paints the desert in her head as a classicist she is also eloquently opposed to romance and romanticism. she said she never met anybody who wasn't searching for love. she thinks this is a great mistake. she described a time of her own enslavement in this respect and how she became definitively done with it. the voices of perfection. of being alone with your self. of everything being the same. of not having any verticals. of lots of time to herself. of not much time for other peoples problems. of solitude and loneliness and contentment with one self. the union of opposites without trying to do so. a zen sort of person who never studied zen. a woman perhaps who's endured many insults, and who forgives everybody—and nobody. a woman who doesn't believe in influence unless it's you yourself following your own track. a woman it seems to me absolutely fearless of saying what she thinks. after all she doesn't depend on people. the work is what counts and the work is so fine and the people like the work so much that they pay her to live without any people. once she took a freighter around the world and someplace in india they took her off the boat and confined her in a hatch because she'd gone into a trance. no doubt the people on the boat were altogether too much. the boat in the desert is a beebee gun a .22 and five vehicles in perfect working order and i'm not without a little remorse that i went to see her myself. do we have to give honor in person to our sages standing outside the affairs of the world. or bother them with ideas of themselves that they don't have themselves and be bothered ourselves by ideas of ourselves they may have that we don't or bother at all. i don't know. in albuquerque after she drove us out and we were having lunch in la placita i asked her if she didn't think she was leading an exemplary life and once again she knocked the whole thing. oh my no, i'm a murderer, i'm a this and a that, i'm working out the hairy ape in myself, i'm just beginning, and so on, and i remembered how she leaned forward intensely in the adobe and said somewhat incredulously and you realized how mean we all are and i nodded yes, so how could i exempt her from her own conclusions about life. the work is the thing. the grid is still because the whole can be grasped by the eye and mind at once. the value she places on the known rather than the seen suggests innate ideas which she sometimes calls a memory of perfection. agnes martin: a study in the memories of perfection. "the ocean is deathless/ the islands rise and die/ quietly come, quietly go/ a silent swaying breath/ i wish the idea of time would drain/out of my cells and leave me/quiet even on this shore."

september 20, 1973